Wildgoose

WILDGOOSE

A Tale of Two Poets

Sally Evans

Postbox
PRESS

First published in 2021 by Postbox Press,
the literary fiction imprint of Red Squirrel Press
36 Elphinstone Crescent
South Lanarkshire
ML12 6GU
www.redsquirrelpress.com

Edited by Colin Will

Cover image: Gallinago_media/Shutterstock.com

Typeset and designed by Gerry Cambridge
e:gerry.cambridge@btinternet.com

A CIP catalogue record for this book is available from
the British Library.

ISBN: 978 1 910632 08 3

Red Squirrel Press and Postbox Press are committed to
a sustainable future. This book is printed in the UK
by Imprint Digital using Forest Stewardship Council
certified paper.
www.digital.imprint.co.uk

'The product of the artist has become less important than the fact of the artist... In our society the person is much more important than anything he might create.'

—David Mamet, External Magic,
in *A Whore's Profession*. Faber, 1994, p.138-9.

'The odd conceit of those who write that words written are shared.'

—Virginia Woolf, *Orlando*.
The Hogarth Press, 1928. Chapter 3.

WILDGOOSE

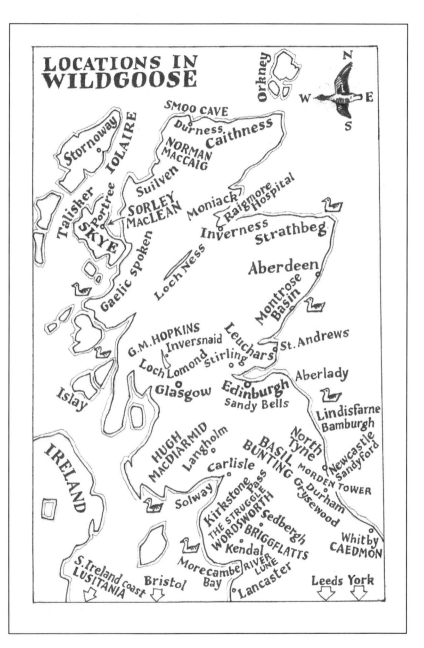

Map drawn by Geoff Sawers

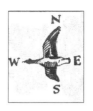

Chapter One

MAEVE SETS OUT   (1955 /1965)

THERE WAS TO BE A guided crossing of Morecambe
Bay on the morrow. The great heaps of tree branches
on the foreshore were higher than Maeve. The branches
would be planted in the sands for markers as the morning
tide drained, before walkers assembled to follow the official guide, from Silver Sands to Morecambe over the wet
Sahara, as it was called. Maeve's parents' friends had told
her family about it.

She had run away from the seaside garden. She could
be missed any time, when her cousin Eric told on her, how
she'd climbed over the gate and scooted away round the
corner. She'd better get on with it.

She wanted to walk on the sands.

There were safe routes. There were also places you might
be sucked into the sand up to your neck. This could even
happen to grown-up people, as it had once to a carriage,
though the horses and travellers had escaped.

She could see a tractor's tyre marks leading from the beginning of the wet parts. A safe bar of sand. She could see it
raised up above the surrounding channels, that were part of
a river that ran into the bay. She did not know the name of

the river. Her uncle said the bay was so big that more than one river ran into it.

She ran ahead in her small Clark's sandals. Clark's was a local factory in Kendal, she knew that much. Her mother took her to buy Clark's sandals for school. Sand oozed water into the gaps in the toes, the heels made a smacking sound on the wet surface. The tractor was far away. It looked tiny, heading for the distant shore.

She ran on. She felt free. Then she noticed the water creeping up the sides of the pathway, coming up nearer to the impressions of the tyres, that continued out into the bay.

She turned and looked back. She couldn't see the way now. Was that Morecambe promenade, all that way over there?

Where was the way back? She wasn't going to cry, she wasn't a cry-baby, but she must think of something to do. If she simply splashed on, she might come to a part of the sand that would suck her in, like the Victorian carriage.

She looked round the wide bay, shielding her eyes against the sparkle of sun on the waves. The small, fenced garden she had run away from was tiresome and dull compared to this, but there'd been nothing to be afraid of. A necessity hit her, to get back to the shore.

Three wild geese were coming towards her, flying low over channels and sands. They came almost up to her, working their wings, flap, flap. The foremost one definitely looked at her, then they turned their direction towards the shore at an angle. She followed them.

The waves came in faster than the geese.

There was no time to be frightened. She ran towards the geese and that part of the landscape where they had gone. Her feet and sandals, her knees and waist were wet when she stumbled onto the dry edge in front of the promenade. She was crying from exertion now, not from fear. There were people on the promenade, her father, her uncle, a policeman, and others she didn't recognise. She could see them, hands at their foreheads, squinting against the light, scanning the bay with its incoming tide for the sight of a seven-year-old girl. Grey sea surged back onto the massive sands. The light, too, was turning grey.

A shout from her uncle was followed by her cousin's loud soprano: *Look, it's her!* The policeman ran along the promenade, and her father came down some steps into the sand. The heaps of branches still lay waiting.

'Maeve, Maeve, what possessed you?' cried her father, picking her up and hugging her, at the same time as he burst into tears.

'Well, Mr Carter, it's a good thing that ended happily. It might easily not have done,' said the policeman.

'There were three geese,' said Maeve. 'They showed me the way back. Where have they gone?'

The little crowd had gathered round them. Eric began jabbering about Maeve being lost in the sands. His father took hold of him, and told him to be quiet.

Maeve looked up round the sky. 'Where have the geese gone?' she repeated, but no-one answered.

They trooped back to the holiday house her uncle's family had rented. She was bathed in the unfamiliar bathroom, dried in a hot thick scratchy towel, and given a jersey belonging to Eric to wear instead of her frock.

> *The water rose*
> *between my toes*
> *and then I chose*
> *where the goose goes.*

She had made up the rhyme. It wasn't very long, but she could sing it again and again.

She was seventeen in 1965. Ten years had gone by, that had turned her cousin into a man of twenty. The Beatles and other pop musicians bleated from plastic transistor radios; young people were suddenly wised-up. Even in the country you could feel the changes these lads from Liverpool had brought.

Maeve was staying on the remote western moors of County Durham, a guest of her uncle's family at Grysewood Farm. She no longer wore Clark's sandals, but neat heels that weren't much use in the country, or fashion boots with chain-store lookalikes of Mary Quant clothes.

Two or three Faber poetry books from Kendal library lay in her suitcase, open by the bed; her schoolfriend had told her she was 'square.' She'd left her *Caedmon* label poetry records at home, two of Dylan Thomas and one of Wordsworth.

Caedmon was a poet from Whitby, long ago. No one knew what he had written, but he was a poet.

Moonlight fell on the pillowcases and carpets, bounced off mirrors and patterned rectangles of windowpane gently round the walls. She went to the window. She wondered who else in the house was looking out. Her aunt and uncle would be used to moonlight. She couldn't imagine Eric would be immune. He would surely be awed by it.

She buttoned a cardigan over her nightclothes. The light was so strong it showed colours; she could write if not read by it. The moon could be 'as bright as day' after all. What boys and girls, whose children were they, in what unreal world were children the moon's playfellows?

Faint, muffled, irregular wingbeats echoed across the sky. A small detachment of geese passed over the house, east to west, bearing the magic, urgent language of their voices. They would fly far over to the Solway estuary, perhaps to Morecambe Bay. The moonlight shone as far as the geese could travel. Glittering the surface of lakes and tarns, lochs and lochans, far into Scotland, the moonlight shone.

Night creatures, fox and hare and hedgehog, kept by instinct to the shadows. Grey and white pebbles, late red and pink roses, tree leaves on their moonlit side, glowed round the green. No pop music, no shipping forecast crackling from radios, no youthful fashions on a city street.

Beyond the farmhouse the country stretched away like a folded sea, hedges breakwaters thrust into pale white stillness. A tree-trunk lay over to the right, a barge in a pool, an ark on an ocean. She saw a snowscape, the tree-trunk was, oh, a dying giant, in the imaginary chill of snow. She turned the giant in her mind back into the tree-trunk, awaiting the farmer with his saw.

As she watched, a figure moved along the hedges and over the grass. Her cousin. Eric knew this farm-ground blade for blade. Yet he was abandoning it for the city. He would make his life among the pavements and buildings. He had boasted thus to her.

She stayed where she was. He might see her.

Footsteps sounded in the corridor; a knock on her bedroom door. The house was full of family, so she was unafraid. She opened it.

There stood Eric.

The corridor light was paler than the moonlight that streamed through every window.

'Was that you outside?'

'Magnificent, isn't it!' said Eric.

Eric had his pyjamas on under his coat. Maeve instinctively tugged her cardigan closer.

'Will you write a poem about it, Eric?'

Eric seemed to hesitate. 'The Muse is out there.'

Divided as she felt from him by a gulf of teenage years and gender, her inevitable girlishness, she was aware of the huge thing they had in common that was poetry.

They'd been pals when younger. She could clearly see them, in their early teens, sitting on a haybale outdoors, here at Grysewood, reading Robert Burns' *Tam O'Shanter*. Eric knew the Scottish words (Scots words, he called them). They laughed together at the mare losing her tail, at sour old Kate at her fireside. Maeve thought the best poems told stories. Eric had said *Not necessarily*. As always, he was confident he was right.

As they stood in the old farmhouse corridor, with its thick wooden doors that separated people, its wainscots, its thin strips of carpet, he seemed to revert to the haughty older cousin, the one she could never emulate, already almost a poet, already conversant with others who called themselves poets, urbane and familiar with city ways.

Above the farmhouse, the moon slid under a thin cloud.

'So romantic! You must come up to Newcastle soon, and meet some of my poetry friends.'

Maeve smarted at the tone. Why had he come in to talk to her? To pretend he was better than her, a more suitable poet who was not concerned with the 'poetic?' Wasn't poetry about the White Goddess? – but a bird in the hand... her Eric.

'I'd love to. When?'

'Why don't you come up in October and I'll introduce you to some real poets?'

'And who would they be?' Maeve asked doubtfully.

Eric pulled himself to his full height in his damp pyjamas. 'Hugh MacDiarmid.'

'Hugh?'

'MacDiarmid, the Scottish poet.'

'Fab. October.'

A door opened further down the corridor.

'Your Mum!' she whispered, and shut her door.

She slept, and the dark geese sang in her dreams.

Dark geese, far flung, hear our voice –
douce the goose or harsh the gander
we will come, beware, rejoice!

Dark geese, far flung, hear our voice,
love us when we cackle thrice
as round the wetlands we meander,
dark geese, far flung. Hear our voice,
and never flee the sands we wander.

The invitation to Newcastle, made in moonbeams, was formalised when Maeve returned with her family to Kendal. Maeve's mother said Maeve was too young to stay in her cousin's student flat. She saw her daughter, correctly, as a well brought up and innocent young girl, whose natural progression should be to go to a nice university where she would take a nice, difficult course until she got sick of it and married a nice, well brought up young man. But Eric's father came to the rescue in a telephone call. The young men his son knew at university (*Durham* university) were perfectly suitable company for an innocent, well brought up girl.

Maeve had heard that King's College had become the brand new University of Newcastle.

She kept quiet, and the trip was on.

She climbed out of the steam train at Central Station, with her light travel bag, including notebooks, and came into the bustle of city streets, the racket of Tyneside: pigeons, whining trolleybuses and banter.

Crowds jostled. She pushed along narrow pavements, trying not to fall into the roadway where buses, vans, cars and occasional horses and carts edged forward in cheerful disarray. In the entrance to the covered market, flower sellers stood beside buckets of sweet-scented flowers. She bought some freesias.

At Grey's Monument she stopped to gain her bearings, first looking into the windows of Mawson, Swan and Morgan, the smart shop for requisites of big houses, from fire-irons to wonderful framed works by northern artists. Next along was the Theatre Royal, like all the other buildings a homely smoky black – the coaly Tyne. The Theatre didn't have big shop windows: she noticed the soot.

She moved on up the wider, populous Northumberland Street, past Fenwick's to the Haymarket.

She caught sight of herself reflected in plate-glass windows, an eager young woman of good average height, country-fresh in her new trouser suit, dark brown shoulder length hair swinging free in the breeze, curiosity brightening her wide-set eyes. She envied the young city women in their town clothes who moved coolly by.

She was to meet her cousin by the Angel at the Haymarket. She assumed the Angel was a pub – she associated poets such as Dylan Thomas with pubs. But soon she saw the ungainly bronze statue of an angel, between the bus station and the church.

Eric was chatting to a tall, thin student in an enormous duffel coat. He introduced her to the student – *My cousin Maeve.*

It didn't take long to walk down behind St Mary's Church to their flat, the ground floor of a house off Sandyford Road. A yard or two of land lay in front of the houses, low flowering bushes shared at their boundaries, low walls, here and there a hedge or bench.

'It's nice,' said Maeve, looking round at the street.

The student, Johnno, took off his duffel coat. 'Ain't bad. That way's Jesmond. Eric'll 'ave to show you round.'

'She can get on a trolleybus.'

Maeve couldn't believe Eric had said that. She pretended not to hear.

Johnno fetched mugs of tea. He made toast with a toasting fork in front of a small gas fire. A divan shared the room with guitars, a record player, and music speakers. Maeve wondered what the sleeping arrangements would be.

Eric turned to her as though reading her mind. 'This is

Johnno's room, but tonight I'm moving in here too. You can have my study. Later we'll go to the poetry society. You can dress up if you like.'

She was dressed up already, but she let it pass.

Eric's room was small and cosy, lined with history books. She spotted a shelf of poetry, and more along the window-sill. She lay down on the bed, reached over to the window-sill and pulled out a small grey paperback, *Beat Poets*. She dipped into the crumpled pages. The poems were gripping and exotic, with their new ways of saying things, all the way from America.

Eric had a Poetry International poster on his wall. Po-ets' names were strung together in lower case blue and green letters: *holub popa bly*. Earlier this summer he had gone down to London to mingle with these exotic guys, and Ginsberg, Michael Horowitz, everyone. He'd had a whale of a time, but he hadn't invited Maeve. She was too young to look after herself in London, which was a kind of travel-ling abroad. It was terrible being too young for things. But Newcastle, with Eric, was 'paradise enow.'

She shut her eyes, gathering strength for the excursion that Eric had promised.

Chapter Two

AMONG THE POETS   (1965)

IN THE DARK AND ECHOING Students Union, Maeve was signed in as her cousin's guest. She gazed around, entranced by this contorted fairyland. She'd never cope here alone. Young people rushed by or lounged about. Some wore jeans, long scarves, corduroys, casual shirts, others had smartened up with suits or rock fashions for the evening. Even the young men who didn't have moptops wore their hair longer than before. The few girl students had skimpy dresses, hems above the knee, loose hair like hers, occasional beehives. The building throbbed with life.

Eric pulled her aside as two heavy, noisy men came down the wide staircase, chatting as though they were alone. 'It was your idea.' 'I copped it from Eliot too.'

A third man pushed past and greeted the duo.

'Good evening, Chris! Basil! Round here!' He led the way back up the stairway and they all followed to the door of an oak panelled room.

'Are they the visiting poets?'

'Obviously.'

'But neither of them is Hugh MacDiarmid. They were called Basil, was it, and Chris!'

Eric sighed. 'My dear girl, Chris *is* MacDiarmid. Come on in.'

Twenty or thirty students were gathered in the room, nearly all young men, with a few lecturers or arty types. Eric nodded to a friend at the window.

'Tony! Big turnout!'

'Oh man, everybody's here. There's Jon Silkin.'

Maeve had heard of Silkin. Dark-haired, in a sheepskin coat, he stood authoritatively at the back with a group of students round him. Others gossiped at the door, expectant and alert. Had they all been to poetry readings before? Was she the only first-timer? She was grateful to Eric – she needed to be part of this.

Across at the front, the visiting poets sat chortling at their private jokes. The compere, who had greeted the poets on the stairs, put a bottle of whisky and some Students Union glasses on the table. The audience settled in curved rows of chairs and fell silent. Maeve was squashed between Eric and Tony on the window-seat, Eric's shoulder and thigh pushed cosily against hers in the limited space.

'Welcome to Hugh MacDiarmid from Scotland. And the distinguished Basil Bunting, discovered in Throckley descanting on the tenor tune of a braying bull.'

An old man, perhaps a professor, sitting near the front, took his pipe out of his mouth and said, '*Briggflatts*.'

'These well-acquainted poets –'

'Recently acquainted,' corrected Basil. 'A re-mingling of the currents of rivers that had gone their separate ways.'

MacDiarmid snorted in amusement. 'You make out your bull is at Briggflatts.'

'Of course it's at Briggflatts.'

'Your ravings on paper. Your visions –'

'Words in my mind, transferable to paper. Music notation.'

'Order, order,' called someone from the back.

Basil wasn't stopping now. 'A few lines a day! Two note-books! 2,000 lines reduced to 700. I'm *not* selling them to Austin Texas.'

Maeve saw a green sloping field, a bull across a beck. Who was Austin Texas? MacDiarmid looked ready to explode.

The compere stood to regain control. 'We'll pour out the article and Basil can begin.' He sloshed whisky into the glasses while everyone looked on.

Basil calmed down and started to read. He read musically; sound was clearly important to him. He said these were older poems: his new poem was nearly ready.

After fifteen minutes MacDiarmid started clapping.

'I'm still reading,' protested Basil.

'That one's good. You should read the whole ode again.'

'It's just Pound cake.' Basil was referring to his former associate Ezra Pound. Maeve had read some of the Cantos. She giggled. Eric frowned. Bunting looked across at her pointedly, and read the page again, making it even more deliberate and musical.

A burst of applause came from the audience, along with murmurs from Jon Silkin's acolytes at the back. Maeve was glad Basil had read the poem twice.

Hugh MacDiarmid was fidgeting. His turn.

'I will recite,' he barked, 'from my *First Hymn to Lenin*. Then we should have time to consider the *Drunk Man*, who looks at Scotland' – he glared round the room – 'the Thistle, the great country of the north, which resounds to our music' – and he was off, in a language that became more and more another as he continued. Maeve was at a loss, though glancing round, Eric and the others were following fine, like those at a church service who had hymn books when you hadn't one yourself.

The forty minutes came to an end, and the leading lights partook of more whisky. Jon Silkin went over to talk to them. Students slunk out to the bar. Maeve listened to their reactions, still too excited to say a thing.

'What did ye think of that?'

'MacDiarmid's definitely got something.'

'I liked Basil Bunting. He stuck to his subject.'

'He's going to be down at the Tower.'

'MacDiarmid, it's all about Scotland isn't it? Must go there some time.'

It made no difference that Maeve hadn't understood MacDiarmid's poems. What was the Tower? Despite puzzles, her first poetry reading was way up to expectations. Her heart was pounding (she could make another joke like Pound cake).

A stranger came up to them. 'Aren't you Eric Grysewood?'

Maeve understood this would be flattering to Eric.

'We liked your poem in *Stand*. See my friend over there with Jon Silkin? He wants poems for his magazine at Leeds.'

The newcomer, an assured young man with particularly long hair, dragged Eric off, deliberately separating him from Maeve. The students argued on. She tried to join in. They looked surprised. It seemed to matter that they didn't know who she was. She hoped her trouser suit didn't seem 'fast.' A few girls, wearing short, simple dresses, clung to their boyfriends. One had seams in her nylons. Could these girls be poets – did they *want* to be poets?

She was no further forward when Eric returned to her side, his new acquaintance still in tow. She smiled at Eric, welcoming him back. Such a fab weekend!

But Eric's life was progressing without her. 'Come down to Leeds with me,' said the young man to Eric. 'I'll be off in an hour, just a dash. Back tomorrow night.'

'Can I bring my cousin?'

'No.'

'Then I'd better not.'

'What? It's your chance. Those poems in your briefcase, that's all you'll want. Nowt else! No room for a girl.'

She couldn't hide her dismay as Eric pled with her. 'Maeve, I'll be back tomorrow. Johnno can look after you.' The floor seemed to sway.

His companion stood quietly waiting for Eric to go to Leeds.

She thought quickly. 'I wanted to look round the library.'

Eric pulled out a card from his wallet. 'Here's my library ticket. Be my guest.' He rummaged further. 'The house key. You see I can trust you with it! It's the only one I have. You'll need to be in when I come back at tea-time.'

Eric turned to his new pal. They immediately left the room.

'He didn't even tell me who that was!'

She had spoken aloud, and the evening's compere replied, 'Did you come with Eric Grysewood? Eric always puts his poetry chances first. To be blunt, there are more biddable young men around... Don't you know any of the other students?'

'I'm not a girlfriend, I'm his cousin.' Maeve sounded petulant. 'I came because I write poetry. This was my first poetry reading.'

'Did you enjoy it?' He was a small, dark haired man with an air of confidence, as well he might have after handling the poets. She relaxed.

'Very much. I liked Basil Bunting. I didn't understand all of Mr MacDiarmid's work.'

'Hmm. Are you all right? Have you somewhere to go?'

'Eric's given me the key of his flat. It isn't far away, but I wanted to move on and hear the poets discussing their work in a pub, as Eric said usually happens.'

'You can still come to the pub. Hang around and follow me.'

'Are you sure?'

'I wouldn't have said it if I wasn't sure. Are you still at school?'

Most of the students had melted away. Only the poets, along with Jon Silkin and several young men, the event organiser and Maeve, were left.

'Where are we going?' Silkin asked MacDiarmid.

'The usual. I'm meeting Peter Ustinov there.'

Maeve didn't even care that she was the only woman as they trooped down College Lane towards Percy Street. She had got what she wanted despite Eric's desertion. She would show him!

They pushed two tables together, in the tiny, dark-cornered, sparkling place, bottles and glasses glinting. Peter Ustinov was sitting in a corner. Maeve hadn't seen anyone 'famous' in the flesh before, but Ustinov had his own party of listeners. After MacDiarmid had greeted him, the poets got down to poetry gossip and everyone except their group faded into insignificance.

Maeve was provided with two half shandies – she was glad she'd known a suitable drink to ask for. The second arrived before she had finished the first. The group's animation was fuelled, silver poets' tongues loosened by convivial drinking. Her shandy mainly contained lemonade, although it looked like proper booze.

She couldn't say much yet, but she listened, genuinely interested in the questions of northern context that were raised. She was almost one of the poets!

They sat and sat, and talked and talked. Most of them drank far more than Maeve's two shandies. Finally Jon Silkin said he was going back to Jesmond. His friends went with him. Maeve looked up and saw Basil regarding her with what she hoped wasn't too much amusement.

'Maeve, that's your name isn't it? Did that student poet desert you?'

'He's my cousin. I'm staying with him, but he's gone off and left me without supper.'

'You must eat with us,' Basil offered immediately.

Chris glanced up. 'Yes, we are due to eat. The University is treating us.'

'Can we include this young lady?' asked Basil of the organiser, the college lecturer who had taken care of Maeve so far.

Maeve was disconcerted. She had felt part of them during the discussion. But they didn't know her and she had no idea how things stood. She hastily backtracked. 'I can get chips.'

'Nonsense,' said the lecturer. 'I'll add you in, no bother. My cheque will be reimbursed by the English Department.'

'We might have brought ladies with us,' added Basil.

'Don't worry about it,' Chris told Maeve when he had stopped laughing. 'When food is needed, it is needed for all the company.' The lecturer smiled at her, and Maeve was reassured.

From outside, Jim's Inn looked shabby, but once inside they were in a lush world of warmth, good food aromas, and a small team of waiters and manager. They were seated at one of two refectory tables. Three diners were finishing their meals at the other table.

Maeve was placed beside Basil and opposite Chris. Everything seemed large – poets, heavy cutlery and napkins, carafes of red wine on the polished board. She glanced warily at the host. MacDiarmid undid the buttons of his jacket and then of his waistcoat. She put her hand nervously up to her neckline.

'Make your choices, gentlemen.' The manager indicated typewritten sheets tucked into folded cards. He didn't say *Ladies and gentlemen*. He could hardly say *Lady and gentlemen*.

Chris and Basil were busy ordering steaks. The cheapest thing was seafood medley, but she didn't want seafood. The host ordered a half duck and vegetables. She followed suit. Basil leaned over and filled her wine glass to the brim. As they relaxed with their excellent platefuls, they began to talk of poetry again. She'd had nothing but a piece of toast since breakfast. She wondered about the duck and where it had been swimming. It tasted delicious.

The wine level went down in the carafes. More was supplied, along with dishes of vegetables. Maeve drank her wine very slowly. Basil was discussing a place called Briggflatts. 'I took Sima there. She's used to the northern wilds.'

'Tom Pickard told me to go there,' said the host, 'but I still haven't been.'

She'd heard Eric mention Tom Pickard. It all seemed so cliquey. She should earn her meal by contributing talk, but it wasn't easy. She didn't want to say anything stupid. The poets could be her grandfathers by age. The scholar, though younger, looked as if he was married. Unfussed, sensibly-dressed, he kept a benign eye on her, as he had first done when Eric abandoned her. Licking her ice-cream spoon, she caught a quick, scary glance from MacDiarmid as he finished his cheese.

She suddenly saw she might have been invited for decoration, for the flirt value. This shocked her so deeply that she launched into conversation.

'I write poetry too!'

MacDiarmid's face broke into a grin. 'What did you think of my poems, then?'

'What language are they in?'

She knew she shouldn't have said that, but the poet had irritated her.

She felt a *frisson* from the others.

'I write in Scots!' His face became animated, under his extraordinary hair that shot up from his forehead for all of three inches then fell away backwards in a tangle. He was still speaking English. He was in England after all.

She turned her attention to the less intimidating Basil.

'Seriously, I write poems. I have a long way to go but – you have to start...'

'Quite right, my lovely,' said Basil.

'It's been so exciting hearing the poetry tonight, real northern poetry!'

'Have you copies of poems you have written?' Basil leaned closer to her. 'You are right to note that it is northern poetry. We speak for our people, on their behalf. I believe you when you say poems excite you. Where are your poems?'

Maeve paused. This sounded like luck, but was it? She had no poems on her person. She didn't have big pockets in her clothes like the men. My poems are in the room where I'm staying tonight. I must go home. I'm beyond tired.'

Chris was contemplating his whisky glass and had lapsed into silence.

'What a loss not to spend the evening with you looking at your poetry!'

Their host gave a sharp glance towards Basil and herself, and for a moment she was checked, held the younger man's stare. But she went for it. 'That would have been good,' she told Basil.

'I have a suggestion. Join me tomorrow afternoon in a friendly place and I'll consider your poems with you.'

'I have to get a train home tomorrow.'

'Basil, you've exhausted yourself. You have done too much this year.'

Basil ignored MacDiarmid. Home, did you say Ambleside? Come to the bar in the station buildings at lunch time. Tomorrow. I'll be there from one o'clock. I will give you some attention' – he turned to her again – 'which I believe you deserve, my dear.'

Maeve faintly suspected that this was too good to be true. 'I'd like that. Are you sure?'

'Certain. We will be refreshed by afternoon. I will await you, and we'll look at your poems and consider their timbre. *The Station Bar*. As soon as you like after one.'

The poets were on the malt. The academic had black tea with a slice of lemon. It smelt good.

Chris seemed to wake from a reverie. 'Basil, I've read your new poem, the part that you gave me. It's the best thing you've done. It will make you more famous than the output of your classical wanderings.'

'I thank you.' Basil looked gratified.

'Your beautiful unknown hideout will be your redemption. You'll be remembered there. You'll make the place famous. Poets will take the narrow roads to your door.'

'Maeve, you shall take the road to my door,' Basil repeated, beginning to sound half-cut.

Maeve said she would have to leave, she'd have to break up the party. She rose to her feet. Basil tried to give her a kiss on the cheek.

'A bientot! Domani! Tomorrow, Miss Maeve!'

'Thank you.' Maeve had no wish to seem star-struck. To her seventeen years Basil was an old man. This was about her poems. She half-hoped one of them might insist on accompanying her, but they let her go. She had assured them her cousin's flat was 'just around the corner.'

It was different in the dark. She threaded her way through lamplit streets among neat terraced houses, through the urban half-light, a dim and livid sky across the city. Down here. That street. Or was it the next?

She was a long way past it before she was certain she had missed the street. She passed an open door where a woman stood smoking in a nightdress. She thought that a little odd, then she saw a second open door, a second woman. She shivered. She shouldn't be down here. Her Mum would think of Eric beside her, protecting her, if she was out this time of night.

The man walking towards her was a policeman.

'You're out very late, miss. Are you going home?'

Embarrassed and relieved, Maeve told him the street name. 'I think I've come too far.'

'Yes you have. It's back there, past that church. Is that where you live?'

'I'm staying there tonight.'

'Well hurry along.'

She turned and hastened back. She knew why the two women were standing in their doorways. One door clicked shut as she passed it.

Eric's flat was quiet. No sign of Johnno. But she was safe. She dashed into the bathroom, drank a glass of water to offset the red wine, and fell into Eric's empty bed.

She subsided into sleep, unaware of a faint feathery pattering on the windows.

Light came from the window but it wasn't normal light. She sat up, reached for the curtain, pulled it back, and started in wonder. A full-scale blizzard was sending folded snow-flakes downwards, pages from a million tiny notebooks.

Across the ground was a deep carpet of snow, so deep you couldn't see where the pavements stepped down to the road. Traffic was completely grounded and if your boots didn't come up to your knees, snow would get into them. Astonishing – this wasn't December or February, but October!

Her head cleared. The long and different day that was yesterday flooded back with the light.

Eric had gone to Leeds. What a cheek. Perhaps he knew she wouldn't tell her parents. She tried to imagine him in Leeds, and failed – she'd never been there. She'd had a successful evening without him. She'd wind him up, if he was home in time, about her dinner with the poets. Something told her he'd have given quite a lot for that experience himself.

An eerie muffled silence accompanied the scene. No cart, van or human was moving. The few cars parked beside houses were hooded in snow. She wasn't used to being alone. She wanted to shout. She dressed, stepped into Eric's loose-fitting slippers, and went out into the passage.

Not liking to disturb the other student, she made her way to the scullery and kitchen. A kettle stood invitingly on the cooker. She lifted it, sloshed it around, lit the gas underneath. A mug upside-down on the draining board. She made Nescafe and a wee plate of Ryvita and marmalade. A cheap tinplate clock had wound right down: it wasn't ticking.

In Eric's room, she pulled back the curtains as far as she could. She found a match in the Bluebell box on the floor, reached over and lit the fire. It went *whoomph*, and the greenish flames were soon heating the firebricks. Her cuppa beside her, she started to write her vision of the snow. She loved a chance to write alone, but the more she thought about Eric's absence, the more it annoyed her. She moved on from the snow scene, intending to jot down notes on her evening for later.

She'd forgotten the furled paper packet of flowers in her bag. She went back to the kitchen, found a jam jar, half filled it with water, and set the freesias on the windowsill.

> *I leave the freesias here to die*
> *till warm above these snowy ledges*
> *a winter room-mate wonders why*
> *I leave the freesias here to die*
> *where lost and saddened poets cry,*
> *ever disturbed by hopeful pledges,*
> *I leave the freesias here to die*

– she was stuck with the last line

> *where giants' corpses leer from hedges.*

A telephone rang in the passage.

As she pulled back Eric's door, the living room door opened and the other student, Johnno, rushed out, stark naked. His chest was covered with a star-shaped pattern of thick black hair – she'd never seen anything like it – and the star pointed down to where she wasn't supposed to look. He'd probably forgotten she was there, but still she was horrified and shot back into her room. She'd thought 'hair on your chest' was a figure of speech.

She hadn't stopped shaking when a knock came on the door and Johnno's voice called, 'It's for you, it's a woman.'

This flummoxed her even more.

She went to the phone, trying not to look straight ahead as Johnno's rather neat bum disappeared back into his room.

'Mother, I'm fine. So's everyone. The blizzard was over-night.'

'You sound a bit taken aback?'

'I've not been awake long. I'm fine and the poets were good.'

'That wasn't Eric. Was it his flatmate? What's he like?'

Maeve wasn't saying. She might be shaking, but she wasn't drooling.

'Is there snow in Kendal?'

'None. Your forms for Oxford have arrived.'

'Who sent for them?'

'The school, I think.'

'Hmm.'

Her mother persisted. 'Are you coming back tomorrow?'

'I'll do my best. Have to go, Mum.' She put the phone down. She suspected her mother of sending for the forms.

She wanted to leave school and stay put, here in the north.

Johnno was from Essex. He had come here to college. People could move the other way. It struck her that *north* could be rhymed with *south*. The vowels sounded different, not alien. The words were parallel. They responded. Eric had told her *paradise* rhymed with *lost*. He'd got that from a poet in the south, called Sebastian. In Eric's study, the valiant little gas fire, the ragged comfortable chair, the blank paper on the bed, her lines about the whiteout beyond the window, all were comforting.

She finished dressing, as warmly as she could.

Johnno tapped cautiously on the door and opened it, fully dressed.

'Do you know when Eric will be back?' they asked one another simultaneously.

'The snow won't help.'

'Snow?' Johnno came further into the room and surveyed the scene from the window.

'Struth!' His face fell. 'I was supposed to play football.'

'Eric's gone to Leeds. Didn't he get in touch with you?'

'No?'

'He was going to share your room.'

'Oh yes, I forgot. Well, make yourself at home. I'll get breakfast.'

'I've had some, thanks.'

Johnno made off for the kitchen. She wrote a few more words. Outside, a small boy and girl, wrapped in coats, boots, and woollen hats, rushed excitedly around. A few adults struggled off towards offices or shops. Someone had a television blaring. Cheery shouts rang around the street.

She cleared up after Johnno in the kitchen – not badly organised for two men. She couldn't see much food. A couple of eggs, Ryvita, a small tin of sweetened condensed milk, tea, coffee and half a drum of milk powder for drinks. A paper sack of potatoes, dry earth clinging to them.

Johnno couldn't be expected to look after her. There was no point attempting any sightseeing. Meeting Basil gave her something to do, before a train back to Kendal. She didn't feel like staying to confront her cousin.

Footwear was going to be a problem. There'd been no forewarning of snow. Her 'court shoes' had low heels that didn't make her look too tall. They'd be hopeless out there. It was her turn to knock on Johnno's door.

Johnno was a normal clothed person again, unembarrassed. 'Come in. Eric's room's poky. I'm thinking of going down to the football club, though the games will be cancelled. You can use my record player and records – there they are.'

She guessed this was a handsome concession. 'I planned to go out, but I've no boots.' There'd be no point asking if he had any she could borrow. She'd noticed his massive feet.

But he said, 'Boots? Hang on, my last but one girlfriend stayed here for a while.' He dived into a gloryhole under the window seat. Triumphant, he pulled out a red plastic boot with a kind of bow at the side, and then its partner. She put them on and walked round the room.

'Excellent. Thank you.'

'Where are you off to then?'

'The station.'

'If you're going home you won't be able to bring those boots back.'

'Not for ages. Is that a problem?'

Johnno hesitated. 'She shouldn't have left them here. She'll have forgotten them. Just take them.'

'Okay, I will, because I need them. They're horrible anyway!'

Johnno laughed.

'How about coming to the college with me? I know somewhere you'd like. Where I met Eric.'

'Oh?'

'His archaeology friends needed a technical genius like me to set up their Museum of Antiquities. Let's go and see it.'

'I'm not wildly keen,' she admitted, 'but Eric mentioned a reconstructed Mithraeum. Any idea where it is?'

'It's there. We call it our 'piece of resistance!'

'Brilliant. I'll come.'

The tiny museum was hidden behind the university gatehouse. Johnno produced a key, and they let themselves in. A case in the lobby held Roman finds: mended red pottery, a brooch, a buckle, rough glass. Johnno was apologetic. 'Nothin' much, but don't tell Eric I said that.' She peered at what Johnno called the 'real Latin' chipped into stone tablets standing against the walls. She couldn't follow the abbreviated Latin. 'Dunno,' said Johnno easily. Eric would have known.

Johnno showed her through a door to the darkened cave of the Mithraeum. Benches and a low wicker fence surrounded a central space. Branches projected from walls. An eerie outdoor enclosure, a walled garden? Johnno grinned.

'A Roman religious service. Wait for it!'

They sat down together at the back. Johnno pressed a switch for the recorded ritual, lights flashing through stone apertures. Music of a sort. Ghostly light played across the tableau. Animals appeared and disappeared, before Mithras the god brought the light back.

They were primitive models, a goat, a cow, a cat (perhaps a lion) and others. A large goose took her by surprise, as it loomed in the flickering light. The spectacle was frightening, and when it was over she asked Johnno to put the light on and show her how it worked. She remained shaken by the goose and its companions, illuminating old, forgotten beliefs. For all that, Maeve was impressed by the Mithraeum. 'Thank you for bringing me here, Johnno.'

'Now how about the football club? You don't need to see them poets again. Come and have a buffet lunch with the footballers. That'll be fun for you!'

This Johnno was a determined fellow, considerate too. She surrendered Eric's house key, and handed him Eric's library ticket. Johnno seemed surprised. He pulled a bar of Fry's Chocolate Cream from his coat, and broke off half for Maeve. She accepted it, laughing.

'See you again some time!' Was she really saying that to Mr Bare-Bum?

She made her way out through the snow to the Haymarket and jumped on a trolleybus to the station. The main roads were coming to life with snowploughs and tractors. Her appointment with Basil Bunting was imminent. She'd have him to herself and he'd talk about her poems in his knowledgeable manner, his musical voice. Eric had discussed his poems with Jon Silkin in Darlington Library. She was catching up with her cousin.

The station wasn't busy but the bar had life in it. She walked in, determined rather than apprehensive, already pulling the envelope of poems out of the top of her bag. Spare seats. A tatty Beatles poster. Older women, waiting for trains.

She bought a pineapple juice and crisps. The barman put them on a tray. There wasn't any change from her half-crown.

She chose a long seat in a nook of the wall. She put the tray on a table and her bag on the seat for Basil. He'd be along any minute.

A poem was coming, about Mithras the sun god. Mithras could fly. She wrote in her notebook, not flamboyantly but secretively. The thin little lady next to her looked over towards her writing, seeming curious, and Maeve hid her page, as she would in a school exam.

'Writing a poem, dearie? Is it for your boyfriend? I bet you've got a boyfriend!'

The lady would guess it was a fib, but what could Maeve say? 'It's a shopping list.'

'Nice red boots,' said the lady.

Maeve looked round. She couldn't see any other red boots. They were the colour of cooked damsons. She smiled weakly. Basil would not remark on her boots. Not that Basil would ever count as a boyfriend. Boyfriends were between sixteen and twenty and not interested in poetry. She hoped the lady would go for her train before Basil arrived. The clock above the bar was so big she could see the minute hand shaking as it moved.

Geordies came and went, in work-clothes or outing-clothes, on their way home from shops or shifts. She finished her pineapple juice and she needed a pee. The loo door had a penny slot machine. It wasn't a place you'd loiter. She hurried back to reclaim her seat. At another table, two old guys spread out a box of dominoes which started to click quietly and went on clicking.

She put away her writing. The prying woman went, and others came, with narrow shopping bags, their spoils sparse, some with an evening paper sticking out. Evening papers were sold from mid-afternoon. Later came teenage boys. The barman refused to serve them beer, but they sat round a table and offered her crisps from their packets. She took some. 'Thanks.' The boys giggled.

She knew by now she had boobed. It couldn't be that lovely poet's fault! And going out to catch the final, five-thirty train, she made an appalling discovery: there wasn't a five-thirty train – that was the weekday timetable. The next train was eight o'clock in the morning.

Crestfallen, she went back to the little bar to decide what to do. This time the barman looked at her suspiciously. The domino players had packed up. The bar was smokier and rougher. She pretended to check for her luggage, and departed.

Basil had clean forgotten. She wasn't important enough. His promise was poetic nonsense.

Or perhaps it was the snow... it could have been the snow.

Her feet felt pinched after their day in Johnno's girlfriend's boots. The streets were relatively quiet; people looked tired; shops were closing and pubs were opening. *'When chapman billies leave the street'* – that moment of the start of Burns' poem. Eric had told her about men selling ballads in little leaflets called chapbooks.

Bloody Eric, he had gone to Leeds.

Johnno answered the doorbell at Sandyford. 'You again! I'm getting ready for a gig. Would you like to come along?'

She was flattered. She had already refused his invitation to the football club, all those hours ago this morning. She hoped he wouldn't mind, but she was tired.

'I ain't surprised you're tired. Sleep in my room if you want, or you can take a chance his lordship doesn't come back, and sleep there again.' Johnno grabbed his duffel coat, and headed off, carrying a guitar.

Left alone, she took cheese and Ryvita from the kitchen and ate them in Eric's room.

She worked a little on the poem about the Mithraeum but she couldn't think it through. Too much had been going on. Animals, darkness. Her descriptions were meaningless. They might crystallise later.

She screwed up the paper and tossed it away. What if Eric picked it up from the floor, flattened it out and read it? Wrote a poem about it better than she could? He'd helped construct the Mithraeum, had studied it – perhaps there was a book here discussing it. Her reaction was paper-thin. One word thick. Eric could throw it away.

But she picked it up again. Lines about a frightened goose. Or a goose that could never be frightened, while it claimed the air.

> *Fashioned fatted goose, of geese unrealistic,*
> *doth not thy stone goose lookalike threaten*
> *flying feathers working wings of air?*

She copied her sentence carefully into the back of her notebook, feeling a fluttering hope that this might become the first contribution, not the first line, to a poem she would one day write. Which poets used *'doth'* like that? Pound? Again she tossed the paper ball away.

Before ten she was drowsy. Neither Eric nor Johnno had returned. Her freesias, not left to die, wafted their scent.

The geese were singing:

> *Frozen north I come from north*
> *I am the north I am not leaving.*

But geese couldn't make north rhyme with south. She'd have to take responsibility for what they sang. She crept gratefully into Eric's bed and went to sleep.

At half past one, Eric, Joe and a Scotsman arrived back from Leeds. They barged through the hallway to the kitchen, accosting Johnno with noisy cheer. One of them, Joe, came crashing into the bedroom and sat on the bed.

'Excuse me, this is Eric's room and I'm his guest!' Maeve complained, woken suddenly. She sat up, putting a hand to her hair.

'Arrgh, help!' shouted Joe. 'There's a woman in the bed!'

This brought Eric running.

'Good Lord, Maeve, haven't you gone home yet?'

Maeve could do temper, especially when disturbed in the night.

'Eric Grysewood,' she cried, 'you invite me for a week-end then go off to another city without me. What do you expect me to do?' She felt empowered by the gold silk shift-dress she'd cadged from her mother, feather-light, tossed in her bag. She was a fierce, sparkling little sun.

'Cool it, kid. We've been stuck in a snowdrift near Durham for hours, or we'd have been back sooner to sort this out,' responded Eric. 'Now we need the room. There are three of us!'

'More fool you.' She snuggled down, sun under blanket cloud.

She wouldn't budge.

Johnno appeared, wearing dark pyjamas and a jacket.

'Come on lass, you can sleep in my room. The other three need to sleep somewhere.'

'But I can't share a bed with you!' The image of Johnno's hairy body came back to her.

More muttering in the hallway. 'Just a case of putting up a few friends, why is everyone making such a fuss?' She wasn't going to be drawn. Eric was making the fuss. She wasn't afraid of him.

'Johnno, couldn't you sleep in the kitchen?' yelled Eric.

'Fuck you, no!' said Johnno with unexpected spirit. 'Why don't you sleep in the car? I bet the car was good enough for you last night.'

By now Maeve was almost on Johnno's side. She called out, 'All right Johnno, if you split the mattress from the base, I can be in the same room as you.'

'Good,' said Eric.

'Braw,' said the Scotsman.

'Will do,' said Johnno, 'and then you can go back to sleep.'

Richard, the Scot, busied himself making a large pot of tea in the kitchen, and Maeve grudgingly went for a cup, while Johnno reorganised his bedroom. She nabbed Eric's slippers again. The shift wasn't warm. She slung the square-knit coloured rug from the kitchen chair over her shoulders.

Eric beamed at her as though nothing had gone amiss.

'Knew you'd be all right, Maeve. What did you do with your weekend?'

'Nice of you to ask! How did you get on in Leeds?'

It looked, from the way Joe and Eric were sitting leaning against each other, they had done something very secret in Leeds. But Eric said, 'I'm having a book published. Joe here took me to see his boss.'

Maeve was impressed despite herself. 'A book of poems? Who's the publisher?'

'Poets from the North. A poet from York University, and two from Leeds. I'm the fourth.'

'So they haven't published any books yet?'

'Shut up, woman,' said Joe. 'It's an excellent start for Eric here. We need more awareness of northern writers.'

Maeve shut up. Eric would have liked her to gush and compliment him – she'd noticed men were like that. She would have liked him to show her some gratitude, give her a quick kiss perhaps, to thank her for co-operating with the beds.

'You asked me what I did, Eric.'

'Okay, what did you do?'

'After you left the meeting with Joe here, I went to the pub with the poets. I had dinner at Jim's Inn with Hugh MacDiarmid and Basil Bunting. Four of us. I'm a proper member of the poets' club now!'

Eric, Joe and Richard stared at her, speechless.

She pulled Johnno's mattress nearer the door of the room, well away from the bed, and rolled herself in a blanket. It was that or a kitchen chair. Luckily she'd spent part of the day with Johnno and he didn't seem much of a 'wolf.' When she was settled, Johnno made for his cushions on the bed base.

'Straight people in this room, queer people in the other

room,' he commented. Perhaps he guessed she wouldn't understand.

She was sleepily sorting out her views.

'I suppose they're good pals,' she thought aloud. 'They'll want wives and all that afterwards, won't they?'

'When they grow up? Ha ha. They won't never get wives.'

'But –'

'That's why we call them *queer*. Dontcha know about it? Oh no, you're not fond of Eric like that, are you?'

Maeve couldn't reply. Johnno clearly thought her silence encouraging, for after a pause he confided, 'My girlfriend's gone home for the weekend. If you'd like to take advantage of the great opportunity that has come your way, you have only to say. You can still sleep on your own afterwards.'

Amid her confusion over Eric, she felt no annoyance or fear. Johnno had been good to her all day. He'd asked nicely enough, it was a compliment more than anything, and now he'd told her something important. This was so different from the boy under the damson trees, who wasn't expecting *yes*. Johnno hadn't even kissed her, yet she knew he was offering more. This was certainly a day of new things. She called on her reserves.

'Sorry, I don't want to be your next girlfriend but one. Goodnight Johnno. I'm knackered.' He would understand that. It stopped further discussion, and she went to sleep.

The snow was melting. The sky was clear. She walked to the station, again wearing the strange red boots. She was almost fond of them. Her light shoes were in her bag, along with the notebooks, paperback *Beat Poets*, and the newly-bought *Collected Poems of Hugh MacDiarmid*, which Eric hadn't read yet. She'd borrowed it late last night, having forced this gallantry in front of his friends.

She knew why Eric had gone to Leeds. He liked that odd

young man. And he'd put himself first, as the university lecturer had said he would. What with Joe, and the prospect of a book, it was horribly obvious he hadn't needed Maeve. Yet she'd had successes of her own, even though Bunting hadn't turned up to talk about her poems. There was no point starting a squabble with her cousin. He and his friends had been stuck in a snowdrift, had they? Good!

The train headed west out of the station. She was going to visit Kendal Public Library tomorrow to see if they'd give her a job. Her head was held higher than when she'd arrived in Newcastle, it seemed an age ago.

Her life lay before her. It would be *her* life, not her parents', not her mother's. Seventeen was artificially extended childhood. Sending her to Oxford would be another version of sending her to school. In a smart ghetto for children of affluent parents, she'd be trained to be just like the others. Maeve saw no point in being exactly like everyone else. She belonged to the northern landscape. Oxfordshire, gentle countryside, where still rivers wound among willows, was not for her.

She'd have to live with her parents for the time being. Instead of phoning for her father to fetch her from the station, she walked. She greeted her parents, let them de-brief her a little, and ate some soup.

The Oxford forms were on the dresser, but she steadfastly ignored them and the next day went to see about a library job.

There were a few complaints from her Mum. 'Would you prefer Durham University?'

'No, Mum. Dad said he didn't want me to be a bluestocking. No way.'

'But you've always got your nose in a book.'

It wasn't true. 'Give over, Mum.' She pushed the forms further back on the dresser, behind some cups. In a few days, the letter came from the Chief Librarian, and the college forms went in the fire.

Transformed from schoolgirl to library assistant, she trekked back and forth to the county town library, with its shelves of farming and local history, its novels, thrillers, romances and westerns. She met interfering councillors, retired teachers, shopkeepers, readers who knew her from school. This was real life; she was paid; and she loved it.

Her parents would adjust. She imagined a new respect in their faces, as she worked her way in, meeting people, sorting out catalogue cards, handling all manner of books. She found another Kendal, full of old gentlemen writers, such as Roger Fulford the historian from Barbon Fell. Rural journalists and country men and women converged on the library that fronted the long and ancient street.

A town thronged too with youths and men who knew about motorbikes, sheep sales and the local countryside. By hedgerows and field gates, on fellsides or among apple and damson trees, they sometimes tried for a private fumble and kiss. She made friends over this time, but, still hampered by her interest in poetry, she didn't settle for any of them.

She found Gerard Manley Hopkins' poems. She read about shipwrecks, and all kinds of books, about dreams, the history of Kendal. She wrote and rewrote poems, corresponded with Eric, watched and listened and built up her knowledge of poetry and poets. She placed a poem in the *Dalesman*, two in *Outposts*, a batch in the Leeds students' duplicated *Poetry and Audience*. Her parents stopped commenting on the envelopes of poems.

Eric was still her cousin. She loved him. Predictable letters arrived, boasting of successes, describing his literary experiences. Maeve read and commented on many of his poem drafts and kept him *au fait* with what poetry gossip she could glean. She didn't send him her poems. She could show him them when they were together, but he never made quite the right comments for her. She was afraid he might steal from them, not deliberately or systematically, but because he thought his work was more important than hers.

Chapter Three

MIGRATIONS   (1969)

A S THE GEESE FLEW north-west over Newcastle town moor, Maeve walked home from the Central Library. The geese had no fixed places but what was inside their inscrutable heads, necks stretched forward as they navigated the turning northern world.

She sometimes came along the Great North Road, on the streets behind the Civic Centre, or by a longer route from Northumberland Street through the university buildings and Exhibition Park. The library was brand-new, part of the city's revamping. Everything was bigger than in Kendal: more books, more staff, more challenges.

She looked plumper and a little taller. She'd been ready for a move across the fells and wildness to this new and exciting but still northern place.

Eric had gone to live in Scotland.

She popped into a small corner shop for a Ski yoghurt and a loaf of bread. She was renting a room from Johnno. She had become Eric. But Eric's three years' advantage over her still left too great a gap, which should surely be narrowing in their twenties. He loved to help her as long as he could stoop to help.

It made sense for Eric to go north. He had fallen out with Joe, and taken up with the Scotsman Richard. Maeve approved of Richard. Less ambitious than her cousin, happiest reading and writing in his own corner, Richard didn't hanker after recognition, as Eric did, or perfection, as Maeve did.

Eric's job in Scotland was in a quango concerned with archaeology. He was a historian-archaeologist, not a digger, and Maeve could see the historian rather than the digger in his poetry too. It was elegant. It had a perspective of time and place.

Acclimatising to life in Newcastle Maeve came closer to Scotland. Her first weekend in Edinburgh brought surprises. Richard used strange Scottish idioms: *messages* for groceries, a *rammy* for a fight, and *Glesca* for Glasgow. Eric showed her the sights, the National Library, the University and Princes Street.

Eric was a WIGLIE – he Worked In Glasgow, Lived In Edinburgh. He'd discovered Sandy Bell's on his way from Waverley station to Tollcross. They pushed open the door to the small corner pub, packed with guys standing round the bar. *Edinburgh's finest*, Eric whispered as they went in. The room was dark, deep and oak-panelled, in yellow light. A notice board was crammed with folk music notices and adverts. The few tables were filled with people quietly gossiping, some in a language that wasn't English or Scots. 'The Gaelic community; the literary Gaels come in here,' Eric told her.

The level of alertness and creativity, the high culture of the place was as pronounced as the yeasty smell of beer or the warm fug of smoking. A fiddle session was in progress, two or three fiddlers in the murk with their own absorbed listeners. Scottish dance tunes; tunes she'd heard back home.

A young fiddler finished his turn then came to the bar beside Eric. 'A good group that. Hard work.'

'You kept it up for twenty minutes there,' observed Eric.

'That's nothing,' said the fiddler. 'These fellows play weddings in the Western Isles, all day for two days or more, from the middle of the week till Saturday midnight when glass coaches become pumpkins for the Sabbath!'

The fiddler caught the barman's eye and turned to Eric. 'I've had a good day busking – what's yours?'

Eric indicated a twenty-shilling.

'And your lady?'

'My cousin.'

'What will she drink? A half, my dear?'

Maeve nodded, hoping twenty-shilling wasn't too strong. The fiddler went on talking about dances on the Islands; like his fiddling elbow his tongue wouldn't easily stop.

A large man came over with his pint, nodded to the fiddler and addressed Eric. 'You look like someone who could sing.'

'Not where I'm a stranger.'

'Grysewood is one of the poets,' said the fiddler. 'He was talking to Hayden Murphy the other day.'

'For my sins,' muttered Eric. 'I thought Hayden had gone back to Dublin.'

'Tomorrow,' Hayden answered, hearing his name. 'I've collected some Scottish poems for my next *Broadsheet*. Including one from Grysewood here.'

'Are you from England?' the large man asked Eric, with interest.

'I haven't come from outer space. I'm from Durham, and I've met poets from Newcastle, Leeds and Lancashire, as well as London you know.'

'We were discussing mutual acquaintances,' Hayden agreed.

'Ever come across Norman Nicholson?' asked the big man.

Eric remembered Maeve talking of Nicholson. 'Yes, once in Kendal, with my cousin who's a poet too.'

'Your cousin – who's he?'

'She! Maeve Cartier – here with me, visiting.'

Despite the introduction, Maeve felt invisible. The company seemed unaware of the concept of a woman poet. There was a short silence. The fiddler addressed Eric. 'If you've heard that joke about splashing your beer and drowning ten poets, this is the pub it's about.'

'Well, welcome to you both,' said the big man genially. 'Your welcome is assured as a poet, or a musician, or a Scot – preferably all three!'

'You shouldn't be anti-English *per se*,' retorted Eric.

The gentleman replied, 'We're absolutely not – but we do like the English who come here to realise they're here.'

Further beers were ordered. More music began, quieter treble notes from two tin whistle players. Maeve temporarily gave up fighting her invisibility. There was so much to listen to and watch.

Another dark-haired man joined in. 'You're quoting me.'

'Hello Owen,' said the fiddler.

'It's a wonderful country,' said Owen, and turned to his woman companion. 'This young pup has just told Hamish Henderson not to be anti-English.'

'*Per se.*' Hamish chuckled. Picking up his hat from a small ledge, he added, 'We'll forgive anyone who's willing to learn. Now I must make myself scarce and take my own young puppy' – he indicated a heaving mass of tawny fur under a chair – 'home for our suppers. See you again, Mr Wildgoose.'

At least ten people stood staring at them. The men at the Gaelic table could be heard laughing, the word *Wildgoose* standing out from their Gaelic expressions.

'Holy smoke,' said Eric under his breath, 'the guy with the puppy is Hamish Henderson.'

'Is he famous?" asked Maeve.

'Very.'

'What for?'

'Knowing everybody,' said the fiddler.

'Never mind. Your cousin will live it down, though possibly not the name *Wildgoose*.' The voice beside Maeve was Hayden Murphy. At last, someone talking to her.

Eric seemed surprisingly put out by his non-recognition of Hamish Henderson. He led Maeve out of the pub without introducing her to anyone else. She'd lost her chance to speak to the Irish editor who was collecting poems. Why didn't Eric ever treat her as an active poet?

They walked awkwardly down the busy road in silence. But Eric became talkative again in the trattoria near his flat. She could see why he liked this tiny theatre café, its four small tables with checked tablecloths, the proprietor cooking in full sight and the authentic, simple Italian menu. They joshed with the Italian and chose a fresh pasta. They sat down to it with a pot of tea. Then Eric went off to meet Richard, which gave her time for writing and thinking.

Eric had a whole flat, not just the share that had been enough for him in Newcastle. Moving along for her was generous of him. He was good to her as a cousin and the sort of baby poet he seemed to consider her.

Eric didn't like to miss a trick. A couple of years back, they'd come to Edinburgh for two days at the Fringe. They'd trailed round windy streets between outlying venues because Eric knew the poets in the shows.

This visit was an improvement. Eric had found the poets' roosts among the branches of city pubs.

Great or small, published, outsiders or women, all poets needed to sit down and write. She used Eric's desk as well as his bed in the two-night visit. Often she'd think about him. There'd been poetry with jazz this afternoon. The jazz was better than the poetry. The bassoonist had come up and spoken to her, but she was apparently with Eric.

Dom, de dom, de dom de domdom dom. In the little room the jazz resounded in her mind.

Silence.

Eric's art prints.

The window onto the street.

The kettle, Earl Grey tea – Earl Grey Street was round the corner, named for the same Grey as Newcastle's Grey's monument. Earl was a jazzy name.

> *We sit drinking Earl Grey Tea*
> *while jazz musicians play*
> *and turn to melody*
> *we trip along the pavement*
> *dropped to earth by sound...*

Eric might not think much of that. A bus swished past the window.

On the early Monday train to Newcastle, she thought over these new connections which Eric was soaking up in the poetry world. Train travel made her feel fortunate. She gazed out on the countryside, Dunbar's sea cliffs, and, later, Holy Island shimmering in shallow tides off the coast. A small deer stood in a wood near the track. Autumn was coming, when the geese would leave the far north, chasing the light.

One day she would write something different, a poem with space and movement. She would make a leap. She stepped carefully down from the express train.

She went straight to her morning work, leaving her small rucksack in the staff room, gossiping with colleagues about their weekends. Tyneside enfolded her as she readjusted.

Certain writers in the cities had never heard of the *Times Literary Supplement*. Such writers were not librarians. All librarians looked in the *TLS* for its pages of library jobs, giving them a pipe dream of possible places of work as they whiled away coffee breaks in their familiar, unexciting, smoky staff rooms. These adverts appeared at the back of the *TLS*, like the racing pages in newspapers.

Maeve grew into her work. It was civilised work. Librarians could dress nicely and stay clean. They could wear jewellery without bashing it. They met hundreds of readers, and it stood to reason some of these were writers. Friends were appearing, like small desk-lights switched on in a reading room.

Her chum Karen was a library assistant who left to have a family. Karen hadn't been a library assistant for long. She was in the children's department, and the only books she knew anything about were kiddies' books. That didn't stop her trying her hand at poems and stories. She came round to Maeve's of an evening now and again, having met Maeve through Bev.

Beverley, or Bev, practically lived in the library. This openly camp young man would come in armed with notebooks, and sit perusing politics, newspapers, poetry and local history, often until reminded of closing time. She saw him in the streets walking to and from Jesmond. Soon they were friends.

Maeve went on typing out her poems. She sent them to magazines, usually in London, and had occasional acceptances, or encouraging rejections, from distant editors, all men. Karen was working on a local magazine called *Tynescript*. Helping with *Tynescript*, Maeve began to frequent Ouseburn Library, and *Tynescript* began to grow.

Basil Bunting was to headline again at Morden Tower. Maeve had heard how he read his new poem *Briggflatts* at one of the Morden Tower meetings, soon after her youthful encounter with him, the winter she started work in Kendal.

Everyone admired the poem. It had been published and already sold out.

Maeve had long forgiven Basil – she seemed to think of him by his first name – for that snowy morning he'd failed to meet her at the station. She could see the joke. How different she looked now, no longer a schoolgirl. She put the date in her diary.

She ordered a copy of *Briggflatts* for the library. It couldn't be obtained right away. She read Bunting's earlier poems and suddenly saw how handicapped he was by the wandering, fragmented experiences that figured in them, and how a good solid poem about a good solid place would have given him an answer.

She read *Briggflatts* in the University Library in the meantime. Hidden cosily in a basement stack, she read it twice over. How alluring to write a substantial poem of her own – even longer than *Tam O'Shanter* or *Briggflatts*. *Tam O'Shanter* fled like a river down its course, a banked rhythmical flight, while *Briggflatts* flowered and opened into a strong gale at its centre, blustery then gone. Bunting wrote a powerful bull into his poem. Burns had the mare. Hers would have geese.

> *Geese migrating high | glinting eloquent species | united angels.*

A throwaway haiku. Another:

> *Home from Syria | the bull by a riverside | tenor in Throckley.*

When the poster arrived at the library, Maeve read the details with surprise. Eric had been angling for months for an invite to read at Morden Tower. He was the third poet, the less important one after Bunting and Norman Nicholson.

Maeve asked Johnno if he knew of Eric's visit. Johnno didn't. Eric generally announced his exploits in plenty of time. These days, he'd want more than a shared room. Well, she'd be seeing him at the event.

A few days before the meeting, however, Eric telephoned Maeve. He'd had a last-minute invitation: Linton Kwesi Johnson, a young tearaway from London, had been obliged to pull out. Eric and Richard were coming by car. They had booked a B&B of their own persuasion, where they could share a room. He was taking Richard on Saturday morning to see Grysewood Farm, and he wanted a chaperone, or was it a gooseberry. Could Maeve go with them to reduce the glare of his relationship with Richard?

'You're still afraid of your mum and dad? I'd like that.' She put the phone down, pleased.

She arranged a swap for Saturday of the bank holiday weekend. She'd have Saturday till Tuesday free, and she thought of Kendal. She sent a postcard to her former English teacher, Mrs James.

It was the usual crush in the little rounded tower. Basil arrived with Norman Nicholson, the Cumbrian poet whom Maeve had studied at school. Eric and Richard came in behind these poets on the hour. They nodded and smiled to Maeve across the room.

Norman Nicholson's poems were droll and contemporary and just as northern as Basil's. Maeve floated away on one poem describing his fear of geese, how one particular goose hated him, how he would walk round the village to avoid their pasture, until finally he went by aeroplane far afield, only to be greeted by his old goose adversary at the other end of his journey.

Maeve listened, thinking how once, in Kendal Library, Mrs James confessed she'd asked their headmistress to arrange a school visit from Nicholson, but had been firmly rebuffed: 'I don't want my girls swooning over poets.' Physically, few would swoon over Norman, by his own admission a crock who had battled with respiratory problems since youth. Maeve loved these quirky anecdotes that made poets so interesting. Norman Nicholson finished his reading.

Eric was the wedge in the middle. He gave just the right amount of patter on the Scottish scene. 'Norman MacCaig liked this one,' he claimed of a poem about climbing down a mountain. 'Sydney Goodsir Smith thinks my Scots is getting there.'

Now Basil was reading, mainly from his older book, *Villon*, then the first part of *Briggflatts* as a conclusion. Maeve listened in a kind of trance, words streaming into her head as though she herself was composing them, images filling her mind until finally the bull in the field in Throckley merged into Yorkshire may blossom in *Briggflatts*. She came to with a start as he finished reading. This was better than most poetry. Maeve slid back into her own identity.

As she greeted her cousin and Richard, she felt a hand on her arm. Basil was gazing into her face.

'If it isn't my friend Maeve, whom I met in a snowstorm. You're still writing poetry, aren't you? I know you are!'

Maeve felt a rush of emotion. 'I'm glad you remember me.'

'Of course! And I'll come and listen when it's your turn to read here.'

She stared at him.

'She's a very good poet,' said Bev, 'even if she is Eric Grysewood's cousin!'

Eric caught her eye, and she sensed their usual mixture of love and loathing. Or better, say, approval and exasperation. But they hadn't met for some time, and their glances turned into smiles.

Poets have good memories. Basil looked closely at Eric. 'Her student cousin!' He departed, waving, as Nicholson and Tom Pickard dragged him off downstairs.

Richard tapped Bev on the shoulder. 'Bev, could you take me to that crazy secret bar you told me about? The one where the men –'

Bev shushed him hastily. 'I can only take one guest.'

Richard asked, 'Eric, would you object if ...?'

'Okay. Don't be ridiculously late. I'll walk back with Maeve.'

Eric remained in a very good mood. As the company dispersed down the steps of the town wall and out into Tyneside, he and Maeve headed for the fish shop with the longest queue – the best one – then wandered along eating their suppers from newspaper. They went through the Bigg Market with its earthy pubs and cheer, and up past Grey's Monument towards Sandyford. He told Maeve what poems he'd had published in Scotland and England over his last productive months, and how many literary men he'd discovered in Edinburgh and Glasgow.

'Some of my poems are waiting to be printed. There's a printer's works up there.' He pointed along a back lane, not far from her library. 'And you? It's time you got a few poems in front of some readers!'

Rejections she wouldn't mention. *Jazz on Earl Grey Street* was waiting its chances at *Stand*. She told him a story from Westmorland. 'I sent a poem to the newspaper for a book they were going to publish. The book idea fell through, but they put my poem in the newspaper. My father ragged me about my pen name.'

'Maeve Cartier? That's brilliant. We can't all be Grysewoods.'

'That's what I said. It infuriated him.'

'Do you like being away?'

They had reached Maeve's door. She had delayed cadging the lift she wanted. 'I haven't been back. I'd like to go to Kendal after Grysewood tomorrow but it would be a long way round by train.'

'Richard and I could run you to Penrith. We won't be all day at Grysewood.'

She smiled. That was wonderful. 'Johnno's out,' she remembered. 'He's playing guitar. He said hello!'

Saturday dawned breezy, soft and warm. Eric was as sunny as the weather. The Ford Anglia was in good shape, taking the hammering Eric gave it. Maeve had to sit in the back. She handed round Sharp's toffees, but this was a mistake; it stopped conversation. They headed west, past carefully kept fragments of Roman Wall, streets of houses built over its route. Eric recited Auden's poem about the Roman soldier. The toffee in his mouth impeded him.

Beyond hidden dips, hedges of gooseberry and redcurrant bushes, farmhouses and hamlets, glimpses of wall on the sweeps of green, they turned south into Durham.

Richard made up a couple of haiku. They were fashionable this year.

> 'Traces of the wall | birdsong above the temple | at Brocolitia.'

Maeve's turn.

> 'Wild geese migrating | over an unknown village | the glove box rattles'

Maeve gave Richard the bag of toffees to put in the glove box. 'They'll stop that noise.' They were approaching Grysewood. Turning in through the front fields, scattering hens, and setting the dogs barking, they jolted home.

Beneath her aunt and uncle's welcome was a hidden air of resignation. Maeve inspected the new deep-freeze with Sibyl. Jack quizzed the men on the countryside they'd passed through. Cousin Sal came rushing in from the byre, fizzing with excitement about her Charolais calves.

Maeve was overwhelmed by memories of family visits to the farm, the gangs of child cousins, the pastures scattered with violets and mushrooms. Barns that held kittens and hay, animal food, tractors and ironmongery. The horse and working dogs watched everything. Richard stared round, looking puzzled. He was from Kirkcaldy after all.

A spread was prepared, pork pie, ham, potatoes, green peas, salad and hard-boiled eggs. Maeve was obliged to keep Sibyl company in the kitchen, preparing salad, shelling peas, cooking eggs. Sibyl made mayonnaise in a small butter churn.

'Do you like Newcastle, dear? I always thought you were a country girl. You didn't want to go to college like Eric?'

Maeve had long settled this argument with her mother. 'I like my job, and there's my poetry...'

'Yes. Eric likes poetry, but a man must make his place in the world. It's all right for a girl.'

Her aunt stood among the clobber of her farm kitchen. Maeve felt like asking, 'What's all right for a girl?' but she thought better of it.

After lunch, the visitors followed Sal to the byre to see the Charolais calves. The young men stood back as the calves stumbled onto their legs in the straw, nuzzling towards Sal and Maeve with the bottle feeds, all knees and hooves and mouths and furry hair.

They went back for a pot of tea with Sybil. Jack had gone outside. After Maeve's move to Newcastle, Eric's job, and Richard's occupation, which he was reluctant to discuss, they ran out of things to say, but Sibyl was a comfortable woman, glad to see her son, his cousin and friend on any terms, and happy they liked the farm enough to visit.

As they drove away towards Penrith, Eric remarked, 'Isn't poetry just the invisible elephant in that farmhouse?'

Richard laughed.

'They don't mind me,' said Maeve, 'They think poetry is

a nice little hobby. Your Mum practically said that in the dairy.'

'She'd better get used to it. I'm serious.'

'It's because you want to make it your career. So do I actually but I don't think I'm in with a chance.'

'Nonsense, believe in yourself, Maeve.'

Richard said nothing. He was a peaceful man. They shot along the ridge of the moors in silence. After the exhilarating drive with its views and switchbacks and moments of feeling almost airborne, they descended into Penrith and dropped Maeve at the station. They invited her warmly to Edinburgh. She paused on the platform.

> *A small Brent goose flew on alone*
> *across your skies and past your doorway,*
> *her fate unclear, her route unknown,*
> *the small Brent goose flew on alone,*
> *battered, exhausted and windblown.*
> *Can this be Ireland? Is this Norway?*
> *The small Brent goose flew on alone.*
> *Here is the Solway and your soulway.*

The train for Oxenholme pulled in and Maeve was in Kendal by four-fifteen. Mrs James hoped to meet her in the Library. Maeve walked into the too familiar scene, books muddled in the shelves after a busy Saturday, air slightly stale, staff beginning to think about going home.

Mrs James was there. 'Lovely to see you dear. Immediate plans are altered: I've been invited to Grasmere by Dr Woof and a poet who's staying up there. I couldn't miss it. I hope you'll come.'

'Dove Cottage? Won't it be shut?'

'Near Dove Cottage. Dr Woof's coming over from Newcastle.'

More travel! But it wasn't far. Maeve had met Dr Woof

with the Chief Librarian at the opening of a local exhibition on Wordsworth, before she left.

'Who's the poet?'

'From Lancaster University. Adrian somebody? Aidan?'

'Adrian Mitchell?'

'That's right. My mini's outside. Come on!'

Elsie James drove into the car park of the Prince of Wales Hotel on the left of the road into Grasmere. They walked up the opposite bank towards Dove Cottage, among buildings of the same traditional stone. Maeve had been here as a child, and again with Eric in the summer before he went to college. They rang a bell on another building and were let in by a custodian.

'I'm off down to the hotel. There are just the three of you here,' he said, indicating the private library room beyond, as he headed for the door. Maeve looked at the Yale latch and the big keyhole, hoping he'd return and not leave them in charge in the wild country with Wordsworth's manuscripts. Dorothy's journals, were they here? Eric had told her about them. Eric would imagine her, Maeve, as a kind of Dorothy, his scribe, his faithful supporter. Her companion led the way through the inner door.

'The ladies from Kendal?'

'And you're the poet from the new university.'

'Adrian Mitchell. Lancaster University. No Dr Woof yet. Come in.'

Elsie James tutted, and looked at her watch. Maeve followed the young poet into a shelved, windowless room, secure, like the room they had at Newcastle for Thomas Bewick's woodcuts. There were folders and boxes on the shelves, a heavy safe in the corner.

'Isn't it wonderful,' said Adrian. 'I'm waiting for Dr Woof before I touch anything, though it's frustrating. He's promised to show me the Wordsworth manuscripts.'

Maeve knew she couldn't touch. She was overawed. The

thought of Wordsworth's poems being here, as Wordsworth had written them down, in the quiet country region that was her heritage too, was almost crushing. Adrian most likely felt the same.

She took a seat at the central table with Adrian. But Mrs James said, 'I think I'll go back to the hotel and look for Dr Woof.' They heard the outside door click.

'Something will have happened and Robert will come breezing in... Elsie said you do poetry. Have we met before?'

'Yes,' said Maeve, suddenly realising where. 'At the Edinburgh Fringe, two years ago. You were talking to my cousin Eric Grysewood in the bar after Sorley Maclean's reading. And you were at the Poetry International readings before that. My cousin was there but not me.' She wouldn't say she'd been too young. 'You all had a beano in London.'

'A beano is just what it was,' agreed Adrian. 'Now tell me – briefly, because the others will be here any time – you write poetry too?'

'I'm in Newcastle. I keep up with Morden Tower. I've had bits and bobs published – but mainly there's Eric, who's had a book published by the people in Leeds...'

Adrian was good at not watching the clock, which was over the door. 'Are you at university in Newcastle?'

'No, the libraries. I was impatient to get out and about.' She leaned back in her chair. 'And now I couldn't go back to being penniless.'

Adrian laughed. 'Then I can't think why you want to publish poetry. There's no money in it – unless you're Wordsworth – and then it's two hundred years later.'

'I don't want to *publish* poetry. I want to *write* good poetry.'

Adrian looked up sharply. 'You must publish it too. He pointed to his guitar case, which she hadn't noticed. 'There's the money. The Beatles, the Rolling Stones... Bowie ... I bring poetry to the students with music.' He looked round.

'It's chilly in here. Constant temperature for documents. I'm doing a revue with my students in Morecambe. Theme of Yorkshire and Lancashire.'

Maeve had really got Adrian Mitchell going, or perhaps the wait had. What was her old teacher doing in the Hotel?

'For Yorkshire there's Caedmon and the Lyke Wake Dirge. But what about Lancashire? Isn't it all hotpot and witches?'

'That's why we've opened a university,' said Adrian.

The outside door creaked. Mrs James appeared with the chap who had let them into the archive.

'A disaster!' called Elsie. She bustled in. 'Kirkstone Pass has been blocked by a petrol tanker that should never have been up there at all. It is slewed over the road, and the afternoon traffic is stuck behind it, we suspect including Dr Woof. All I can suggest is we go back to the hotel and get you two warmed up a bit. Drew here has come to lock up.'

'Fraid I have,' said Drew, banging his key which was too big to rattle.

The hotel was brightly lit, warm and busy. If Adrian was disappointed by Dr Woof's absence he was playing it calm. Mrs James, who had already had an alcoholic drink and still had to drive back to Kendal, declared she would need a bar supper. She would therefore stand Maeve a bar supper, and Adrian joined them.

At the roaring fire beside their pub table, they ate their scampi in baskets. Mrs James kept watching the bar where the local bobby was leading a discussion of the events on Kirkstone Pass. She excused herself and went across to join in.

'Your teacher is kind to you. Everyone likes poetry, but it's different learning to write it. It's one of the definitions of a poet that they have friends who are poets too. You exchange poems with your cousin?'

'He sends me his – some of them – and I comment on them, but I only show him mine if we're together. I was with him today. I had some poems, but we forgot.'

'You have them with you?'

The poems were typed onto quarto and folded. Adrian pursed his lips and read them. Maeve looked out of the windows. No lake – they had passed the lake.

What a rush these days had been. She was tiring. She jumped when Adrian spoke.

'I like this one.' He was looking at the top poem, her sonnet about Kendal's damson harvest.

'I've heard of the damsons. Though not with horses and carts.'

'I've seen a cartload of damsons.'

How nice to hear another voice, Adrian's voice, reading it out.

Damson Saturday, Kendal

He brings a cart of damsons into town,
a long haul for the old horse; at the train
his money counted, a harvest of his own,
the hard red plumlets shaken down like rain
from high trees in his orchard by the field.

'You have the hang of the rhymes,' he said. They mulled over the poems. He jotted down some addresses of suitable editors, and gave them to her. He went back to the damson harvest. 'I'll give you a tip,' he said. 'If anyone shows you a batch of poems, the top one's always the best.'

'Why?'

'I don't know.'

The wives lay by for winter famine's yield.
Kitchens reek with warmth as crimson juice
darkens to jam and chutney. Rolling loose,

> *weighed and sold on the pavements, hard and sour,*
> *and sent by rail to Manchester and south,*
> *this country's effort to fill the city's mouth*
> *serves Kendal's taverns till this late crowded hour*

'Could I have this one for the revue in Morecambe? Lovely ending!'

> *with tales and beer and fresh-made damson tarts*
> *while eighty horses wait with emptied carts.*

He wouldn't suggest this just to be kind to her. 'I'll let you know how the revue goes. And don't get discouraged. This is good work!'

Mrs James was seated on a bar stool, talking animatedly to two of the firemen who'd been up the Pass. The tanker was stranded at the junction with the Struggle, the steep hill down to Ambleside, so that neither road could be passed. The details were relayed round the room. Drivers waiting up by the Kirkstone Pass Hotel had decanted to the tap room where many imbibed too much alcohol to move their cars when the opportunity arose. Those held up on the north side were just beginning to come down. Adrian and Maeve were the only people who'd talked about anything else.

The door opened. In walked two men, one about forty and a younger one. The elder was Dr Woof. He came up to Adrian, ready to apologise. Clearly, everyone knew of the hold-up. He carried a briefcase and a travel bag. The younger man was sniggering.

'I should have got the train,' said Dr Woof, 'but we ended up coming in this idiot's souped-up car. We've been up there for hours.'

'In the Kirkstone Pass Hotel. One of those *Highest Pub in England* outfits... you could have come on from there on your roller-skates.'

'Too steep,' answered Woof, as if that were a sensible suggestion.

The idea of the Wordsworth scholar traversing the scenery on roller-skates reminded Maeve of the Scottish clergyman skating on Dunsapie Loch. Eric had sent her the card from the Gallery.

She'd been over the stony desert of Kirkstone Pass with her father, but only once down the Struggle to Ambleside. Eric and Richard should be in Edinburgh by now.

When Woof had acquired a tray of tea and his usual room, everyone calmed down. Adrian would see the manuscripts in the morning. Elsie and Maeve said their goodbyes.

> *Then hopeful to your cottage came | invited in to see | your written words... but they | were under lock and key | The book | in which you had been writing*

She couldn't turn *manuscripts* into the right sort of language. She sleepily remembered Eric making a joke about 'cottaging' at Grasmere, which she hadn't understood. 'What a cock-up of an evening,' Mrs James apologised.

Maeve hadn't considered how late she would arrive at her parents'. They wouldn't be impressed by her walking in at ten o'clock at night and expecting a bed. Of course she'd get a bed. She thanked Mrs James before they reached the house, and ran straight to the door.

Her father was standing at the bay window looking out.

'Hello dear, what's kept you?'

'I've been up in Grasmere at the Prince of Wales talking to a poet called Adrian Mitchell. I'm not sure I will even dare tell Eric!' She hadn't thought about tactics.

'You mean Eric wasn't with you?'

'We went to lunch with Auntie Sibyl and Uncle Jack, then Eric took me to Penrith and I got the train then I met

Mrs James in the library and we headed up to Grasmere, and I met... Kirkstone Pass was closed and Eric's gone back to Scotland.' This jumble of facts would probably appease her father.

'You'll be tired out. Come on in. You can have a cup of cocoa or something. There's a casserole in the oven, though perhaps you've eaten.'

'Yep.'

'I should talk to your mother about Jack and Sibyl, if I were you.'

Her Mum was plating up the casserole so Maeve ate it anyway, and told her about the Charolais calves and Eric's parents.

'I'm ready to go upstairs. Your bed has a hot water bottle in it, but it's probably cold by now.'

'Maeve, come into the study with me.'

She went through to her father's cosy den, warm with the embers of a fire. They sat down in the armchairs one each side, as though the comfortable fire of the Prince of Wales had somehow transferred itself here.

'How is your poetry going?'

'I thought you'd ask how my job was going.'

'I know you can handle your job. But you also write poetry and it's important to you. How's it going?'

'It's a good moment to ask me. I've had some encouragement today. A real poet told me to send poems to some editors he thinks would like my work. Eric – '

'I thought Eric was a real poet.'

'He is but Eric's different. He's family.'

'You're very close to Eric, aren't you?'

'Yes.'

'And he seems to be doing better than you?'

'He's marvellous. He knows hundreds of people – he's had all these poems published – '

'But he's three years older than you. Hasn't all this happened in the last three years?'

Maeve was taken aback.

'And you have moved into his house in Newcastle?'

'He's moved to Edinburgh. I've got his old room and he's given me some books.'

'Ah, I have some books for you too. I have to say Maeve, I believe you have a great gift for language. Naturally you think I'm an old fuddy-duddy but I can see what's in front of my nose.'

She squirmed.

'I suppose you know Eric is a homosexual?'

'Oh Dad, what next? He's my cousin. As for being – as for preferring men – he understands it himself, that's what matters.'

'It's becoming more accepted,' said her father, 'and I believe it's now legal or nearly so, which will greatly help them. As long as you understand.'

'Yes I do.'

'And don't go thinking this man Eric is better than you in any way. You always idolised him. That can be quite convenient for a man, even one like Eric. Doesn't he ever annoy you?'

'He annoyed me terribly once,' she blurted out. 'But he never found out. I didn't tell him!'

'You needn't tell me.'

'Oh but I want to! There's this poet – ' she didn't give herself time to think, 'this poet called Edwin Morgan.'

'Yes, I've heard of him.'

'... this poem by him, *Message Clear*, was on the front page of the *TLS*'—she knew her father read this, or at any rate saw it weekly – 'set out like a concrete poem. Nobody could understand it and people wrote in complaining. But I understood it and I wrote to the paper explaining it. But guess bloody what?'

She paused and her father said nothing.

'When the next *TLS* arrived in the library I looked to see

if my letter had been published. My letter wasn't there but there was a letter from Eric saying exactly the same thing.' Recounting the story to herself, she became agitated again. 'Practically word for word. It could have been anybody but did it have to be Eric?'

Perhaps she'd overdone the confession. 'Is that all?'

'Only that I hope you'll find time to catch yourself the right husband amidst all this poetry.'

She couldn't reply. The problem with what he had mentioned – *What he had mentioned*? She couldn't even put it into words.

Such an awkward question. Everyone except poets seemed to be watching her for signs of an impending *husband*. Was that why she liked poets?

She suddenly saw it. Nothing to do with husbands. *She didn't want to be a wife.*

> *Wildgeese need no one on their side,*
> *from shell and sand, from seed and stubble*
> *in slanting skeins they rise and ride.*
> *Wildgeese need no one on their side,*
> *where we, our riddled paths denied,*
> *seek skies in dross and realms in rubble.*
> *Wildgeese need no one on their side.*
> *Far from our fear they fear no trouble.*

But something was on her side, fate, luck, destiny, or was it destination? She bade her father goodnight from the doorway. They were not a demonstrative family.

She crashed out for half an hour without properly undressing, and briefly slept.

When she came to, the lamp was in the wrong place. This was her old bedroom of childhood and schooldays. She was visiting, between long, mad, exhausting days like the one just gone.

The men she had spoken to today, Eric and Richard, Uncle Jack then Adrian Mitchell, then her father, came back to her, all intellectual, nothing of men as partners, nothing of attraction. Though Adrian was nice. Married, he'd said so. They were careful to say so, when you got talking. The women were different, Elsie James and Sal.

She passed by dishy men. They didn't keep her interest. She got more of a buzz from those well-guarded folders of Wordsworth's handwritten poems.

She wrote her poem about the Charolais calves, with pen and notebook, under the goose-necked study lamp, still with that smell of hot paint on its metal shade. She finished very late. The poem was short, twelve lines with five beats, rhythmic not metrical. She'd imagined herself straight back into the byre where she'd picked up the calves from the straw and where Sal bottle-fed them. They were irresistible to her and she got something of that into the poem.

When she had done, she titled it *Charolais Calves*.

After the weekend, back in Newcastle, she typed it and sent it to the poetry editor at the *Times Literary Supplement*, one of the people Adrian Mitchell had suggested for her 'more sensitive' poems.

Three weeks later it was accepted and printed.

The librarians didn't see it because it wasn't in the 'sports pages.' That didn't worry Maeve. She got hold of an extra copy of the *TLS* at the library, and sent a newspaper cutting to Sal at the farm. Sal was not the most literary of ladies but she wrote back to thank her, complaining in passing that the *TLS* had misprinted Maeve's name as *Cartier*.

Maeve smiled.

She knew Eric would hear from Sal about the poem, and she later learned that he had.

Chapter Four

BRIGGFLATTS   (1973)

From about this time Maeve had a friend called Ollie Northold. An interesting though stubborn scholar of English literature, he had once been a research assistant in the university, but now lived apparently on nothing, haunting the college precincts, the bars, library, bookshops, eateries and cafes, as though he were still in his early twenties, not his mid to late thirties. A large chap, untidy, all hair and beard at first glance, he was observant and original.

Ollie knew everyone. Eric, of course. He claimed to have seen Maeve as a school leaver on that long-ago visit to the Poetry Society: he'd been in the Percy Street bar she went into with MacDiarmid and Bunting. He'd been at Peter Ustinov's table, otherwise he might have met her back then.

Maeve was to learn he never lied.

She went to see Ollie on her way home from work.

His extraordinary pad was up one flight of stairs in St Mary's Street. Bookshelves surrounded two sofas. Cheese plants and rubber plants rampaged along a window wall. Some of these potted monsters reached the top of the window, giving the room an air of a forest clearing. Beyond the window, the arched stained-glass panes of St Mary's, lit from inside the church, glowed against the darker street.

Ollie was reading Henry James. He put the book away and offered her a glass of sherry, medium and very nice. They started gossiping and she told him when she'd last seen Eric, how he had settled down with the poet Richard, and how Dr Joe had rejected Eric's second book.

'Serves him right.' Ollie laughed. 'What else has been happening?'

'I saw Basil Bunting last week. He was at the station with Jon Silkin and a guy who looked like Che Guevara. But I didn't feel I could hang around all that male camaraderie.'

Ollie looked thoughtful. 'It's radical chic to look like Che. I wish Silkin would stick to poetry. But Basil's *Briggflatts* is a very great achievement, just as I said it would be. I don't travel much but I'd like to visit that place in Yorkshire.'

'Briggflatts? My parents went via Sedbergh on the way to Durham.'

'Sedbergh, that's right. A corner of three counties. That's what makes it remote.'

'You'd like to go there? I would, too.'

'Shall we do it?' said Ollie. 'Will you come?'

'Neither of us drives.'

'What do you mean? Of course I can drive.'

Maeve was astonished at the idea of Ollie driving, and said so.

'Do you want someone else to drive, shall we take someone else?'

'No, let's have a special day out!' Maeve thought for a moment. 'I have a friend who would love to go with us. Would you drive a party?'

'Depends who they are. I mean she, or he...'

'Janey Hogg,' said Maeve. 'I told you about her – she works at the bookshop on the quayside. Janey thinks she's

Basil Bunting's granddaughter. She might or might not be, but certainly she looks so like him it gives you a start. She's in one of the writing groups and she has taken to Bunting's work, well only *Briggflatts*. I admit I don't know too much about her, but she would love to go down.'

'Oh, I know her from the bookshop. That's fine. I'll take it your motive is not that of being chaperoned. We'll pick a day, take a chance on the weather and on your friend being able to join us.'

Ollie said he would acquire a car. He lent her his copy of Basil's poem to reread before they went.

The night before they were due to set off, Maeve's telephone rang. Janey had never phoned her before – she'd found Johnno's number in the book. Maeve didn't recognise the voice at first.

'About tomorrow. I'm bringin' Alice. Me friend Alice.'

Maeve reckoned two Janeys would be not much different from one. Ollie wasn't on the phone: she couldn't alert him, but he would drive three people or four.

Janey and Alice were to meet at Maeve's flat before Ollie picked them up by car.

When Maeve opened the door to Alice, both Alice and she were thoroughly taken aback, for they knew one another. Alice was the librarian known as Miz Martin, one of Maeve's bosses at the Central Library; and to Alice, Maeve was the librarian poet Miss Maeve Carter.

Alice spoke first. 'Oh Maeve, I had no idea.'

'Me neither.' Maeve was trying to visualise this lady as Janey's friend.

'Would you rather I backed out? We weren't expecting this. I wasn't given a name.'

Maeve's good manners came to her rescue.

'Good heavens Miz Martin. If you want to go to Briggflatts, this is your chance... well let's do it! But I shall have to call you Alice.'

'Good thinking, we are not on the job now. I sort of thought...'

Maeve recovered herself. 'Well, it's perfectly all right. Come in for a moment... oh here comes Janey.'

Janey sauntered in. 'Have you two said hello?'

'We work together.' Maeve was smiling.

'Oh aye, I forgot you were a library wife,' said Janey.

They hadn't long to wait for the next surprise – the car Ollie had obtained. When the massive Humber drove into the street Maeve could hardly believe Ollie was at the wheel. But it had to be him, it *would* be him, and it was.

They crowded round, grinning. Maeve felt she wasn't dressed smartly enough, in her coat, gloves and walking shoes. Alice was similarly dressed. Maeve indicated their extra passenger and Ollie said, 'Oh I know you from the library! Then we're all friends!'

They climbed in, Maeve at the front and Alice and Janey into the capacious back seat. They purred away, curtains twitching as they went.

Maeve hesitated to say it, but Ollie said it for her.

'You're thinking, isn't this a bit extravagant? If I did it every week it would be, but this is a one-off. It will eat petrol. I need to watch the gauge. And we've absorbed your friends without any problem. Perhaps I knew you'd gather more passengers. Don't worry, I'm going to enjoy this.'

By the time they crossed the Tyne Bridge, Maeve had stopped worrying. Ollie could drive.

On the open road, cars slowed down when they saw the Humber, and edged out of its way. The interior was palatial. They could have got several more folk in the back, and there was a hamper, which looked as if it might be full of food.

Ollie had clearly driven regularly at some time. He was steady, quiet, proprietorial of the borrowed car. She looked out over the northern fields, mildly wondering about Ollie's motives for the trip. With two unexpected passengers, she might never find out.

They filled up with petrol on the A1 and Alice insisted on buying them coffee. Back in the car, Ollie started the conversation.

'What would you have done today, Maeve, if you hadn't come along with me?'

That was easy. 'I'd have been writing.'

'Poetry? Sending things out to be published?'

'I'm not that fussed.' She *was* that fussed.

'How old are you now my dear? I know I shouldn't ask. Shouldn't you be thinking about your future?'

'Should I?' Maeve answered sharply. 'Do you ever think about yours?' And they had listeners in the back!

'Oh but I am a servant, I don't live for myself but to observe all around me. I should like to find someone to serve.'

'I've never thought of life like that,' replied Maeve nervously.

'You ought to marry someone and have children.'

She couldn't believe this. In the car with others!

'That's very sweet of you Ollie, but – what do Alice and Janey say about that? I bet they'll say...'

'Oh, not me,' said Ollie. 'I don't think I'll ever... want to be a member of a club that wouldn't have me... you know what I'm like. Where's my house? Where's the family support, my mother, my cousins, the chit-chat? Where's my normality?'

Maeve wasn't surprised to hear a loud giggle from Janey.

'Stop the car somewhere, you soppy old duffer. You're doing my head in. I'll swap seats with Alice or Janey and you can lecture them on... you can ask them what they'd be doing today if they hadn't come out for a drive. I'd quite like to know!' She peered out at the passing water and trees. 'We just missed a clearing.'

'I telt you Ollie was hilarious,' said Janey to Alice.

Ollie obediently slowed the Humber and presently found a place to stop. They were looking over the River Tees, near a village called Crook. Alice and Janey promptly disappeared down a little path to the water level, leaving Maeve alone with Ollie. She could have killed them!

'Ollie!' said Maeve. 'If anyone else had said that rubbish to me I'd be black affronted!'

Ollie laughed. 'I couldn't offer you a normal life because I am not normal.'

'You tell me! I'm not normal either.'

'Dear Maeve, not being normal is a state of play, not an achievement. Why is a nice young lady like you cruising the sticks with an old shambles of a fella who can't even move out of his student digs? Let alone entice you with freedom to write all day – a couple of ideal kids and an ideal nanny, a beautiful kitchen, posh friends, a conservatory full of plants –'

They were sitting on a wooden bench and Ollie put his arm round her. His right hand strayed onto her knee.

What was Ollie thinking of? He didn't want these things for himself, yet he wanted them for her? He was reasonably fond of her, sympathetic, but... but...

Trust Ollie to include a conservatory full of plants. The picture of his extraordinary room came back to her, staid and exotic at the same time. His rubber plants were dull like him, but thriving. He had a flair for their quiet needs.

She sat watching the Tees ripple by, brown water singing ditties to itself, almost too low to be heard. This was real country, where an otter would come by, on land or in water, where finches would gather, a kingfisher streak from tree to tree. Someone from the library was moving into a swanky housing estate near Gosforth. All glass and sculpted gardens, too far out of town to walk, yet it wasn't country. Yesterday at work, when this brash property owner asked,

'Wouldn't you like to live there?' the exasperated Alice had replied, 'On the whole, I'd prefer a farm cottage.' There'd been smirks behind hands.

Maeve's mind came back to her seat by the riverside. This was her day off from the library, yet somehow Alice was around. Ollie was beside her on the bench, waiting for a response. What had he said? 'Oh, basically you mean, don't you, that I become an ideal wife with an ideal husband and ideal kids etcet'ra, and we *all live together in a crooked little house*? Where does that rhyme come from?'

'*There was a crooked man and he walked a crooked mile*,' began Ollie.

'That's right, *a crooked sixpence upon a crooked stile*. Well, you're not a crooked man, Ollie.'

'Thank you, my dear.'

'You've made my point. Conventional life is not for me. That sort of becoming well-off is a game in my view. A game I don't much want to play.'

'It would be different if you fell in love.'

'I know why,' she said. 'I want to write, more than anything, it's my game if you like, but love is one of the things we write about. Perhaps it's the main thing. To deny love for poetry would be wrong. But it would have to be love, not convenience.'

'And it might never happen.'

'It's sure to happen, but by no means likely to be convenient.' She smiled brightly at him, convinced this was true.

Alice and Janey came back along their path. They were unfazed and looked comfortable together. Maeve found herself wondering if they were a lesbian couple. Why hadn't she thought of it before? Himalayan balsam flourished beside the river, shining stands of pink flowers. Bees cruised among them.

Driving the Humber down the narrow lane to Briggflatts

seemed inadvisable. Ollie edged into a gate off the main road, if it could be called a main road, that ran past the Briggflatts lane. An iron signpost stood among the grasses: *Brigflatts*.

'Only one *g*,' said Alice. 'Basil Bunting spelt it wrong.'

'He preferred the double g, and he's entitled to, having written so much about it.'

'So *well* about it,' corrected Ollie. 'I prefer Basil's version. He's earned it.' He smiled at Maeve. They started down the lane.

The geese sang her a poem. It wasn't like Bunting's work, his organ chords of sound, but she always listened to the geese.

> *In folded fields beyond the Lune,*
> *this secret, stone-clad cave of meeting*
> *with oaken pew and pillar hewn*
> *in folded fields beyond the Lune*
> *where stone inscribed with name and rune*
> *suspends the streams and rainfall fleeting,*
> *in folded fields beyond the Lune*
> *this secret, time's eternal greeting.*

The geese were poets too, but you couldn't always read their work. If she needed a name for a goose, she'd call it Caedmon.

They continued between the hedges. Even if these visions never changed, poems could carry them to people far distant. Bunting had made words out of this hidden place as Eric said Hopkins had made them out of Inversnaid. Maeve had never seen the burn fall into the loch at Inversnaid, but Eric had travelled there from Glasgow. She was now to see Briggflatts as she knew it from the poem. That was why Ollie had gone out of his way to bring her here.

Basil had made his poem with hulking, solid, chiselled

words, whose music sang without rhyme. Hopkins had hit the twentieth century too, with the spring and sound of every word, not only the end rhymes.

Both these poems were implacable records, of the dell and the waterfall.

The guest ladies disappeared down a different path at Briggflatts and came back looking very pink and happy. Ollie and Maeve walked in the sloping graveyard, then they all invaded the carpentered shrine of the meeting-house. It would hold a hundred; it was crowded with thousands from the past.

The others let her be. She sat in the sanctuary, intently listening to imaginary voices, seeing the visions of two hundred, three hundred years. Early Quakers, in hats, with tracts, their horseback travels, the women, silences, secrecy, their dark clothing. Early Quakers were a very large clique, a conspiracy of outsiders. Writing poetry was outsiderish too, the distancing, observation, the attempt to grasp life which was otherwise meaningless. Like this moment, that small bird passing the skylight, the old, cared-for panelling and strong wooden benches and pillars.

She wanted both the hidden magic and the ordinary life.

She wasn't an abstainer. Ollie was right, it would be good to have a bedfellow. She didn't crave the trappings of courtship. It sounded bleak put like that, time to put your arms round somebody of the kind who attracted you in a personal way, to enjoy them and let go. Parents, sometimes friends wanted it for you, but they couldn't bear to put it so crudely. They used phrases like *tying the knot*, or *going steady*. Even poetry described it as a big deal. She supposed she could go unsteady. She would still be picky. Because there was something about it mysteriously connected to who you were – to who you *really* were.

Basil Bunting had sat here and reflected, many a time, on

love, life and poetry. She knew he wouldn't come often now, from Hexham, but he still had places to stay in Sedbergh. The poet Maeve sat in Briggflatts and meditated on, not poetry, not *Briggflatts*, nor the ineffable secret at the heart of our being, which Quakers sought in silence, but this, the allure, the pull of sex. What man, what poet, what woman even, had never allowed their mind in that direction?

Alice and Janey came smiling in from the meeting-house garden. Ollie strolled back from where he'd been looking at the tributary river Rawthey running deep towards the Lune.

Before they left they had an astonishing picnic out of the hamper in the car. Someone had put together a banquet of ham and salad sandwiches, Scotch pies, tomatoes, eggs, fruits, chocolate gateau and apple juice, amounting to a substantial meal with cutlery and plates. They ate sitting in the meadow at the head of the lane.

Late and tired they dispersed in Newcastle. Dropped off at her door, Maeve put the Vesta chow mein with crispy noodles back in the cupboard. She didn't need it.

Back in this invigorating city of long, curving streets, where its library was her living, its poetry her life, she relaxed as her coffee cooled. There was no sign of Johnno.

She wrote to Eric of their pilgrimage. She was pretty sure he hadn't been to Briggflatts. She even swanked about the Humber Super Snipe.

No conclusion was reached between Ollie and herself, yet before too long Maeve and Ollie were having a proper affair, a slow and quiet affair indeed, not because either of them had answers for the other but because they agreed there were questions.

Chapter Five

WORK EXPERIENCE   (1976)

BEYOND HER OPEN WINDOW, high and early, they headed west and north. She dressed for work, swallowed a half cup of coffee, and made for the town moor. The sky filled with lines of geese. Above land and cities, they freely crossed the skies.

An old guy hobbled towards her on the grass. She pointed up. Skeins thickened, thinned as they watched. No one goose led them. Wide arrow-tips altered in the air, as they pushed in turn into the headspace.

By afternoon they'd be way north and west, in Scotland, or Ireland, by fresh or salt water, who knew?

When the geese had departed and the sky was white again, paper not written on, a dozen people were watching on the moor, separated from the roads by lines of trees. Along with Maeve they turned back to their lives and the coming summer, walking away as though disappointed at staying behind.

> *As Tyne flows down from peaks to town,*
> *through vales and plains of Pennine rivers,*
> *as Lune, as Wear, as Tees run down,*

as Tyne flows down from peaks to town,
Lancaster, Sunderland, Stockton, frown
in floods a seasonal storm delivers,
or dry and drown as Tyne flows down,
geese wander and the landscape quivers

The summer became hot. Maeve alternated two dresses she found cool and comfortable enough to work in. One was a blue dishcloth cotton with a wide skirt, two deep pockets, and sleeves that covered her arms (she wasn't one for soaking up too much sun), the other fine cotton, patterned in lemon and grey. These clothes were easy to wear. She slept in them sometimes, lying on top of the bedclothes, and rinsed and changed them round every day or two. They dried almost instantly in the heat.

She was sitting with Bev in their favourite café in Jesmond.

Mad Women Press at Durham were compiling an anthology of poems about clothes. The publisher was a playwright, a costume fanatic, and actor – no one was allowed to say actress. They had already accepted one poem of Maeve's and two of Beverley's. They thought he was a woman.

She and Bev lingered after the women writers had fled back to lunches, children and domesticity. Bev was a great dresser, clad for the heat in a bright pyjama suit, sandals and panama. He could carry this off. Other friends had simpler dress philosophies. Eric had worked in Glasgow long enough to look businesslike and smart in a quiet way. His good shoes set him apart from other writers.

She thought next of Ollie. Ollie didn't have an outlook on dress. He disliked hot weather. He was wholesomely, untidily, drably clean.

Maeve was beginning to wonder about her friend. She'd had a quiet relationship with him for three years now, that is they had sex when she was up at his place talking, or when they had been out to eat, or occasionally when she had returned from poetry meetings and wasn't following them up in a pub.

She looked across at Beverley.

'Penny for my thoughts. But I'm not going to tell you them.'

'You'll be thinking about your Ollie,' said Bev.

'He's not my Ollie. That's the point.'

'Or the problem.'

'Not a problem. But I said I'd go and see him. He doesn't always get up unless I call around early afternoon. Which I can't do when I'm in the library.'

'I get the impression he'll be a better friend than a lover,' said Bev.

'You're wicked. What business is it of yours?'

'I'm tuned in. And I'm right. Off you go then and do your alarm clock duty.'

She put her light jacket round her shoulders, bade Beverley farewell and walked through the sunny streets to the Haymarket and Ollie's.

Ollie was up. He'd been out, to the Hancock to see some drawings of birds. He'd fetched milk. He didn't normally use his place for eating or drinking, and seldom used his shared kitchen.

'It's so hot,' he explained, 'that if I don't drink tea I'm certain to be back on the beer. Without something to drink here I'd hardly be in the house at all.'

'Fair point.'

'I hoped you'd come. I'll make you a mocha.'

In a few minutes Ollie returned with a warm drink for each of them. 'Mocha' sounded a strange drink for the heat. He poured a white powder into his, from a narrow tube.

'What's that white stuff?'

'Sugar.' Ollie laughed.

After all that effort to organize a simple drink, Ollie put his down and leaned close to Maeve. 'Come on darling.'

Maeve put her mug on the table. She gently shrugged off her jacket and put her hands inside his coat. 'You wear too many clothes.' They giggled.

'Hey, put the light off if you're... I don't like this glaring electricity!'

'People will see in from the Church roof!' Maeve switched off the light. It was not much different.

Despite his extra clothes, or perhaps he drank the mocha more quickly, Ollie was undressed first. Maeve had got as far as her bra and slip. He embraced her.

'You're still wearing your socks.'

'O romantic poet lady, Maeve, the light in my life, and she talks about socks,' murmured Ollie, affectionately.

'Socks or sex?'

'Both!' He assisted her over the remaining few feet to the sofa bed. They lay down, two close nude bodies, one with socks and sex in evidence. Maeve lay looking up among the cheese plants, contented with Ollie's contentment. Over his shoulder she could see his books by and about Joyce; she would not think about Mollie Bloom, but she did recall briefly a moment in her school's cloakroom, thirteen year old girls crowded round the knowledgeable one, saying *How long does it take? – about fifteen minutes!*

Ollie's kind of sex meant she had to co-operate passively, and it did take about fifteen minutes. She cried out when he squeezed her too tightly. He ran his fingers through her hair – she quite enjoyed that though she never did it to him. He didn't seem to *want* her to do things to him, but expected her to be laid back (no doubt the origin of that term). He managed to bring it to a pleasing end for both, and they lay there, giggling a little as they often did. 'Sex is comical,' whispered Ollie.

He was about to go to sleep, and the bed was too narrow – this had happened before. She would move to the other sofa in a minute.

Ollie was quiet and Maeve crossed the room, where she

picked out a book from a bookshelf and switched on the table lamp. This was something she enjoyed, the temporary ownership of her friend's room, with all its eccentric charms, and the sense of trust as Ollie slept and she relaxed. She had read two chapters of Naomi Mitchison and a recent reprint of a Sylvia Plath, the one with the bee poems, before Ollie stirred.

They were ready to eat. They drifted to Maeve's via the Indian takeaway, and settled at a corner of the kitchen table to enjoy red tandoori.

Johnno was there with a woman Maeve didn't know. Maeve accepted some of Johnno's salad though they had nothing to trade for it. They all chatted about the hosepipe ban, which didn't much affect them, then Ollie departed for the privacy of his home.

'Glad you happened to bring Ollie,' said Johnno when his guest was out of hearing. 'She was suspicious that I shared a flat with you.'

She put the debris in the dustbin and rinsed a few plates. *Better friend than a lover.* She was twenty-eight and he was forty. Perhaps Bev was right.

At last, she went to her writing table and turned to her papers. Eric had sent her three poems for a look-over, and unusually, one of Richard's. Richard was coming on well, Eric wrote. Eric considered himself a better poet than Richard. He probably thought he was better than her, too. It was enough for her to be included in his circle, both as a poet in her own right, and as family.

She read her cousin's poems and commented, as invited, on their structure and content. One poem was about a young woman: the old high heels and lipstick stuff. Maeve felt if it wasn't already out of date it would be soon. 'I didn't believe in her,' she wrote. She'd be no use to Eric if she didn't tell him the truth. She made points about Eric's other poems and thanked Richard for his.

She turned to the book she was compiling for Deirdre of Mad Women Press. She hadn't told Eric or Ollie about Deirdre's offer. She was being secretive even to herself about this round-up of her work – effusions, sonnets, screeds. She had always had this wish to write a major poem – silly perhaps. Yet she was nearly there with Deirdre's book. A few more poems, a matter of theme. She meditated until some connecting lines began to come. This moment of conceiving the poems was the best thing about it.

Eric came to Newcastle the following week. They would meet along Percy Street, where Ollie had chosen a café without the temptation of booze. Maeve arrived after work. Ollie was waiting at his corner table where they could see the whole café and the street. The café was half full: lone men, a woman with kids. The tables and dishes were clean. It wasn't far from Thorne's Bookshop, and Ollie had a handful of new books he had purchased there. 'I like a good novel,' he said. Maeve shuffled through his choices. The door pinged and Eric walked in.

They already knew about Swing Bridge Press and Eric's book. Maeve had not met this publisher, though Ollie had.

'How did you get on?' asked Ollie.' 'How was Buddy?'

'Different from what I expected. Not the bow-tie type.'

'Are there bow-tie types in Scotland?

'Sure. Yes, I liked Buddy. Forthright and interested.'

'He will sell your books. Whether he can get them reviewed in the *Guardian* or the *TLS* is another matter, but which would you rather – guys actually reading your books, or posh people pretending they've heard of them?'

'That's roughly what Buddy said.'

'The democratisation of poetry.'

'The Library is going to stock Swing Bridge books. I've been arguing the case for them.'

'Maeve here is pulling her weight in our cultural battles.'

Maeve looked towards the counter. 'Bacon and cheese rolls?'

The men sprang to their feet. Soon there was a platter of hot, savoury rolls among the teapots and teacups.

'Tell us about Buddy.'

'He's from Teesside. I recognised his accent, though he denied it.' Eric laughed. 'Entertained me in a pub he seems to own. The Lorikeet. Is there some Geordie joke about parrots?'

'Definitely. He has the flat above that pub. Smart fella, quick decision maker.'

'He read my manuscript while I drank a pint of beer. He'd had recommendations, of course.' Eric was forthcoming, confident now the book was accepted. 'The oddest thing he said was, *Is Maeve Cartier your sister?*'

'Where did he get that idea?'

'I admitted to being your cousin. Can't do us any harm – a poetry dynasty, my dear...' Eric tried to make a joke of it.

'Did he say anything else about me?'

'He said you were popular – those were his words.'

Maeve wondered if those were all of Buddy's words, but it was good enough. 'I have an envelope with your poems and Richard's from last week.' Maeve kept quiet about her own news, the proposed book from Mad Women Press. It might not come off, and besides, right now it would be stealing Eric's thunder.

'What will your book be called?' she asked him.

'*High Tide Bamburgh*. We had a long discussion why it wouldn't have a comma. I wanted a comma: *High Tide*, comma, *Bamburgh*, but he said it was better typography straight out.'

'That day we were in Bamburgh? Is your book about that?'

'It's everything, Scottish and English. Buddy said I should appeal to everyone. Buddy said...' Eric waffled on. Surely a poet could boast of his second book.

Maeve recalled the day she'd spent in Bamburgh with her cousin.

After the time they went to Grysewood with Richard – no, *she* went to Grysewood with *them* – there'd been a catastrophe. On their return trip, Eric flipped the Ford Anglia off the moor road to avoid a horse-drawn caravan. They landed in a bog without damage to himself or Richard, but by the time the garage pulled the Anglia from the bog, it was a write-off. Maeve wasn't supposed to hear about this but she did, via the parents. While Eric gossiped with Ollie about Buddy and the Lorikeet, Maeve drank her tea and mused on. It would be the day the tanker skidded on Kirkstone Pass.

She'd had an outing in his replacement Hillman Imp. In the sweet, quiet village of Bamburgh they'd had a long talk about Grace Darling and the ship that broke, a coaster with passengers. They'd had tea in a tearoom with curtains, cushions and tablecloths. Didn't Eric write some lines about the high tide? Scones on bone china. Coastal birds: it wasn't the season for geese.

It came back to her, how she asked Eric about the wreck of the *Deutschland*. The Dutch ship bound for America never made it past Harwich, but perished there in 1875, a generation later than the *Forfarshire*.

She looked up at Eric reading her far-away face. 'The Hillman Imp is still going well,' he said, showing he guessed the course of her reverie.

She and Eric had laughed over the consternation in Grasmere about the hold-up on Kirkstone Pass. They loved the bleak grandeur of the pass, a few stray humans in the bowl of rocks, the brooding sense of disaster diffused in the landscape... The North Sea had on their outing shown cold blue; soft sand, eider ducks, puffins, a spring tide; the massive backdrop of the castle high above.

'How's Richard? He wasn't with us in Bamburgh.' Eric had devoted that day to her, had left Richard to other occupations. 'But he was with you the day you knocked out the Anglia.'

'He's fine. Always asks how you are.'

There were signs the café was closing, the evening bright and inviting. 'Have we time to go to the coast?'

'There's a fair in Exhibition Park,' said Ollie. 'A few rides have got the date wrong for the Hoppings.'

'Let's walk round there. Maeve, could I stay over?'

'No problem. Johnno's away. Do you still have a key?'

'A hoopoe was seen in Exhibition Park last winter,' Ollie said as they headed up the road. Maeve could picture the big, red, incongruous bird in the bare green space, unwitting precursor to the razzmatazz of the fair. They walked round, watching gaggles of kids, families and students, keeping to the flattened-grass paths through the shows. Caravans, lorries and tents stood behind tacky rails, flashy entrances, carousels with painted animals, fair organs churning out gaudy mechanical music.

The friends drifted back to St Mary's Street with their spoils – a coconut, a cellophaned packet of fudge, and two odd knitted gloves Maeve had picked up separately from the grass. A red and a green, each with coloured touches of Fair Isle.

'They make a pair,' said Maeve.

'You'd better wash them.'

They looked clean. She pocketed them.

Ollie smashed the coconut, tied a large piece onto a string, and hung it on a nail outside his window for the birds. Wherever their nests were, the birds had gone to them and wouldn't be back at Ollie's window till morning.

Eric and Ollie started discussing Ollie's new purchases of novels. Eric was over-excited, Ollie his usual self, able to gossip all night about literature. This was a bad combination. Maeve was tired.

'I'll head off and do a spot of food shopping on the way home. Eric, see you later.' She picked up her coat.

Eric smiled. 'I'll catch you up, if you're going to get some food in.' He handed her two notes. 'It's my turn.'

Her library salary wasn't bad, but she accepted the contribution, and left. She picked up breakfast things in the tiny shop. Eric arrived later, faintly sloshed. She hoped he'd found a pub on his own, without Ollie.

High Tide Bamburgh was a good poem. This was sure to be a good book. Maeve turned to it when her copy arrived in the post. It brought back the minutiae of that day. After admiring the shore and the high castle outlined on its rock, the poem went into the old, sad shipwreck from which few had survived. A rowing-boat race between dangerous rocks had become legend. Eric was good at legends.

> *Father and girl rowed hard, rowed hard through bully*
>   *waves.*
> *Dark, tilted bulk of the Forfarshire*
> *Rock snarled the paddles till she broke.*

They had sat on the sea wall watching the high tide stutter and turn.

> *Two poets swing by the harbour wall.*
> *speak of the past where no words latch,*
> *seen under splashed cold glass.*
> *Hope in Easter weather, tide's turn*
> *and return, sun's answer. Eider-duck,*
> *sea-geese, puffins, ply daylit sea.*

She was in this poem! What the hell was a sea-goose? She leafed to the front. Her cousin was two books ahead of her. Soon she'd start catching him up.

She dug out her poem about the odd gloves found at the fair. It hadn't been cool enough for gloves since then, but imagination helps composition. She was fond of the poem already. She finished the last grouping, poems at the start and in the middle that gelled the book together, and packed up her typescript for Deirdre with a letter. She could find a few more poems if necessary. She posted it on Friday and went to Edinburgh on the Saturday morning.

The Fringe had started. Eric took her again to Sandy Bell's, more crowded with unknown visitors than last time. He still managed to introduce her to several characters, all seeming very Scottish to the Sassenach. Nobody called him *Wildgoose* this time. They went on to Eric's trattoria near his flat in Tollcross.

'You poeta?' asked the old chef. 'Wildgoose is poeta. I am busy in Festival. I find you meal.'

And he found them meal, genuine Italian pasta for the smallest of prices. She could eat there every night. Eric left her at his flat, armed with the shiny Festival programme. It listed dozens of poetry events ranging from high status visiting poets to local and Edinburgh groups. Maeve could find her way round, trying to get into pubs at the last minute, talking to poets before or after shows.

Eric met her for a drink the third day. She had the option to turn up at Richard's flat, but Eric was so busy writing reviews of literary events in order to get free tickets, and Richard had such bad hay fever because of the warmth, that she took to her own agenda. She had another meal in the trattoria and chatted with the chef. His Italianised lingo was part of his game.

'Where is Wildgoose tonight?

'Do they still call him *Wildgoose*?

'It just his name – Wysegrouse or whatever. Me, I like the wildgeese. I go to see them.'

'Where?'

'Aberlady. Village on coast. You go in winter!'

Maeve went back to the flat. 'Aberlady – go in winter,' she wrote.

By morning there was a good draft of a poem.

She needed to visit Aberlady. She called the bus station. It could easily be done in a day. She bought a takeaway picnic in a cardboard box from the trattoria.

Where you going? asked the chef.

'Aberlady.'

'Ho ho ho, you have wonderful day but no geese! No goose and no geese!'

'But the sea,' she said.

'Sea and space, big beach. You walk. You tell me tomorrow!'

She waved goodbye and went for the bus. After the journey she walked miles on grass, asked locals about the geese, ate her picnic beside the sands, bought postcards and a small book on the geese in the tiny shop.

She went home after her holiday bearing a new sense of Edinburgh life. Independence from Eric was part of it. She would go up to Scotland more often. Her Aberlady poem was revised and finished. On impulse she sent it to Mad Women Press, with a note that it might make an addition to her book. Within a week, Deirdre replied. She would publish the book. She wanted *The Geese of Aberlady* for the title poem, and she was sorry, *Odd Gloves* didn't fit with the rest. Maeve's first book of poems was on its way.

They were aware at work that Maeve had published poems and knew the poetry world, and the local writing scene. Not everyone liked this. Jon Silkin's *Stand* had stood her a couple of placings among its almost all-male repertoire. Her second poem in the *TLS* – a while after the early one about Charolais calves – had also been noticed. Others of her poems were not in such generally known journals, but local readings and activities were covered in the *Chronicle*. Morden Tower had a pretty good publicity machine. Maeve had her turn there, on a quiet winter evening, on the strength of her poems in *Stand*.

Thus she was summoned to Miz Martin's office one morning, to help draw up a programme for the Literary Initiative, a series of literary events in the libraries.

Both had ideas and they hammered them out: a talk by Harry Sutherland the novelist, Sid Chaplin who would do a discussion on how to get published, and an actress from the University Theatre willing to read Shakespeare's Sonnets and poems by Sylvia Plath. Maeve thought this should be two separate occasions, and when she asked about the copyright on Plath, Miz Martin said it was a matter for the Theatre.

Maeve suggested a visit from Catherine Cookson but Miz Martin said there wasn't a big enough hall. She asked if the Women's Writers Group meeting at Ouseburn could perform their poetry. Miz Martin didn't see why not.

A secretary would be brought in to send invitations and proposals to all these people.

Then Miz Martin's phone rang, and, not being asked to leave the room, Maeve sat quiet while Miz Martin dealt with it.

Or didn't.

First she said she couldn't take the call right now, then she listened for a minute, then, 'But that's impossible, you can't – Why, why now?' She wailed, put the phone down, looked at Maeve across the table and burst into tears.

Maeve had seen library juniors crying at times, but never someone like Miz Martin.

The senior librarian tried to pull herself together. 'I'm sorry, Maeve, that was little Janey, she's had enough – no oh oh.' More tears. At least Miz Martin had a posh hanky.

'I can't really talk to you, not here, it wouldn't be right.'

'If it helps you can talk to me!'

'But promise you won't put it in a poem.'

This appealed to Maeve's sense of humour. She started laughing and couldn't stop. Alice joined in.

'There's only one thing for it,' said Alice. 'Come out for lunch.'

In the sandwich bar, Alice talked about Janey.

'She's distantly related to Basil Bunting. She's from the same part of Scotswood. She wants to go and stay in that little town Sedbergh.'

'What, ever since we went there? That's years ago. I admit Sedbergh is a place you don't forget.'

'That's it. It's insane.' Alice sighed.

'Has she met Basil Bunting?'

'Yes! Since we went to Briggflatts. She took this notion to him and went up Hexham way looking for him. She's mental, is Janey. He can't help being nice to people. She just likes him!'

'Is it about poetry?' asked Maeve. 'I came across her through Beverley's gay writing group.'

Alice sighed. 'It's not about her tendencies. She's, you know, Sapphic. I can't make it out!'

Maeve said *Yes* and *Oh*, and Alice began to cheer up. In the end Maeve said, 'As long as you know I'm not like you in that way – I couldn't be reduced to tears by a Scotswood lass.'

'Divvent talk daft,' said Alice.

The Library's Literary Initiative was well received and events mostly fully booked. Shakespeare's sonnets were very successful at the Theatre. The Sylvia Plath reading was to be free, to circumvent copyright law, and advertised only to members of groups. It was ill attended, and Maeve and the Theatre found this disappointing.

The poetry at Ouseburn Library was fun and amusing, the amusement not altogether intentional. The readers included some mildly disastrous ones who hadn't been advised or prepared to speak slowly and raise their voices to an audible pitch. Karen, the group's leader, brought her children, and a last-minute request was made for poets to remember the audience and keep their language clean. One young gentleman withdrew his act.

Following on from the Literary Initiative was a Conference in Durham on Libraries and the Arts. Alice sent Maeve as a delegate. No one was suspicious of her outside-work non-relationship with Alice. They were Miss Carter and Miz Martin to the librarians.

Maeve thought Ollie might accompany her to this event. He was a Durham graduate from the days when Newcastle University was Kings College, Durham. But he'd said, *Not for me, Maeve. It's for younger people who still hope to change things. Find yourself a young Lothario*. She smiled. She would enjoy it, a change from Saturday in the library, with extra readers and schoolgirl Saturday staff, the regular library assistants squabbling about trifles, the caretakers who knew everything before anyone else; and the top brass who rationed themselves to an hour in the morning.

The conference was highly organised, though not well organised. Maeve picked up her programme at a reception table in the Castle. She was directed to a student room that wouldn't lock. She admired the view of trees, sorted out her small case, and hung up her dinner dress.

There was a name card: *Miss M. Carter, Newcastle City Libraries*. She took a biro and wrote *MAEVE* on the top of the clear plastic cover.

In the assembly area more people stood around – mostly men. She spoke to the nearest one.

'I'm from Newcastle. I hope this is going to be good.'

'Northern Arts,' said the man, dismissively.

A group of younger delegates came in through the wide doorway. Three or four men and a girl. She joined them.

The girl read Maeve's name. 'What a good idea – we haven't got name tags or I'd put Sylvia on mine. We're writers from P.E.N. up from London to support our speaker. That's Sebastian and that's Edwin Brock over there.'

'And that's Barry Cole,' said Maeve.

Barry Cole had had a two-year post with Northern Arts. She'd met him at Morden Tower. He came over.

'Hello Maeve! How's the writing going?' Not waiting for a reply he added, 'I didn't know you were a librarian.'

'I don't need to tell you I'm not making a living from poetry!'

'No, you don't,' agreed Barry. 'I've only got till September, then it's back to begging.'

They lined up for coffee and biscuits, Mr Northern Arts at the head of the queue.

'These are Librarians' Biscuits,' said a novelist. A librarian from Stockton-on-Tees looked back disapprovingly. Sylvia laughed. 'More librarians need to discover Smirnoff!'

The conference opened with a talk about managing the arts. Barry winked at her. Then the main opening: dinner. Maeve sat between Barry and a friend of his, a novelist who wouldn't give his name.

'I am quite open about my name, and I write poetry. Can't you be open?'

'You're a librarian,' someone across the table reminded her.

'Haven't you heard of librarians writing poetry? There's one at Hull.'

'Philip Larkin?'

'Are you a real poet?' asked Barry's friend.

'Course she is,' said Barry. Maeve smiled gratefully.

'You look like one,' said Barry's friend.

She turned to him. 'Come on, what name do you go by?'

'I am the silent unknown. I am the writer. Only my novels matter: it is of no consequence where I come from or who I am!'

'You've practised that, it's a prepared speech. Tell me the truth.'

'Nobody ever tells the truth. It's a false concept.'

'How can there be false things if there aren't true things?'

Barry's friend didn't look pleased. Maeve didn't usually feel so challenged. She looked to Barry for guidance, as did the friend. Barry grinned.

In the bar after dinner, she found two librarians from Glasgow. They were friendly, sleepy and married. She asked them about Scottish poets, whom they had heard of but weren't wildly excited by. The conversation turned to Durham City.

The young, unnamed novelist came over to her chair.

'Please come and cheer Barry up – he's crying!'

She followed mystery man over to a small table in a corner, where Barry was indeed weeping, a tumbler of whisky and half a glass of beer in front of him.

'Here's Maeve. You need some more writer friends. You can't live in the past, Barry.'

Barry looked up at her. 'Sorry Maeve. But my friend...'

'He means B. S. Johnson.'

Maeve knew of B. S. Johnson, who had famously published a loose-leaf novel.

'I can't bear it!' sobbed Barry.

The other writer, not more than a lad, pulled her away, his hand on her shoulder.

'B. S. Johnson killed himself last year,' he told her, 'and Barry was first at his house. They were friends. Barry is not recovering.' He attempted to drag her. Barry was in a collapsed heap, the picture of poetic despair.

'Hang on,' said Maeve. 'Barry's a novelist, B. S. Johnson's

a novelist, and you're a novelist. I'm going no further unless you tell me your name!'

Barry looked up from his weeping.

'Tell her your name for Christ's sake, and let her come and talk.'

Barry pulled a handful of nametags out of his pocket. 'We weren't going to wear them.'

Maeve looked over the names. Sebastian Barker. Edwin Brock. Sylvia Graves. Barry Cole. The others were managing without them, somewhere in the company.

'That just leaves yours, where is it?' said Barry. He dug again. 'Here it is!'

She grabbed it. *Mr U. Maverick*. 'What sort of name is that?'

'It's my pen name. Underground Maverick.'

'You can't go by that name officially.'

'P.E.N. accepts me by that name. Not everyone does.'

'Ask him if he's published any novels,' said Barry, with renewed interest in life.

'Of course I have. I'll get you a drink, Maeve. What'll it be?'

'Port if they have any, please.'

'You're beautiful,' Barry told her as soon as his friend had gone to the bar. 'I wish I wasn't married!'

'All right, I don't wish I wasn't married,' he added, seeing her face.

Maverick was back with a glass of port, and whisky for himself.

Barry said, 'Come on Maeve, we'll go and meet our friends.' He rose and led them in an unsteady beeline towards tomorrow's speaker, Adrian Mitchell.

Sebastian Barker recognised Maeve out of the corner of his eye.

'Oh Maeve, how lovely to see you!'

Gazing sternly at Barry, Mitchell declared, 'Barry Cole! Newcastle and Durham to the fore!'

Sebastian was asking after Eric Grysewood. 'Is he still in Scotland?' Adrian looked at Maeve and shouted, 'Dove Cottage!' Maeve could see librarians collapsed on chairs, walking around unsteadily or disappearing toward their beds, not always singly. She gave Sebastian Eric's news: he was working on a gay poetry anthology and living with the poet Richard Calm. Adrian hadn't realised Maeve's cousin was Eric Grysewood.

Barry and Maverick sprung their little plot, insisted Maeve had promised to help them guest-edit their magazine that evening, and bore her away. 'We'll see you at Adrian's talk in the morning,' she promised the Londoners.

Is this the first night or the second night?' she asked.

'You know it's the second. Last night was the pillow fight!'

It was Maverick. Maeve had given in.

'Again, please!' said Maverick, 'I've got another...'

The bed wasn't very wide, but Maverick was slimmer than her and much smaller than Ollie.

The excitement passed from Maverick to her. It had started right away when they got her into their room. In the twin room, all three of them chucked pillows at one another for half an hour. Then she was aiming every pillow at Maverick, and Barry had disappeared, to sleep in the other room – Maeve's.

She could not say she minded, nor whose invitation it had been. Once Maverick was holding her, once they were collapsed together, she knew by instinct how to touch him, how to add to his excitement as he came into her again. This was, what, the fifth time in two nights? She reflected hazily through the flowers that swirled in her mind, rippling round the room with a life of their own. She'd have said this could happen only if you were serious about somebody. It seemed she really liked Maverick. It hadn't taken long conversations or research.

He was moving round the room. She sat up and reached for last night's dress, suitable enough for the warm morning.

'What happens next?'

'There's a plenary session. It won't really be plenary – *plenary* means full doesn't it? We're going to miss it.'

'Will you come to Newcastle another time?' she asked hopefully.

'Hell, no,' said Maverick. 'This is a conference, don't you know?'

Maeve could not find an answer to this cavalier remark, but he turned to her smiling.

'You're coming to see a garden I've found you.'

He led the way down through the building to a hidden side door. They walked along a passage through high stone walls, turning a corner into a walled slope, surrounded by an orchard. In a central space were a stone seat and a quiet round pool.

'Private breakfast.'

She hadn't noticed his tote bag until he sat on the stone seat beside her and emptied it between them. The bag held sun-yellow cherries on tangled stems, two croissants, and a flask of coffee, smelling real and delicious as he removed the stopper and two small metal cups.

She sat looking round at the tall narrow trees. Maverick looked at her indulgently as she sipped at the coffee.

'I don't sleep with poets every night. I've brought you here to write me a poem.' He produced a notepad and pen from the same bag. 'Call it the guest-editing.'

'Damson trees,' said Maeve.

'How do you know?'

'Kendal's famous for them.'

'Will you write me a poem about damson trees?'

'Who says I'm going to write a poem?'

'You are, you will write one for me. What else is poetry for?'

Maeve laughed. 'But not about damsons. This strange little garden – reminds me of somewhere. I'll write you a poem. Did you really mean you wouldn't come north again?'

'I am Maverick, I am only what I write, I exist in no other form.'

Maeve wasn't sure she understood, but the air was special, the place was special – almost as though it had not existed before and never would again, that it had appeared expressly and purely for her and Maverick's benefit. She took the paper and pen. There was something else to write for him now. She knew he was watching, but she couldn't look. Finally she gave him the paper block.

'It's rather long,' she said.

The Sun God

This small rectangular garden reminds me
how a friend of a friend finally took me
to a Mithraeum on a snowy morning
*   in someone else's boots.*
We sat, intruding on the spectacular
demonstration of sunrise in religion,
two of us brought together unwillingly
*   then scared by a goose.*
In secret religions a creator dies
and love is at the heart of it in some way,
Maverick. Sex and religion are dangerous
*   to writers and poets.*
This is a Sapphic metre. It has dance-steps
also a tune. I swore I would not give up
love for poetry. Both are bound together.
*   You have decided.*
The goose will return soon, so will the sun-god.
Life will hassle and always be in the way
throwing me its obligations and delights.

Only gods can fly.
Served by the poets and archaeologists,
these rectangular gardens are our churches,
Damsons fall from the trees, but we won't notice.
We will be working.

His eyes went slowly down the page, reading.
'Thank you. They won't all understand it, but I do.'
'Who are *they*?'
'Oh,' he said, 'readers. When you publish it.'
'I won't publish it. You've got the only copy.'
They were walking back to the hall.

As they checked out, Barry came up alongside the registration desk. 'I'll keep in touch with you, Maeve,' he said. 'I'll be back up north. Remember me to Wildgoose – they called your cousin Wildgoose, didn't they? I met him several times. I knew you were his cousin. You're a Wildgoose too – look how you're flying away. I insist Eric shares his name with you.'

She gave him her best smile.

'My wild goose,' said Maverick.

'She's taking flight,' said Barry.

'I'm a genius at losing things,' said Maverick.

She climbed in a taxi, pushing Maverick away. Barry slipped a packet into her hand at the last minute. She told the driver to go all the way to Newcastle. She couldn't meet these two again at the station.

She opened the packet when they were out of the hilly centre. A novel by Maverick. Paperback, fat and floppy, it bore no noticeable publisher's information and it said 14th *thousand* – a lot for a young unknown writer.

Her library didn't buy this kind of book.

Back in Newcastle, things settled down. Maeve had some

correspondence about a batch of poems. She caught up with gossip at Central Library, paid Johnno the rent, and put in her conference report. She didn't think much would change as a result of the conference. Sid Chaplin was giving another talk next week, at the Central Library. The Theatre was still muttering about the audience it didn't have for Plath.

The Geese of Aberlady would be available in Thorne's. Eric would have a party for his own book in Edinburgh. They might share events, his second book and her first.

Buddy introduced himself to her at the library. She'd recommended his books to her bosses. He knew she had a book coming out with Deirdre. He hinted that he would be willing to look at her next book. More poem acceptances came, and invitations to join in poetry readings, with a few poems after somebody more important (and male). Howard Sargeant, editor of *Outposts*, and Maurice Lindsay in Glasgow wrote letters to her. Her successes were surprising Eric less. Richard, at least, treated her as an equal.

She met Ollie in the street, and he diverted her into a bar. She didn't want to drink, but they sat and talked. He asked her if she'd met any Lotharios.

'Well yes I did, but we won't be meeting again. He's in London.'

'Did people come all that way? I hoped you'd find someone interesting. I'm too stick-in-the-mud for you, Maeve.'

Maeve laughed. Perhaps she was stick-in-the-mud too. She showed Maverick's paperback to Ollie, who scratched his head and said he didn't recognise the genre. They parted amicably at the pub door. They didn't say when they would meet again, but they would.

Bev, the next to see Maverick's book, said, *These books are well known. Young people buy them in newsagents*. Intrigued, she mentioned the author to Buddy when he came in the library. Buddy immediately showed interest and said, *You met him? How did you get in touch with him?*

She left the whole question and lent the book to Bev. She was busy writing, and so was Maverick. Her poetry snowballed. Wild geese flew overhead.

Chapter Six

HOW IT HAPPENED · (1979)

IT ALL CAME ABOUT BECAUSE of *Tynescript*. This magazine, started by Karen and Margo, had been produced
on a Roneo at Margo's branch library for the last two years,
until the Central Library found out, the Librarian of the
Branch was called to order, and the magazine looked like
ceasing publication. Karen and Margo wanted their brain-
child to continue, for all its shortcomings, and were in favour of applying to Northern Arts for support.

There had been six issues, containing short stories from
Margo and Karen, poems from raw beginners, a couple of
bigger names, and occasionally, Maeve. Eric had contrib-
uted once or twice, writing under the name *Wildgoose*.

Maeve was at her table in Sandyford, peacefully looking
over the back copies. With their rough white paper and sta-
ples, garish yellow or blue twisted chessboard patterns on
the front (one colour per issue), they looked what they were
– a declaration of intent by some ordinary folks who had
discovered writing, and wanted to be heard and contrib-
ute alongside more privileged authors. The copies were too
amateur-looking to impress the pen-pushers at Northern

Arts; *Tynescript* was entirely a Little Magazine. But Maeve enjoyed receiving the issues one by one and she had read them from cover to cover. She picked up her mug from the copy she had used as a mat on the table. It had an archaeology of coffee rings.

She looked round, reasonably content. Twelve years had passed since she first moved into this side-room in Johnno's flat, silted and crowded with her books and clothes, scarves, shoes, a coat on a hanger on the door, the single bed covered with a throw. Ollie had last year phased out his lovemaking rather than take precautions when Maeve had told him she was coming off the pill. She was worried about staying on it forever.

Johnno was largely unchanged. His life was centred not around libraries and poetry, but building renovations and women. He did up pubs. He had strings of women friends, two or three at a time; after a few weeks one would drop out and another appear; they hung round him like a plait. There was often one of these women in Maeve's kitchen. They rarely lasted long enough for her to get to know them.

The phone rang. She went out to answer it, noticing how chilly it was in the hall – these were early days of the year and she had the gas fire on. Karen wanted to come round and make plans for Issue 7 of *Tynescript*. Maeve said yes, the time suited her, to ask Margo along if she was free; to bring biscuits if they wished.

She scuttled back into the warm little room. She'd entertain them here, because Johnno might be using the bigger room and there wasn't time to consult him. She fetched chairs from the kitchen. A party was always fun. She found the cups with roses and put the kettle on, to be all set when Karen arrived. She expected Margo too, and she was right. They breezed in bringing cold air with them, cheerful and lively. They started with tea, but she noticed all eyes on the magazines on the table. This was a crusade.

Karen opened her ring binder before she had finished her first cup.

'I've collected these new poems.'

'Who have you got?' asked Maeve.

'Surely you want to see the poems, not who wrote them,' Margo objected.

'Let's see anyway.' They spread out the papers. The writing group was strongly represented, with under-written short stories and overwritten poems. The student literary society had sent some offerings.

They all liked a story about fear of the 'Yorkshire Ripper.'

'I hope they catch that bastard. We can't glorify him,' said Margo.

Margo was right.

Maeve liked a poem in the Geordie dialect.

'Vernacular!' said Karen.

'Me grandad spoke like that.'

They came to a halt. 'Are we ready for another issue?' Maeve asked mildly, meaning they weren't.

'Oh yes,' Karen was fired up. 'I've been up to Northern Arts office. Here's the form to get money to print it. We can have quality printing.'

'And keep the price at 20 pence? I don't think so.'

'I've filled in most of the form.' Margo indicated the page. 'You have to sign it, too.'

'Wait a minute. We haven't got good enough content to go applying yet. We need a few poets they'll know of. They won't be impressed by all these women.'

'Go on, rub it in,' said Margo. 'You put a poem in. They know your name... and get your cousin to send us something, like last time.'

'But he didn't use his real name,' Maeve protested. 'He used *Wildgoose*, which he does when he's slumming.'

Eric had made the slumming comment but it was the

wrong thing to repeat to Karen and Margo. They looked at each other in alarm.

'So you're going to let us down and not sign this?' asked Margo. 'In that case...'

'I didn't mean that,' said Maeve hastily. 'I was thinking about standards. I know Northern Arts has its problems but they are considering giving me a grant and...'

'Oh, self comes first,' said Karen. 'when you're a traitor to the working class.'

'I'm not a traitor.'

'Sign this then.'

'I haven't even read it,' said Maeve with exasperation. 'Let me read it, then I'll tell you what you think.' Why couldn't she say anything right today?

Karen and Margo looked at each other. Maeve lifted up the forms and opened them out. From her library work with Alice, she knew about these applications. 'I can't agree with this,' she said. 'This funding isn't meant for groups like *Tynescript*.'

'I'm not standing for this.' Margo stood up. 'I'm going home.'

'You don't need to ...'

'Yes she does need to. You and your posh cousin are not right for *Tynescript*. I realise that now. You've been condescending all along. You think you're so much better than the other writers in the group... don't bother seeing us out. We know where the door is!'

Karen got up and put her coat on. Margo picked up her long knitted scarf from the floor.

'Don't go,' cried Maeve, 'I didn't mean it.'

'You meant every word!'

Margo's voice was raised. She snatched the remaining half packet of biscuits.

'Look, listen – '

'I've listened enough,' snapped Margo.

Her visitors were storming out of the door as Johnno came in.

'Karen, Karen!' She collapsed in tears.

Johnno picked her up off the floor. 'Whatever happened?'

'I thought they were my friends!'

'Who? Those poets?'

'Yes but...'

She gave up and howled.

'Come on,' said Johnno. 'I don't like this happening in my house. Any more than you like it in yours.'

'I invited them,' she stuttered through her tears. 'Oh no I didn't. Karen phoned and said they were coming round, then they did this to me.'

'What did they do ... don't get so het up about them...'

Maeve was almost choking. 'I said the wrong things... They said Eric and I were snobs... they said I was a traitor...'

'Come on. It's only poets. Not even proper poets, the ones I saw.'

She couldn't stop crying.

'You're too wound up about them, and about all this poetry. It's only words. We all use words. We don't all get so...'

'They haven't taken all their stuff.' Maeve picked up a paper. It was a poem by Margo. She read the first lines and they set her off again.

'This won't do,' said Johnno. 'Leave all this and come into the other room.' He steered her across the corridor. 'Eric gave me this brandy.' He took the bottle from a bookshelf and poured her a small glass. 'Sit down on the bed there.' He threw an extra cushion on the cover. 'Relax. I'll have a spot of this too.' He pulled a second glass from his shelf. She was still shaking with sobs. Johnno took hold of her shoulders, trying to calm her. His strength went into her and steadied her a little: she began to relax. She sipped the brandy.

'I've never seen you so upset before,' said Johnno. 'In fact I've never seen you upset at all. I don't like it. Now you are a little calmer, you must relax.'

He sat down beside her, still supporting her with an arm round her shoulder.

Distracted from the quarrel by the sight of this new, strong Johnno she hardly recognised, she sat more quietly beside him, the contentious words, *traitor, slumming, class, posh, snobs,* simmering down in her mind. She drained the glass of brandy. It wasn't much but it had stabilised her, and she was about to suggest a pot of tea, when something else completely unexpected happened. Johnno had an erection.

There was a look of simultaneous triumph and shock on Johnno's face, a fleeting male Mona Lisa smile. Her lap was so close to his trousers that she had to shift a little. They stared at each other for a moment. Then Johnno made to turn away but she said, 'Johnno, it's all right.'

'Do you feel better?' he asked but she said, 'No Johnno, I mean...' and she put her hand out tentatively towards his groin.

Johnno was now the one to be astonished. He played for time by drinking the brandy (there was more in his glass than she'd had in hers) and stared at her closely. She held her ground.

They went for it, unpremeditated as it was. Johnno pushed the cushions away and tried to pull the thin daytime cover over them. It wasn't particularly warm. Her diagonal patchwork skirt, a wrap-around, came off neatly and elegantly. Johnno didn't seem worried about elegance and threw his clothes down with the cushions. He still had the patterned hairy front she recognised from long ago.

Not much to write home about perhaps, but then this had been their shared home for years. It was almost as though they were making love to the house.

After a while they were satisfied, and perhaps the house was too.

Johnno apologised that he only had stale cigarettes.

'I don't smoke.'

'Oh, of course you don't.'

She went back to her room carrying her stray bits of clothing. She didn't know what to say. Not, 'Good Lord,' 'Good Heavens,' or 'That was a silly mistake,' all of which went through her head. She settled for, 'I think I've got everything.' Johnno said, absently, 'It's not far to come if you haven't.'

Johnno eventually went out to his darts club, though he said he'd be too late to play.

Maeve was half asleep when the phone rang; she went out to answer it. Another of Johnno's women friends. 'No, he's gone out.'

Next morning Maeve packed up her *Tynescript* magazines before work, and went round to see Karen in the evening. Within a week she was friends with Karen again and almost friends with Margo.

Johnno and Maeve crept round each other carefully for a few days, but neither of them seemed to want to repeat the performance. They'd had long enough as flat sharers and they knew the arrangement worked, and things settled back into the same undemanding relationship they had had before.

Maeve wasn't much of a filler in of calendars or a counter of days. She forgot that she'd taken a risk. She had almost forgotten what the pill was for. But when you thought about it, every human on the planet began with a woman noticing a strange taste in her mouth, or unwarranted tiredness or sensitivity, and going, *oh, uh...did I?... have I?... am I?...* , and after a few weeks it was obvious, she was.

Johnno was the dad. One day when they were each getting a snack supper, she told him.

It began with him. 'You look done-in,' said Johnno.

'Erm, actually, well. You know when...'

Johnno sat down.

'Thought so,' he admitted. 'The safest contraception is the sheath plus abortion.'

The grill pan made a spluttering noise.

'You didn't use a sheath.'

'Well, let's not quarrel about it. It's your decision.'

There wasn't a decision to make. She was thirty-one and this was life.

'Do you want pepper on this egg?' she asked Johnno.

She had little idea what would happen next. The doctors didn't want to see her till four months unless anything 'went wrong.' She hadn't even realised this meant four months from the date of conception. She went into Thorne's for a book about pregnancy, but there were none. She asked an assistant, angling to speak to a young woman.

'Nobody sells them,' said the young woman. 'Tell your daughter to ask at the clinic. The clinics dish them out free.'

She left the shop without informing the sales girl of her mistake.

She told Karen, and she wrote to Eric: he was her correspondent and confessor and she'd never before had very much to confess. Karen was more pleased than Maeve, saying, 'Oh, you'll get married now,' but Maeve thought this wouldn't happen. Karen's face fell a mile at first.

But telling Eric was a miscalculation. It really upset him. She had a not very comprehensible letter by return, written on his commuter train to Glasgow, and a not very appropriate congratulations card from Richard, whom Eric had promptly informed. She hid the card from Johnno. Eric wished her all the best and said he hoped wholeheartedly it would not interfere with the poetry. He concluded, 'I was hoping you might come and live in Edinburgh but this probably means you never will.'

Karen was some years younger than Maeve, but her youngest child was already at school. They hadn't much baby equipment left. Karen's partner turned up in his baker's van with what they had to offer. Blankets, rattles, bootees, vests and knitwear were bundled in a cot, a Beatrix Potter feeding plate lodged in the centre of the bundle, like the present inside Pass the Parcel. This really touched her. Excited and terrified by the tiny garments, she thanked him and piled the goods into her overstuffed room.

She began to notice everything about babies around the town, things that would never have come to her attention before. The time she was on a bus, and a woman got on carrying a baby in the new little one-piece garments that were everywhere, and a young girl commented, 'Mam, them's babygrows!' The previously invisible baby food sections in chemists. And the pregnant lassies.

It felt odd being suddenly bracketed with women a dozen years younger than herself.

She wondered how to rearrange the flat. She didn't want to sleep with Johnno regularly and most certainly not for the rest of her life. In the late twentieth century, people went by how they felt. The child would appreciate a father; she had no intention of obstructing Johnno's rights. She would love the child that the world was going to give her – but on her own account she had not lost hope for something better. She thought of Maverick. She was excited as well as scared.

She and Johnno got on annoyingly well at one level, but things didn't work in terms of being a couple. Here he was, coming up through the small gate. She made him a cup of tea and sat down on the kitchen sofa, tired, and asked what he wanted to do about supper.

'This isn't really working,' said Johnno.

'I suppose not. But I'm scared of moving out. The risk is my parents would take over. Welfare of their grandchild.'

'They mean well,' said Johnno.

'But they're not far enough away. They're not next door either. They are the worst distance.'

'Every distance is the wrong one,' said Johnno, 'if people are in your way. But this is what I'm going to do. I'm going to move out, on condition I can visit whenever I like. Don't worry, I'll pay for the house. You can't have the costs bumped up when your income is going to go down.'

Maeve was astonished. 'It's good of you, but can you afford it?'

'It's because I'm buying a second flat. I was going to sell up for a house if this hadn't all happened, but it has, and I'm not in the least sorry about your baby.'

'Nor am I, and with that sort of help I'll manage fine. It has to be fair though. You can't be financially responsible for me.'

'No, but I'll be responsible for the baby. Why don't I put the house in the baby's name?'

Johnno then solved the question of supper by saying he had to go out. 'I'm grateful to you for not trapping me.' He paused at the door before delivering this accolade, and departed. Relieved, but still jumpy from being pregnant at all, she ate the heel of a loaf with a tin of tomato soup, a piece of cheese and an orange. She wondered what would have happened if Johnno had bought a house.

In the dark, the doorbell rang: a messenger with a cardboard box. 'I'm dropping this off from Ollie Northold,' he said, and went away. Maeve pulled the box over the doorstep. It contained a long set of *Proust* in English, the Chatto & Windus edition with light blue and red dust covers. Ollie had scrawled a message:

Congratulations – baby gifts are not my scene, but you might have some time to read.

Ollie thought her deserving of Proust! She was trying to make space for baby things. Where would she put these extra books?

Her parents found out when, unusually, they came up to Newcastle for lunch. She could have got away without telling them yet, but it seemed as good a time as any. They had asked her to meet them in the restaurant at the top of Fenwick's.

This wasn't an inquest: they'd heard nothing via her cousin. But the soup hadn't even arrived before her mother said, 'You're quiet today, Maeve. Is everything all right?'

'I hope you'll think it's all right.'

'You're moving to Edinburgh with that cousin of yours?' asked her father, still unaware what was going on. She already knew her mother had guessed.

'It's more important than that,' she said. 'I've just found out that I'm pregnant.'

'Oh that's marvellous,' said her father.

Her mother actually smiled. They waited. So did the waitress, surreptitiously.

'You met Johnno, the guy in the flat. It was him.' She realised as she said it how accusatory it sounded, as if it wasn't both of them.

'You'll be leaving your job.'

'Are you going to marry this Johnno?'

'I won't be marrying Johnno.'

'And the job?'

Incredibly, this was the first time she had faced up to the job. 'There's good maternity leave these days, and I hope they'll give me part time work afterwards. They run all the branch libraries.'

Her mind raced round her options. 'I've been going to a group of women writers,' she told her parents, 'as well as the main poetry events. Some of them are feminists, and some are just women. Some have children. There could be childminding opportunities.'

'The baby will be your top priority,' said her mother sternly.

'But it doesn't stop you living. Men need to help with the children.'

'Will Johnno help with all this?' asked her father.

'Oh yes, he is quite pleased about it.'

'Well, that's something,' her mother conceded. 'What's his family? Where's he from? What work does he do?'

'Oh he has work, and he owns my flat and one other. I'm not going to be destitute.'

'I hope your new way of life won't stop you doing your poetry,' said her father at last.

She looked at him thoughtfully. It wouldn't stop her, but it could hinder her. How had women got themselves pushed out of poetry in the first place?

'Poetry is only a hobby,' continued her mother. 'It won't make you money. Bringing up a family will be your priority.'

While her mother was in the cloakroom, her father whipped out a cheque book and hurriedly wrote her a cheque.

'Put that away, and make sure this man looks after you properly. I'm glad you think that he can.'

Her mother came back. Her father again used his cheque book to pay the bill. 'I've added a tip for them giving us privacy to talk.' He pocketed the chitty.

'How will you keep in touch?' asked her mother. 'We have to know you are all right. Can you come down for a weekend soon? You don't always need to change at Carlisle.'

'I'll keep in touch. I'm going back to the library now. Thanks for the lunch. You've got the sunshine!' and she left the expectant grandparents to the rest of their afternoon.

A wild goose swooped down the middle of Northumberland Street. Maeve stopped dead on the kerb. It passed her close, and flying on, winged its way northwards. While low, not far above the people – lower than a double-decker bus, children saw it and women turned their heads. High again, it joined a great skein heading towards the town moor.

'Swans!' someone said.

'Geese,' replied others, as they all gazed up at the skies.

Maeve savoured the outdoor air of the city street. Though not lifted by grass and hill, this was breathable air. She breathed it, and went back into her library, where the changing shape of her body might or might not yet have caught the notice of her colleagues.

She remembered the geese her father failed to see when she was a small child.

She entered the library and went up to Alice's office.

'Maeve! I thought we were keeping to out of work hours?'

'I have something to report to the management.'

Alice indicated an easy chair. Maeve sat down.

'I'm pregnant. I'll have to adjust my work arrangements.'

'Oh Maeve, you silly blighter!'

'Well, thanks!'

'Did you do it on purpose? Are you okay?'

Maeve smiled at her friend. 'I didn't do it on purpose, but I'm pleased.'

'In that case, congratulations, my love. I'll see 'admin' about the leave we can give you... you've got continuous service from Kendal, haven't you?'

'I suppose I have.'

'Leave it with me. And you're not to worry. Look after yourself. What about Sunday, can I come round on Sunday afternoon? I have some news too, actually, but it's something I cannot yet discuss in here.'

'Sure, Sunday is good,' answered Maeve, relieved she had raised her situation with the library, and wondering what her friend was about to divulge to her.

On Sunday Alice came with her news. She had landed a fabulous job in London, as a senior manager at the London Library. She'd written to the Librarian on spec and had been appointed to a position that hadn't then been advertised. Alice explained how the library in Jermyn Street had at least three gay men on the staff. Openly liberal, it was the origin of the joke about gay men liking quiche. On her interview visit Alice had heard two men discussing their supper that night, quite blatantly.

Alice would enjoy the cosmopolitan lesbian scene. 'An improvement on summer evening trips to the coast,' she told Maeve.

'And Carter's Ladies Bar,' said Maeve. 'I always noticed it had my surname.'

Another enticement to Alice was the clientele. Half the famous writers in England were members of this library. She had bumped into Iris Murdoch at the issue desk, and the singer Millicent Martin – her own namesake, in the entrance foyer the moment she arrived. She'd seen a small handwritten request for books from Sacheverell Sitwell, received on the same day.

This was to be Alice's great adventure. Maeve was glad to see her happy and excited. Alice was giving two months' notice and would be away before Maeve had her baby. She spoke of buying a flat at Covent Garden and inviting Maeve down to the London poetry scene.

When Alice had gone, after so much one-sided excitement, Maeve sat down and howled. The chances of her visiting London with a young child were small. She'd be losing her best woman friend when she needed her most.

It seemed odd that the leader or teacher of the pre-natal course was a man. It wasn't an all-female group; one of the women had her husband with her, but in this first session, Maeve felt self-conscious and prickly, as if men were having their hair coiffured in the next chairs at the beauty parlour.

She herself seemed slightly out of place. She could almost have been the mother of some of the first-time pregnant women in the room. She shared their apprehension and excitement, however, as they all listened carefully to the leader.

'When Baby's ready,' he was saying, 'your bones will loosen, your pelvic bones, your whole frame comes apart enough to allow the delivery of Baby into the world. That's why having a baby hurts. But we will show you how you yourselves can make it easier. You must remember it's perfectly natural. Your bones come apart that little bit.'

They were sitting in a circle, wearing easy clothes, because for part of the session they would lie on the floor and learn exercises.

Maeve's life was coming apart too, it seemed, as the weeks progressed. She found it harder to be calm and collected at work. It wasn't like her to be easily upset by library users. A man who was doing an Open University degree wanted constant nannying and had taken a liking to her personal attention. She started hiding when he came in, and he noticed this and complained. She took it personally. Was the man stalking her because she was pregnant? Alice had to intervene, and put her on cataloguing duties, where she wouldn't be seen by the public. Soon enough she was off work – signed off sick by the admin lady until her pregnancy leave began.

'A boy,' said the nurse. Shocked, sore, jubilant, Maeve gazed up at him. The new human being looked back at her and yelled. A nurse lifted the baby into the cot, while Maeve was sent to have a salt bath. A young girl was crying because she had a girl baby and wanted a boy. Someone who had had a 'bad time' cursed and screamed *Butchers*! in the corner of the ward. Amid such turmoil, she and her son began life together. As an 'elderly' first-time mother she was here for a week.

Johnno came the second afternoon, bringing a gift of a teddy. Maeve was impressed, not only that Johnno had organised himself sufficiently to buy it somewhere, but that it wasn't too large, too small or too garishly coloured, but the right sort of teddy for a young child, and in Maeve's opinion an essential. Thus Johnno's first act as a father succeeded with Maeve.

While Johnno was there, Karen and Margo turned up. She had never whispered to them their part in the baby's existence, but she noticed Johnno looking slightly askance at them. They didn't stay long, and when they had left, Johnno commented wryly, 'But for that pair pitching into you, neither you nor I would have had any offspring!' 'Speak for yourself,' said Maeve, but she wasn't displeased.

Her father was on jury duty so her parents couldn't visit yet. Parcels of new, pressed, pastel knitwear in the smallest sizes arrived from her mother. 'I'm sorry I couldn't knit like this,' she wrote. 'I got them at Hawkshead sale of work.'

A card from the library was signed by a couple of dozen staff, including the large, generous signature of the Chief. A letter came from Alice Martin in London, in the envelope a slim-boxed silver bangle. Had Alice anticipated a baby girl? A card from Eric, alerted by the parents, said he would be in Newcastle staying with Buddy at the Lorikeet the following week. He and Buddy were working on a new magazine of which Eric would be editor. She wasn't surprised that Eric could barely remember to add his congratulations. She'd had a tiff with Eric last autumn, but it had blown over.

At the next bed a gang of youngsters, the older kids, were greeting a new-born, with family chatter and exclamations about the baby's small fingers and toes. That was the poetry to new mothers. She began to compose a line or two, but had nowhere to write them down. Over the week Maeve was unable to attend to anything except herself and the baby. Rushed in suddenly, she had no reading matter nor even a notebook. She hadn't picked up a pen or pencil in days. As she grew familiar with her baby, and the days extended, she couldn't wait to get out of this humming, relentless, powerful asylum, from under its muffled, almost feathery Maternity Wing, into the rest of her world.

After the sterility of the hospital, the house looked untidy. It had been cared for in her absence, in a masculine way, but its proportions seemed changed by the presence of the baby. Johnno had been round putting various items in place, a cradle, a baby bath. A friend had called with flowers which were on a windowsill against the light. She moved them to the table. There were more baby cards, still enveloped. She opened them, leaving them for the moment in their heap, with the funny dog picture from Sal Grysewood on top.

The brand-new family allowance book had arrived. She looked it over with interest. Like the other mothers who'd been in the hospital, one way or another she would be all right. She could think of nothing she was extravagant with, except postage stamps, which were going up to 10p for second-class next month.

The baby's name was Giles Grysewood Carter. She'd always admired the name Grysewood. No one denied it would make a great middle name – an invisible middle name as most people's were, something to pull out of the hat when required, or cause a giggle at a wedding.

She couldn't remember where 'Giles' came from, except

it suited him perfectly. The minute you saw that baby you thought, yes, Giles. He looked self-contained and determined from day one. He had a shock of sandy hair, under which his firm gaze looked out at his mother and everyone else. Maeve was incredibly proud of him. If you were going to interrupt your life with a baby, you might as well have a baby like Giles. She didn't say that, because every woman liked their own baby, but she also believed quite strongly in the feminist tenet that having a baby messes up a woman's life, but it doesn't mess up a man's life.

That was the difference between women and men.

On the other hand, if you didn't have a baby at all, you might be resented for not messing up your life like the other women, many of whom despised you for seeing this greatest experience as a messing-up.

Eric turned up the next week, tripping through the chaos with a wrapped vase, a poem for the baby, a bottle of whisky and a bunch of flowers. He proceeded to stand in the way drinking the whisky, but he admired the baby, complimented Maeve and behaved well enough. There was to be a Morden Tower meeting before he was due back in Edinburgh, and he asked whether Maeve could leave her baby for a few hours to attend this event with him.

'You're still calling him the baby. I think of him as Giles.'

'Well, Giles is the baby. How about it?'

'Yes if Johnno will come.'

So Johnno came.

'I'm surprised you trust me with Giles,' said Johnno.

'He is asleep and he'll probably remain asleep, as long as you don't play loud music.' Maeve gave Johnno instructions including the clinic emergency number. There wasn't a telephone in Morden Tower.

Maeve felt delicate, soft and sensitive like a creature

without its shell, but she was determined to meet the poetry crowd and be reassured that her life would carry on. The maxi-dress style was more or less finished but she felt comfortable in her greenish-blue maxi-coat. Fashion had become more liberal lately.

Eric took her arm as they headed out to the bus stop.

'Have you forgiven me for forgetting to tell you about Hugh MacDiarmid's funeral?'

'Is that still on your mind, Eric? You must have felt guilty.'

'I thought your Newcastle mob would know.'

'You intended to get drunk. I heard you managed it.'

'We didn't get drunk until afterwards.'

'Someone who should have known better said you were all jockeying for position after the top poet had gone. But you know what?' she continued. 'That was months and months ago. Last autumn. I'm a different woman now, I have a baby. I can't go running round the country and getting drunk to prove what a dedicated poet I am! When some woman poet merits a poetry funeral, then I will want to know, but not till then!'

The bus slowed down and they boarded it.

Close again, and she liked being close to him, they arrived at Morden Tower.

'How's the baby?' everyone asked, quite disappointed she hadn't brought him along.

It was great to hear the poets. Tom Leonard knew Eric from Scotland and was surprised to see him in Newcastle, but he didn't remember Maeve.

They didn't stay too long. She felt an eagerness to be back with the baby, as strong as her wish to be part of the poetry scene. Eric suggested going drinking with Barry MacSweeney and Jackie, but he didn't get his way.

They found Johnno asleep fully clothed on the divan, Giles sleeping quietly beside him.

'Johnno, that baby is supposed to be in the cradle,' declared Maeve, and took up the baby but did not put him in the cradle.

'He's fine,' answered Johnno. 'I wasn't asleep. Was your meeting a good one?'

'Thank you, Johnno. I needed the change of scene,' she said, still holding Giles. 'Johnno, could you please put a kettle on the stove for me. Eric, you should be off to the Lorikeet.'

Eric picked up his briefcase.

'Mind you, Giles is an odd name for a baby,' said Johnno. 'It will be fine when he grows up.'

'You can choose a name for the teddy.'

'Goodnight Maeve. Glad things are going well. We can make this work.' Johnno strolled away after Eric.

Maeve put Giles in his cradle beside her bed. From tomorrow she'd be a single parent, but she wouldn't lack friends, nor, it seemed, would the child lack a father. She'd had little time for poems, but one came from the geese.

> *How fast they fly to raise their young,*
> *their new-grown goslings soon migrating*
> *trails of which former flocks have sung,*
> *how fast they fly to raise their young,*
> *lifted in air, on currents flung,*
> *when springs emerge from winters waiting,*
> *how fast they fly to raise their young,*
> *how old their need, these wild geese mating.*

Chapter Seven

THE LONELY MUSIC   (1980–1985)

THE HALF-DECADE FROM 1980, while Giles was under five, was a very practical time. Maeve felt as if she'd gone to sleep a certain gender, a robust woman, liking men, wanting also to vie with them, to argue on their level, to take stands on art and politics and information. She wasn't a sissy, she wasn't delicate. She liked many things men liked, a walk, a pie and chips and beer, a challenge, to speak in public.

It seemed she had woken into another gender, a fussing, serving, cuddling and dependent gender. If she had ever considered she might have more children, she was changing her opinion. She hadn't decided on Giles. She had become accustomed to not having babies. She had let things slip.

On the other hand she loved her baby, this was something she wanted to be doing with. She and the baby hadn't reached a testing time yet.

She'd been writing poems again, while he slept. When he grew, sleeping less, she still managed a series of poems about places, the weather, and birds, and about geese. You saw geese if you drove north (she hadn't been in a car for a while), or went to their haunts – Druridge Bay, Montrose Basin, the Solway Firth – but you had to go in winter. They made themselves totally scarce in summer, obeying their inbuilt call to rise into the sky.

She was finding it harder to send her poems anywhere. The palaver of envelopes and stamps, the trivial costs being left for a day or two, the physically longer distance to the stationery shop when you had to take a small person with you. She knew some Scottish magazines and had a poem in one called *Cencrastus* on a facing page to one of Eric's, by pure chance. She hadn't been writing to him. Like him, she was busy. He was engrossed in his magazine, which should have been called *The Lorikeet* but was only called *Poets Plus*. She was waiting for an invitation to submit to it that hadn't come. Maeve knew the score.

The geese raised their wings, creating currents of air in the bigger air around them, lands and interminable oceans passing beneath their numbers in flight. They abided in sky or on wetlands and meres, up the east coast into Scotland, near Tyneside where water stood over abandoned mine subsidence. If there was suitable terrain the geese would find it.

She sought out somewhere local. She took Giles, while he was light enough to carry on her person, using a fashionable baby-carrying harness for her accessory, a baby. She wasn't getting out enough. She couldn't, until the baby's life started separating from hers.

The geese were abundant in early spring. They went, every one of them, later, as if none could miss the annual festival of nesting, hatching and feather-growing on far, inaccessible shores.

They seemed ungainly, clumsy in contact with land, these creatures of the sky and water. She walked near and among them, watched them on the lake surface, or grubbing around the mud. She saw landings and take-offs with splashing and noise, heard the cackle and burble of their conversations. The baby stared, waving and imitating goose-sounds, which drew amusement from other walkers around the paths and trails.

This sunny morning, she went into the little café where there was a chair in the ladies to feed the baby, then had coffee and a sandwich surrounded by wildfowl posters, showing the various colouring of the greylags, pink-footed and barnacle geese. She gave Giles a piece of the sandwich bread, which he chewed and spat out. She looked forward to him being old enough to talk of such simple, definable matters as ducks and swans, geese, egrets, goosanders. He was burbling again, waving his arms as if conducting the weird music of geese.

That could have been the day Maeve decided she would make a long poem about geese. Freshened by their outing, Giles sleepy, she sat among her papers and books. She would start one day, perhaps soon. She was preparing to do it already. She went to the library, carrying Giles, and sought out the bird books. She needed to know where the geese went in summer, Greenland she thought, and how they nested there. The best books were too heavy to carry. She sat and read them for a while. There weren't many answers to her questions.

Librarians nodded and smiled to see her with the baby, but they did not disturb the quiet study area.

The seasons passed, like those of the geese. It wasn't easy to get along to poetry readings. Johnno was a willing babysitter, but Giles as a toddler was more lethal, no longer an angel face seen in sleep of an evening, but a dynamo of worrying action. She was free for some events, for Johnno wasn't simply a babysitter, he was the child's father. Sometimes she felt she was wandering the town alone to give Johnno his turn with this dangerous little human, and would then return to chaos at her home.

On this occasion she met Sandie Craigie and Elizabeth Burns, two young Edinburgh poets. Sandie warmly invited her to go up to Edinburgh the following week on an 'exchange.' They had come from some outfit called 'The Diggers' and there was so much female poetic camaraderie at the Old George Hotel, where they met, that Maeve was very, very tempted.

'But I have a baby, a two-year-old.' `

'Bring her!'

'He's a him.'

'You could stay over with us.' Sandie Craigie didn't see a problem.

Maeve saw the problems too late. She and Giles made it to Edinburgh, to Sandie's High Street place. They had a memorable weekend. She couldn't go to the intended poetry, because the Diggers turned out to be a downtown pub named after gravediggers. When some of Sandie's friends offered to take care of Giles for the evening, she felt obliged to decline their well-meant offer for reasons they would have taken amiss, connected with the smell of marijuana on their clothes. She said she would take Giles sightseeing, and wandered down the High Street till she came to an old house, the Netherbow. It had a café. She took Giles in and settled down with him. He was peaceful and sleepy.

Some young women came in. One of them was Elizabeth Burns, whom she'd met last week. They crowded round and it transpired they were all poets. They had come to hear a poet called Liz Lochhead, here in the Netherbow. It seemed amazing that there was such a range of poetry on in Edinburgh that she could walk away from one event (at the Diggers) slap into another, at the Netherbow. But the girls laughed and said their friends were all in poetry groups, it could happen. More and more young people piled into the café, then they set off upstairs. Since Giles was deeply asleep on her shoulder, Maeve went up with them to a room for the reading. It was crowded out. No space for a couple of dozen more men and women on the stairs.

'Oh dear,' said Liz Lochhead to the organiser, 'Would it help if I did two sessions?'

Maeve was at the top of the stairs near the cut-off point. 'Let that woman with the baby in,' said the organiser, 'and the rest in the second house. Half an hour each session.'

Maeve sat at the back while this woman poet wowed the audience. She realised that what she'd been fighting for was happening in front of her eyes. Women were poets; young women aspired to be poets. She was so affected that, far from her toddler crying, she was almost in tears herself, and she scurried out as Giles began to wake at the end of the session. She pushed her way downstairs against the tide of the second sitting, hastened back to Sandie's flat, and settled herself and Giles on the sofa she'd been allocated for the night. She was exhausted.

The dark-haired, cheeky, welcoming Sandie brought a retinue back from the reading at the Diggers. Maeve revived and enjoyed their conversation. Everyone seemed to be a poet. Given she had Giles with her, she was lucky how the visit turned out. She didn't contact Eric; she had begun to see there were echelons in poetry, and for all its vivacity, this echelon did not overlap with Eric's. There was a late-night, unplanned, inspired recitation of poems exploding with expletives, Sandie's the most poetic ones. Giles then woke and did some yelling, but everyone was too spaced out to worry. Maeve reckoned she'd done well to catch the Netherbow reading, then this.

She thanked her host and set off for the station next morning with a strong admiration of Sandie and her world, and a new friendship, which would round out the Edinburgh of Eric and Richard. She arrived home to find

Johnno upset that she'd taken off with the baby to a poetry weekend, and a few days later, Eric expressed his annoyance that she'd been to Edinburgh without informing him. Stuff them both, she thought.

And yet, she felt faintly ashamed of her trip. It had somehow failed. All the young women were running around being poets, while she was vegetating – was that the word? – with her dependent child. She was being left behind. She must write.

The seasons of Giles' development wore on. Speech, walking, questioning, socialising with other tots: Maeve was responsible for everything, despite Johnno's interested support.

Her own 'development' was irrelevant. She was beginning to see she couldn't do everything. With the child, she could either make time to meet poets or time to do her writing. She was at the limit of what could be done.

Nor had Eric deserted her. Here he was in Newcastle again, to see Buddy, his publisher and now hers too; his feet were well under the table at Swing Bridge Press and he was staying in the Lorikeet helping to edit a book. *Poets Plus* was limping a bit by the sound of it: Eric said it had too many cooks.

Maeve and Karen had a table set with a swish chocolate cake from Karen's partner's bakery. 'Surplus to requirements.'

'That's a good perk,' said Eric.

'You know the best perk? He works from dawn and is finished and in when the kids come in from school.'

'So working mothers should marry a baker.'

'I'll bear that in mind,' said Maeve.

They set about the tea party, including Giles, but Maeve made him eat a sandwich first, while they all waited for the cake.

Eric remembered something. 'Oh Maeve, well done for winning that competition. What a lovely poem. *Odd Gloves*... fun.'

'Thank you. What a surprise! The gloves I found at the fair.'

'Red and green with Fair Isle! Yes.'

'I wrote it long ago. Like the gloves, it hung around, had a few outings... no one took it, but I still believed in it...'

'Quite right,' said Eric. 'People who think publication in some wee magazine validates their work, drive me crazy.'

'Or they think they are better than you because they have Arts Council grants.'

'I've got an Arts Council grant! I thought you had one once?'

'I did,' said Maeve, 'though it nearly came to grief because I named you for a reference.'

'I told them I was your cousin. I thought it only fair.'

'What's a grant?' asked Giles. 'What's arts council?'

'Blimey, Giles, eat up your cake.'

'What's blimey?'

Maeve took him through to where most of his clobber and amusements were, and presently came back.

Eric was showing Karen the poster he'd filched from a pub. The pubs were not short of them.

'This is for you, Maeve and Karen. An open poetry reading on Calton Hill in Edinburgh next week.'

'What's an open poetry reading?'

'Anybody can join in. It's on all afternoon.'

'That's unusual!' said Karen. 'I suppose we'll have to take Giles?'

'Of course we'll take Giles! It's an outdoor event at a huge park on the hill. It's ideal for him.'

Karen made a joke of it. 'I divvent knaa, I should've left baby-minding behind. But my Katy's growing fast – it might not be long before I'm on granny duties!'

'You cannae wait!' said Maeve, teasingly.

'Okay, I'm coming! This Sunday? Himself won't like it much, but I've hardly been anywhere for weeks!'

Giles wandered back.

'How would you like to go to Edinburgh on Sunday?' asked his uncle.

'On the train?'

'Yes,' said Maeve. 'And Karen is coming and we'll take the pushchair.'

'Nooooo,' began Giles, 'I won't go in the fooking pushchair!'

'Giles!' Maeve was horrified. 'Wherever did you learn that word?'

'From Johnno's floozy,' said Giles complacently.

'Well! You don't say that word and you don't say floozy! Ever again!'

'I thought you called Johnno Daddy,' said Eric tentatively.

'Yes but he *is* Johnno. You don't call him Daddy, only me does!'

'Oh well,' said Karen, 'we'll need the pushchair if you get tired.'

'Nooooo! I won't get tired! I don't get tired! NOOOOO!'

Maeve pulled out a paper and pencil from under the chair. 'Here, you can...'

They didn't go. Giles fell over and scrubbed his knee. It stiffened. Terrified, Maeve took him to the doctor. The doctor treated him and said, 'They are India-rubber at that age. See that he rests over the weekend and try to have him sit on the sofa, or in bed if he won't sit still.'

Thus, what could have been an exciting day with her cousin and Richard never happened. Life seemed full of plans that didn't quite come off. Soon Giles would be at school, and the library might be interested in giving her a morning job. What would she do then if he was ill?

Huntsmen went for the geese. Great, thoughtless, macho guys in cast-off military dress, carrying heavy guns then posing with huge dead geese held by the legs, dozens brought down. To individuals in the multitude the risk was slight. Geese preferred the reservations. They knew these were safe from marauders bar a fox or a poacher, ragged, disguised, at unheralded times. The geese descended to mingle with lesser birds, warblers and sandpipers, cormorants, dunlin, goosander. Awkwardly shaped on land compared to their comfort in water or streamline in air, they used the three elements constantly.

Farmers locally went for the geese. The marauding of crops was a serious matter. You could lift a goose, though they were heavy, and strangle it. Or you could take the farm shotgun on your own land. You had to be a decent shot. Not even the callous wanted to wing a bird.

No wonder country people ate goose for Christmas, and not at exorbitant prices. You needed a scullery for plucking the goose, and a good-sized family to eat it. You would take your bag back to the farmhouse. Your wife or your daughter would pluck and cook, and it would be food, even as your winter corn sprang more thinly after the visit of the flock.

There were so many geese. The one you took from the skies, or coastal fields, was one of tens of thousands. Yet they held to their mates, and some goose in some strange part of the world would be wondering where your goose, their partner, had gone, and wishing ill of the hunters.

Maeve would soon know too much about the wild geese, rather than too little. She would have to distil it. She would make this poem thoughtfully. It would not be in iambic pentameters. It would have the beat of wildgoose wings, the width, the freedom. It would have movements, like music.

'Where's my dulcimer?'

School and a birthday: Johnno was right, these were

milestones. His father had given him the dulcimer, calling round yesterday teatime and braving the jellies, tots and their women writer mums. It was a crowd for a little house.

Dulcimers came in many shapes and sizes, a fact Maeve had not known. This one was on the small side – Giles could lift it and carry it around – but its volume ran to at least as many decibels as Giles in his worst (and fortunately outgrown) screaming fits. Unwrapping and trying out the dulcimer resulted in the other parents deciding the party was ending, and they circled round, young and old, in a flurry of donning hats and scarves, prompted and recited thank you speeches, and a trail of candy, smarties, sniffs and protests.

Maeve thought the hammer dulcimer an extravagant present for a five-year-old.

'It's a bit advanced for him,' she told Johnno, not wishing to belittle the handsome gift, but wondering how it would fare under Giles' ownership.

'It's for children,' said Johnno. 'It's strong. He can't break it.'

She was startled by a bang. The child had taken his dulcimer into the hallway. The back corner hit the door frame, and a chip of wood flew off, not from the dulcimer but from the door. She turned to Johnno with a hint of accusation.

'He's five,' said Johnno. 'He likes it.' He picked up the small chip of wood. 'I'd live with that, it'll look worse if you glue it back on.'

'It says here, for children eight to ten,' she said, referring to the booklet.

She went to look for the dulcimer. Giles had been banging on it from the minute they got in from school until she'd stopped him to eat at the table. He had then turned his attention to scribbling on his cards.

He had tried various batons for the dulcimer: the pair

supplied with the instrument (using both the right and the wrong ends), his toy magician's wand, a wooden spoon, a stick of rock, fortunately wrapped, and a pair of sharp scissors he wasn't supposed to have. Wearily she retrieved the scissors, and the stick of rock, which she threw into the kitchen bin. How had it even got into her house?

The combination of yesterday's birthday, the dulcimer, and continuing school had been exhausting for her, but also for Giles, for by the time she came back with the dulcimer, found unexpectedly in the bathroom, he had fallen asleep on a cushion on the floor. Not prepared to wake him, she carefully put a blanket over him. Now for some time for herself.

Her father had acquired a golfball typewriter from his office, and had driven it up to her on a grandparents' inspection visit. The typewriter was his secret message that he approved of her writing. She was glad, but she would have written anyway. It was also the envy of the writers she knew, including Eric. Its desirable feature was proportional spacing of the letters, as in printing. The typewriter lived in a safe cupboard in case Giles decided to pull out the golfball. And it became the catalyst for the poem about geese.

Arrived for nesting, out of thousands pared to pairs,
Shell dissolves to grit in reeds,
yolk builds feathers, bones and greed,
demand of growth and flight

What was flight? Necessary? Right? These lines shouldn't rhyme. She put them in a thin folder with a roughly drawn goose on the front.

Time was precious. Every day was a rush with Giles. She couldn't leave him sleeping on the floor all night. She lifted him (he was heavy) and put him in his bed. He didn't wake, but said 'Dolcimor,' with an alarmingly Geordie accent, in his sleep.

She could write in the mornings while Giles was at school, but she knew this might not last. She'd go back to work part time with the Libraries if they'd have her. The typewriter came out of the cupboard for now and she returned to the lines about geese.

demand of growth and flight

Should that be *demands*?

Goslings | spikily purposeful, scouring a beach.

The doorbell sounded. Janey Hogg, Alice's young friend and once partner, was standing on the front path. Maeve had not seen her for years. Maeve stepped out into the minuscule garden in the warm spring air, and sat on the bench, giving room for Janey beside her, next to old bluebells and a coral-blossomed quince.

'How are things, Janey?'

'You divvent want me in your hoose?' asked Janey, direct as ever.

'In a minute. I've been writing.'

'Basil Bunting died. I've been at his funeral,' said Janey.

They both remembered their visit to Briggflatts in the Bentley. This would be something Janey would come and tell Maeve.

'You have? When? Last I heard he was in an Arts Council house in Washington New Town.'

'Na! He was back along the Tyne, an' died in Hexham hospital. I've been livin' out there, but...'

'That's sad,' said Maeve, still trying to pull herself together. 'I wish I'd known about the funeral. I might have managed to go. I liked the old man. He was old when I met him, twenty years ago!'

'Funeral last week,' said Janey. 'I seen Eric Grysewood there.'

'Eric?' Good god! Not again. Why hadn't she known? Here was Janey, her uncompromising dialect made fashionable recently by *Auf Wiedersehen Pet*, which even the non-television-watching Maeve knew about. If not Eric, at least someone had brought news of Basil's death: Janey, the real thing, her northern tongue unashamed.

'Ye knaa, wi got on great with Basil. I've been seein' him, till he was in hospital...'

Maeve listened, incredulous.

'You always looked like him!'

'He sez I could be connected with his ancestors in Scotswood.'

'You went down to Sedbergh?'

'I loved Sedbergh and Briggflatts... I came back and found him up the Tyne. Among his dashes round the world's universities, where he got paid to show off – who wouldn't like that? – he'd stopped bothering to write. He had time to gossip. He sez wi looked like him because wi thought like him.'

'And do you?'

'Well aye, I'm political like Bev and like him.'

Maeve wasn't going to get Janey off the subject of Basil.

'I read *Briggflatts* quite often,' she said. 'Tell me about the funeral.'

'He had family, children, wives and what not, and poets – some American. I saw Eric with this Gael bloke and someone else. Gael asked me which poets I knew in Newcastle. I sez you. Eric wasn't too happy to see wi there.'

'I'm astonished Eric didn't get in touch with me,' said Maeve. She stood up and led the way inside. She was appalled by this news, if only because so many years had vanished. She was not desperately sad to have missed the great MacDiarmid's funeral, just miffed that Eric hadn't told her. But this was more personal. She had met Basil only occasionally, at readings or in the street, yet she felt connected to him. Eric knew that.

'I seen Peggy. Her family's from Briggflatts. She was dead chuffed with Basil's poem.'

'I heard you talking about a Peggy.'

'Me nana was Peggy Greenwell, but Basil's lass was Peggy Greenbank, before she was married. I'd have liked being Basil's granddaughter.'

'You're no longer a teen,' said Maeve admiringly. 'When I first met you – '

'It's twelve years.'

They sat over tea and biscuits, both remembering the poet whom no one had doubted was a poet, least of all the old man himself.

Janey put down her cup. 'I'm gannin back to Sedbergh. I promised Basil I'd gan to Briggflatts.'

Maeve looked at this untaught woman and marvelled how she had taken what she wanted from life. Maeve wondered if she knew that Alice was in London, living in Covent Garden and regularly dropping Maeve postcards inviting her down for a fling. But she didn't know how things had concluded between Alice and Janey. She returned to the door to see Janey on her way. 'Tara then,' said Janey. Maeve couldn't but smile.

It was time to fetch Giles.

Chapter Eight

DISTANCE AND LOSS   1988

D EAR MAEVE,

Yes! I have been awarded the Canada Writers Exchange. I will be away all of 1988. The letter from the Scottish Arts Council is hardly a work of literature. Conditions and stipulations but that's it – a paid, expenses covered tour of the country with readings, meetings with Canadian writers and provision for writing! As soon as I had the offer (a secretary phoned me at work to give me the news) I went to see my boss, and he said, 'We will have to consider leave of absence but it's not my decision.' Half an hour later I was summoned by his boss, who said he could not guarantee re-employment after a year, and I should give in my notice. Instead I went home and typed a letter to *his* boss, and guess what, I have been given leave of absence. It will be even funnier if I get a better opportunity beyond the year and can tell them to stick it. My new Amstrad word-processor has paid for itself.

I am renting out my flat. Richard will take the Amstrad and some of my books. He's coming out to visit me during the Canada year. I assume you could not follow suit because of Giles.

Yours in poetry,

Eric

PS. I've told Buddy I can't continue editing *Poets Plus*. I had a penning from Sebastian Barker and I planned to ask you, among others, for poems, but circumstances have intervened – I must give my all to Canada.

Dear Maeve,

Toronto is extraordinary. The University is an enormous place, old stone buildings founded when the city was designed, plus huge recent development. The bearded founders could hardly have foreseen the diversity. A cosmopolitan cross-roads, rather like Oxford – you haven't been there, sorry. I have accommodation in an old college and an office in the Department. I'm winging it in many ways.

I've met dozens of people, but know none of them well. Everybody seems young. Research students everywhere. I'm meeting some poets tonight at a reception arranged by the department. Must hurry to be there on time.

Yours Aye,

Eric.

Dear Maeve,

Life goes at a great pace. I have some teaching, to groups of new students who, wait for it, all want to be writers. Nothing diffident and tentative, as in our day. They are so eager, with their fountain pens and thick new pads of paper, and their bland faces, some serious and silent, some talkative, some inquisitive. None of the other staff cares what I teach, so I teach what I like, what interests me. I talk about the difference between Scottish literature and that based in London and Oxford. I invite them to think how Canadian literature differs from that of America. Something like that keeps them going for a week or two and then I plan something else.

The social life is a whirl of invitations. I never know which to accept. A tea at the chaplaincy led to a delightful evening with wildlife experts and a chance to go out in the wilds in a camper van – seeing moose nearly as big as our van, walking calmly away from a bear, birdwatching where I would not have enough information to go unaccompanied.

Yesterday I was invited to a poets' party. We trailed miles through the suburbs – the pavements were so clean, people took off their shoes. We didn't find the place they were looking for, and I never even found out which of them were poets.

In one of my classes there's a curious lad who rather attracts me. And a woman who is absolutely bonkers. The whole class considers she is crazy, and whatever she says, she has everyone laughing out loud. I told a research assistant I'm quite friendly with about her and he said, 'Sounds as if she's more likely to become a writer than any of the others,' which could well be true. But it doesn't tally with departmental principles that most of its graduates expect to be readers, teachers, administrators, or take any occupation where clear communication is of value – then it's actually the duffers who end up being writers! We've survived without educating writers in Scotland and England up to now, but I warn you, it's coming.

I have had no time for any sustained writing.

I don't mean to moan, because Canada is rich and wonderful.

Your mad cousin,   Eric

Dear Maeve,

Richard has arrived, with the news of your postal strike. We're having a great time, despite poor weather.

R brought me over a couple of books by an Aberdonian writer, Nan Shepherd. She died a few years back. She wrote books on the countryside, mountains, and there's a piece about wild geese you would like. I am including wild geese in the background of my poem about the *Lusitania* sinking – we spoke of it once. The geese fly all over Ireland. I think the idea of the geese travelling and the travellers not quite making it – do these ideas clash or support one another? Not sure. You said you were writing something with geese in it. I assume not exactly *about* them. Good idea. Keep on with it. I remember how you loved them when you were a bairn – the geese are your call.

The gay and lesbian community here is rather down in the dumps because of this modern illness AIDS. It's widespread here – many are dying, and the malady isn't understood, let alone curable. It isn't something that would threaten you, but it has seriously disrupted our 'shadowy world' – is it shadowy? It certainly was, within living memory! Even if we avoid this awful disease, our lives are diminished by it. Richard and I are old enough to be a married couple, but it's not how we're made, and it's not our belief to be 'faithful.' And we can't even take pride in that, because it isn't faithfulness, it's fear.

All we can do is carry on, exploring and writing. By dint of midnight oil I'm getting some observations down, and providing poems for literary editors in Canada. They don't seem to mind my English spelling. They either print it as is, or correct it to American, but they don't come back to me and fuss.

What's going on in Newcastle? I heard Tom Pickard fell out with Northern Arts – or more likely the other way round. Are you enjoying Jesmond Library? Are you WRITING? Giles will be nine now? Still playing guitar and drums I bet, what fun. Do you ever see Ollie?

Here's the poem about the *Lusitania*. Unfinished. With geese. Richard says hello.

Yours aye,   Eric

Dear Maeve,

My tour of Canada is scheduled. We take off alternate weeks from Toronto, myself, liaison officers, and academics varying with the location. The best was a creative writing session on First Nation lands. Savvy young men and women were printing work onto a concertina pack of computer paper. The old guy who oiled and serviced the computer said, 'This communication is going to change our lives! It's like telex, we can talk to the government and print it all to keep. It is far better than telephones – you have a record of what was said.' How surprising to go to the most remote and deprived of communities and have the world's future paraded to one!

Next week we go to Montreal. I haven't heard more than a sentence or two of French in all these weeks. Perhaps I'll be airing my Edinburgh French in Montreal? Then back to the Department here. On a scale out of ten, it is Experience 10, Writing nil.

Save my letters.

Eric.

It seemed her cousin was having a great time in Canada, while she was having not quite such fun at home in Sandyford. There had been a long postal strike, and his letters had not arrived in sequence. Now the strike was over they were turning up in dollops, all at once. At Maeve's end, the letterboxes had been taped shut; they were open again but the rhythm of the correspondence was all to pot. Her replies would not be very interesting to him and he wouldn't keep them even if they were.

His unexpected geese poem troubled her. She didn't keep

the poem. It wasn't one of his best and it annoyed her. The *Lusitania* had come not from Canada, but all the way from New York to perish just south of Ireland. And there were those non-scientific sea-geese again. She'd pointed that out to him after *High Tide Bamburgh*.

Maeve hadn't told him she was writing *seriously* about geese, but in one of her letters she asked if he'd seen any snow geese. She'd read they could be seen in numbers in Canada. Despite the delays of the letters, it seemed only a week or two later, the Snow Geese postcard arrived. The outsize, elongated card was slightly bent by the postman pushing it through the door. She forgot her annoyance in gratitude. Behind the laminated shine, a great lake curved away (not a Great Lake, somewhere called Middle Creek). The air above the lake was white with rising geese.

Although only a small picture, it was better than an ordinary postcard. She could see right into the wide area of water. She could feel the flow of thousands of geese, every one a snow goose, intent on reaching the tundra of northern Canada or further for their summer breeding.

The postage stamp was American, the postmark Pennsylvania. She read the small printed panel: *Geese can fly 800 miles in a day*. Eric had added, *Weekend over the border. This is the spring migration – they go back via the coast, we were told. E.*

Eric had witnessed that wonderful event, the whole air resounding with geese who were not bumping into each other, so balanced and controlled were they. The geese mesmerised Maeve, as though each was a verse for her poem. Line breaks were tricky when you launched out on your own. The lines went smack on the page like lifeboats dwarfed by the sea round a sinking hull. Here were three, two stuck together like a catamaran:

> *above the southern tip of Ireland winged, solid deck*
> *swallowed by sea's smooth roll*

> sun n flurried watersheet in sight of land   all is not
>   well   a child, a feather fall

and the lone line

> frail wingtip of map, wingtip of unreached haven

She wasn't looking at a postcard. She was standing on a grassy shore, above her head the excitement of geese, not women's cries. How had a shipwreck interfered with this moment? The geese on her postcard spoke for themselves:

> A four-dimensional white wall,
> our sunlit hordes, our sky in motion,
> our snow goose din of each one's call,
> a four-dimensional white wall,
> our wings, necks, navigate by all
> our senses, feather land and ocean.
> A four-dimensional white wall,
> there is no end in our devotion.

But wait, she had a longer piece about the *Lusitania*. She would never use it as a separate poem, for it was only justified as part of the experience of migrating geese. She preferred long flowing lines. There had to be clippings on the floor from a poem like this.

> Geese come close, these city dwellers cannot fly,
> Wings and waves ever in harmony,
> What blow has ripped the safety from the craft they ply
> Their normal helpless wish to sail and fly,
> by wicked underwater trickery.
> Adventurous determined voyagers
> goslings not yet able to fly
> parents and partners drift away,

wings and waves ever in harmony.
Short messages, folded paper tokens beg them all to try
to sense their life at some lost point they were before,
siblings shielded safe hatched within.
We could not save them if we would,
but had they copied us in ease of movement?
They would not make it to the coast of Ireland
decked with fuchsias, seashore furze, valerian,
thrift, pink cushions for their corpses, bog rosemary.
Bands of mourning in the sky
we fled on to our loughs, our destiny,
wings and waves ever in harmony...

She liked parts of this, but the style was too like Eric's. It could go in or out. She would have to decide soon. Her *Wildgoose* manuscript was expanding.

Snow geese race north, return by coast
  greylag, pinkfoot converge
    in Greenland guarded nurseries
      heavy marauding swan, fast vixen foe

Sometimes the geese did most of the work themselves.

Ollie didn't call often but Maeve kept a packet of green tea on a top shelf, especially for him. This quiet afternoon had brought him, welcome as ever. Maeve was under pressure. She'd had another phone call from the school. Giles had been present this morning but could not be found after lunch. 'A child of nine shouldn't be wandering the streets,' said the secretary. 'If this happens again we will have to call in the attendance officers.'

It wasn't the first conversation of its kind this term, and the attendance officers were a regular threat who never materialised. Maeve promised to phone back if he came home.

Ollie wanted to know how Eric was faring in Canada. She held up a letter, with the extravagant postage stamp. 'He's telling me about his CW classes.'

'What is CW?' Canadian something?'

'Creative Writing. Students sign up to it if they have done no writing at all, but hope to be shown how to start. They begin with, like, How to put something down on a blank page!'

'Good grief,' said Ollie. 'I might want to learn how to write elegantly, but I'd always have something to say.'

'You can read this if you like. He's been getting excited about Sylvia Plath. Oh and *geese*.' She held up the postcard.

'He's on your territory, Maeve. You and I beat him to Sylvia Plath.'

'We talked about her at your house early on,' said Maeve, 'and I read *The Bell Jar* way back in Kendal. Didn't she go to Toronto? Eric doesn't mention it.'

'Tell him,' said Ollie, with a grin.

The phone rang again. Ollie followed her into the hall, cradling his mug of green tea. Not the secretary but the headmistress.

'Mrs Carter,' she began, 'Giles has been brought back to school in a police car with two large expensive-looking drums. His story is that he bought them. He tried to get a taxi, back to your home I understand, but the taxi driver was suspicious, and called the police.'

'Oh dear,' said Maeve, 'he has much to learn. Mainly about waiting till he's an adult to do adult-looking things.'

'Where would he get the money to buy two big drums?' asked the teacher.

'His father gives him money for music, seeing he is gifted.' She added some details, although she had to make them up: she didn't know how much Johnno gave Giles, or when.

The teacher didn't seem to like the 'gifted' argument, but

she acknowledged that the money had a reasonable explanation. Maeve turned to Ollie and pulled her *Giles problem* face.

On the phone she said, 'Could the policeman bring Giles and the drums back here? Not that we're needing more drums – '

'No, he's gone.' Maeve could sense the headmistress looking at her watch. 'Giles isn't due to leave school for fifteen minutes.'

'Spare me a moment, while I explain this to my friend.'

Ollie listened. 'I don't mind fetching him. It sounds as if a taxi may be needed, even with me to help carry drums. I'll be firm with him, don't worry. I know you can be firm, Maeve, but you can't put the fear of Christ up him, and that's what he needs.'

'That's great of you,' said Maeve, 'I wouldn't want to turn you out to go myself.'

She saw Ollie to the door, calling out as he headed off, 'Make Giles pay for the taxi!'

Maeve's poem was developing apace. She had bought herself a book, *Waterbirds of the Northern Hemisphere*, from Thorne's. Comprehensive, lush, with coloured and detailed illustrations, the section on migrant geese was always open on her table or windowsill. It was the most expensive book she had ever bought. She didn't want to wear it out, but it had a purpose, was intended for use. She wanted, she meant, to write this poem about the geese.

Not only about the geese but featuring the geese, as narrators, as seeing eyes, in her poem of ambition about the world she knew, a world in which she was tied by twin demands: the upbringing of a challenging and unpredictable child, and her mornings' paid work in a quiet and pleasant local library.

She had notes and notebooks, first ideas about the poem.

She had thought about it during the lonely time when Giles was very young. The folder of scribbled lines was waiting its time. She had a structure or 'plot.' Her poem on the *Iolaire* was finished. She seemed to have lines for the *Lusitania*. They weren't like Eric's poems, except for that *ever in harmony* business. The geese were her call.

Now her poem was alive she could finalise the start, the traditional 'invocation,' an inspired piece that grew within her. Words crowded in. If she didn't write them down she lost them, or half-lost them and would spend days with some phrase on the edge of her mind, eluding her. She needed time. If she shopped, cooked and saw to the house in the afternoons, she'd have Giles at tea-time and then, say, two or three hours, say, from eight or nine till eleven p.m. most days. It would be in addition to any other writing work or poems she might send out, but she could do it.

She put a new sheet of paper into her typewriter.

She was so excited by her first session, when she had collated fragments and written two and a half new pages, that she set out the typewriter the next afternoon as soon as she was back from the library. She had nothing else urgent to do in the two hours till Giles would be home. She had just rolled the next sheet into position, when she heard a banging on the door. She would ignore it.

But the banging moved to the window of her room, accompanied by Giles's voice.

'Mum, you've locked me out!'

She went quickly to the door, where she found not only Giles but a wisp of a girl, about the same height and age as her son.

'Giles!' she exclaimed. 'Whatever's this?'

'Frippy,' said Giles, 'and you should say who, not what. She's a person.'

'I mean what is this you are not at school?'

'We've had enough of school,' said the girl.

Maeve let them in, but she couldn't be harbouring an unknown child in her home as well as her son.

'I'll have to phone the school,' she said as they crowded into the kitchen. She barely had time to wonder how two small kids could make a crowd.

'Phone school, Mum? Why? That's treacherous.'

Treacherous made her think *sands*. *Sands* made her think *geese*.

'Can't be helped. Unless,' turning to the girl, 'I can phone your mother? Where do you live?'

'I live in Brighton Grove, but my mother's at our house in the Borders.'

The Borders? Did she mean Scotland? Maeve looked at them helplessly. 'I'll have to phone school.'

'My daddy's the boss,' said the girl 'My daddy tells them what to do at school.'

'Oh yes? Perhaps he's the janitor?'

'Ha ha ha!' She had amused Giles, but not this girl. Frippy, was that her name?

'Frippy's father – ' began Giles.

'Shut it, both of you. You can give Frippy some juice, if you like.'

Maeve went into the hall to phone. The school's number was written on the wallpaper in biro near the phone, but Maeve knew it. She was hesitant as she asked for the head teacher.

'Oh, Mrs Carter,' began the head.

Maeve was going to be on the wrong end of this.

'Mrs Carter, thank you so much for phoning. Have you got Giles and Frippy there? We've missed them. Thank goodness we know where they are! I will arrange for Frippy to be collected, someone will come for her. Your son might as well stay home now. What a relief!'

Maeve was astonished. Since when was she in such favour

at her son's school? She said goodbye, heard a click, and was about to put the phone down when the headmistress spoke again. 'Sorry to keep you on hold. Can you let Dr Percival know we have located his daughter? She went to another pupil's house and his mother had the sense to get in touch with us. I've just had this lady on the other line...'

Maeve quietly replaced the receiver, and returned to the kitchen. Dr Percival was the Director of Education. She knew this because she worked in the libraries. 'Are you Frippy Percival, dear?' The girl nodded. 'Someone's coming to fetch you.'

After the car collected Dr Percival's daughter, she lectured Giles but she had trouble hiding her amusement. She knew this wasn't adequate. She would have to speak to Johnno, but he had already sided with Giles on school matters, and she doubted he would take the absconding seriously.

Maeve was constantly interrupted – hers was a life of interruptions – but her poem was now taking shape. She worked on it more days than not and gave it thought at all kinds of moments throughout her day. Her ream of paper shrank in its paper box as the heap of typescript grew, until she swapped them over and the box became the receptacle of the living text of the poem. There was the first page, still at the top: the Invocation. *Goose muse, wild art spur thy retreat...*

Giles didn't bring Frippy home in schooltime again, though he continued to 'bunk off' quite a bit, she realised, from his tales of where he had been. Frippy still appeared in his accounts; she liked music; she went to the covered market with him. Maeve sometimes wondered how the headmistress was coping with her special charge.

In the end, a letter came from the Education Department. Giles Carter and Frippy Percival were being recommended for a new School Refusers' Unit, a pet project of the Director of Education, intended for pupils of promise with a bad attendance record at school.

Maeve informed Johnno, who said, 'Very good.' So she went down one afternoon to visit the Refusers' Unit. She met the manager, an enthusiastic and gabby teacher called Bernie, who seemed to know Giles and Frippy already and who showed her a music room with a piano and stage. The Unit was already open for middle school pupils, but there was no sign of any kids. 'They come mostly when it's raining,' said Bernie. 'We're building it up. We welcome them and give them any education they are suited for. We don't discourage them by treating them as children.'

Maeve looked round with interest and didn't say too much. As Bernie saw her to the way out, he said, 'Excuse me for asking but aren't you Maeve Cartier the poet?'

If Giles wouldn't go to regular school and Johnno thought this okay, then that was it. Giles had free access to voluntary schooling, and Maeve would have to cross her fingers and keep an eye.

Maeve sustained her work on the poem. Her timetable involved mornings at the library, coming back and seeing to food for the rest of the day, across lunch and supper, surviving the afternoon and evening racket of Giles playing guitar or drums, Frippy singing, and an assortment of other young people who turned up shortly after four. These differently advantaged boys were at conventional school. They'd strum around till they went home for their suppers, usually by six. Maeve couldn't deny the visitors biscuits and coke, but she didn't want them there all evening. The gang of music-crazy children seemed to grow and threaten Maeve. She started a rule of no music after 8.30 p.m., which Giles accepted reluctantly, though it often crept to 9 p.m. He read fantasy, comic strips, and books about popular music after nine. Neither Giles nor his mother could be bothered with television. After they grew out of young kids' programmes they packed in watching it, and Maeve stopped paying the license and had done with it. They missed *That's Life* and other programmes people would talk about. Maeve and Giles seemed to be agreed on this, that a dog that could say *sausages* might be amusing in passing, but it wasn't worth the sacrifice of your creative life.

Maeve constructed her poem from 9 p.m. till midnight, with some nights off. She could generally read at the library, and as the work went on, she would occasionally note down a few lines on a memo sheet, transferring it to her pockets for attachment to the poem. The poem was substantially developed from her original scratchings. She swept them up in the ancient folder and dumped them in a lower drawer.

Giles spent Thursday evenings at Johnno's. Maeve had a writing binge then, which little was allowed to interfere with.

She was at the shops in West Jesmond one time and met Karen.

'Maeve,' said Karen, 'Long time no see, how's it going, how is Giles?'

'All fine thanks,' said Maeve.

'Come for a coffee.' Maeve was dragged into their old café.

They sat for a while, Maeve in a complete daydream, until Karen rumbled her.

'What's the matter, Maeve? You haven't said ten intelligible words in twenty minutes! Where are you? Coo-ee!'

Maeve jumped. She tried to laugh it off: 'Sorry, I'm writing something difficult and it's getting to me.'

'Difficult? Poetry?' said Karen. 'A form? A sestina? A villanelle?'

'No, nothing like that, something very long.'

'A ballad?'

'There are two ballads, and other forms, within it, but it is one long poem.'

'And what's the poem about?'

'Everything.'

'Recite me a bit?'

'Okay,' said Maeve. 'This is the Invocation, it starts — *Goose muse, wild art spur thy retreat to tundra, fly beyond fear, let moor spread packed river pearls unopened, beyond human invasion, yearly spin life from rock's barnacle skies, —*' She broke off. Karen stared.

'That's from the preamble. It welcomes you in.'

Karen shook her head. 'You'd better go and have a rest, or go swimming or something to freshen yourself up! That's way out! Nice to see you anyway!'

They left the café.

'I'm sorry,' said Maeve, 'I suppose I do appear vague. My head's woolly. Swimming sounds great but I can't make the time... it's nearly finished.'

'A good thing it's nearly finished, then,' said Karen cheerfully, as they parted.

When she was finished, Maeve asked Giles if he'd like to go down to the coast one evening. She wanted to clear her head and enjoy the sea air. But Giles was busy and didn't want to go. He was trying to score some tunes for the band. Maeve felt sad he was growing up, realising that the days of taking her child to the beach or the park, those parental expeditions, were over.

The poem sat around for a week or two. There was nothing else to fiddle with. All the lines sang. She would learn it by heart. She had learned the introduction or Invocation she had tried out on Karen. She didn't know any of the main poem yet, but with the precious words captured on paper she could take a rest. It had done what she meant it to do. *Wildgoose* was ready for publishing. She might ask Buddy at Swing Bridge Press if he'd like to read it.

Eric had been back from Canada for a while. He was

rushing around trying to fix up another job and she felt she should give him recovery time before visiting Scotland. They'd both become exhausted by their separate poetry adventures.

She took a week's leave from the library. She went out for two expeditions that week, on her own. To Cullercoats and St Mary's Island one day. She sat on the rocks and sang the Invocation to two seals, who watched her politely. *Goose muse, wild art spur thy retreat to tundra...* all the way to the landing in the walnut grove. On the other day she got the train to Durham.

She began to relax and feel the release of the poem, to think freshly about her life. The seabirds and foamy waves at the coast, the steep river banks of trees in Durham City, brought freshness to her tired brain, bounce into her step and her hair. In Durham, she looked round the Cathedral and let her mind dwell on Maverick and her friend Barry Cole. She had met Barry a couple of times since then; she would never see Maverick again. *Packed river pearls unopened...*

On other days she took things easy and cleaned up the house. The noise of guitars and drums and the singing, rocking gang of Giles' friends continued. She noticed it more. A week of rest; a week of holiday outings; of self-sufficiency and earned satisfaction.

On Monday it would be back to her library mornings.

On Sunday she went to get the poem in its box out of her cupboard.

It wasn't there.

Hold it. There was a pit in her stomach. *Try the window-sill, chairs.* She went back to the cupboard. It contained the typewriter and stationery, old notebooks. There was easily space for a ream of paper in its box, but no such ream.

Where did she put it? When? On the table? It must be on the table all the time. It had been on the table, not in

155

the cupboard. That would solve the mystery. Had she had a memory lapse and lent it to anybody, given it to someone to read?

A friend had left her, without notice. They had misunderstood one another. Things hadn't been easy. But they were there. And now not there. She'd had a bad day, made a mistake. The past denied. She looked round the whole house, surfaces with other things on them. She moved cushions, under, behind, checked bookcases. There weren't many places to look. She looked everywhere many times.

She went to the kitchen, made tea in a mug. There was no milk. She heard Giles moving, he was awake. It might be in his room somewhere, among the music paraphernalia, balanced on a drum. It might have fallen off some surface, a ledge, a table, leaves strewn on the floor. She could sort them out, she just needed them in any state, whatever state they were in. She sat down and drank the brown watery tea. She'd blown it somehow. This object, this sheaf of typewritten papers, had to exist. She would ask Giles. She would concentrate her brain, visualise where it had been, till it came back to rights and she would say, *of course, that's what I did with it, why it wasn't on the table, in the cupboard.*

A friend lost. They had been wrong about each other all those years. She had known it was out of kilter. But a poem was a friend known, understood. This friend could not desert her. It had to be somewhere, this heap of paper in a box, with all the words of order and comfort in it.

The world could be physically very strange.

She looked everywhere twice. She pulled out the old drawer of beginnings and went through the fragments one by one, till she was frantic. They were nowhere near enough to recover the poem. She threw them all in the air and then sat on the carpet and wept as they lay around her.

Giles was sorry for her. He helped her look. He was tired, he was going out. He wanted some breakfast and to play his guitar. He played music in the kitchen while she searched through the music room. But it had never been in the music room.

Or had it? Had the boys been in? Had they glanced at it on her table, picked it up as a curiosity to read, then dropped it in a corner?

Giles had gone out. Sunday; she had the library again tomorrow. How could she face things now? She didn't feel like eating, nor anything, a hellish shutter had come down over her, a shutter, a block to her expectations. She pushed the door of Giles' room. The best room in the house, it was filled with music clutter. The window was open. She banged it shut. She felt dizzy, no, giddy, unstable. He had all this, guitars, drums, electrical stuff. She had only one thing she cared about, her poem, and it had disappeared. She looked round the floor, round the skirting. Where else? There was a big drum in the middle of the floor. Giles had recently painted his initials on it: G G C.

Maeve's mind exploded. There was space inside a drum wasn't there? It looked as if the front came off: those were clamps at the sides, to tension it. She grabbed the drum and it seemed to fight with her. She pushed and tugged and then started hammering at the front panel. Some of the fresh paint transferred onto her hands. She took no notice of a voice warning her it would be better to calm down.

She wasn't calm.

She had lost her poem. What else mattered?

The drum nearly fell over but it was held by a stand. She kicked at the heavy stand and pushed at the sides and front. There was a ripping sound, the whole front came away and clanged to the floor. Drums weren't supposed to make that sort of noise.

Inside the drum was an empty hollow. It wasn't a treasure chest, it did not and could not have contained Maeve's poem. Outside the drum was the rest of the world and Maeve. Her poem was somewhere else, and somewhere else was Giles.

She started to cry.

Very fortunately Giles was able to replace the front of the drum, but it wasn't perfect and the episode wouldn't be forgiven. He was furious. He shouted and she said she was sorry but she couldn't explain if he wouldn't listen.

'You can't explain at all,' said Giles. 'Johnno was right, you're a brick short of a load.'

Maeve went into her room, taking the electric kettle, and shut her door. It had already got out of hand when she missed the typescript box.

Perhaps Giles partly understood, or perhaps Giles wanted the kettle, for they were speaking again by the evening.

'Come on Mum, do something else, think about something else, then it will turn up of its own accord.'

Time went on, and she did something else. It was like a bereavement.

Months went by. It never turned up. Had she dreamed the whole thing? Then where did the result of a dream go, for she knew it existed. That was what she hung onto as the disaster receded, as time went by. The words of Eric's latest sonnet came into her head.

> *So much is lost, so much is always here,*
> *a sight once seen, we never could let go,*
> *a power once known – which should it reappear,*
> *the pattern of the universe would flow*
> *around its template –*

She tried to rewrite *Wildgoose*. She listed sections, but the sections objected and clashed. She gawped at the hopeless paper fragments. There had been seven cantos. They wouldn't go back together. She had a copy of one of the shipwreck poems somewhere else. Lines fluctuated and changed, like a jelly that wouldn't set. She couldn't fix the order of anything. She maybe had fifty unconnected lines.

Even the Invocation panicked her. She couldn't get the start. *Wildgoose muse*, no, *Wildgoose thy retreat*? Damn, she was sure of it a little further in, up to the walnut trees. It sounded wrong, broken without its first three lines, and this wasn't the poem, but the pre-poem. She must write something else.

Chapter Nine

PARENTING THE BAND   (1993)

PANCAKES WERE ONE OF HER favourite dishes. She dropped an egg into the well of flour and dabbed it with the wooden spoon, watching the batter congeal with a little milk. Some years had passed since her poem had vanished. A middle-aged housewife, making pancakes.

In walked Giles. She looked up. 'I wasn't expecting you. Haven't you got the club tonight? I'm off to a poetry reading on the Quayside. Two of your pals are in the front room.'

'I heard them.' Giles stood there, fourteen, with the strength of a man. 'Okay, I'll have a pancake.'

She turned to the cupboard and took another bowl, flung some flour into it and flipped open the egg box.

'Hadn't you made enough?'

'Soon put right.' Maeve continued to mix.

Still a well-known poet, she had poems in a recent women's anthology and sonnets in the current *Chapman*. A pamphlet of her favourite poems by others had appeared in the great little series *Poets Choose*. This was high status and put her in a league with Edwin Morgan.

Eric was jealous of that.

He didn't know she'd met the editor and pointed out that he had no women subjects.

The editor had answered, *Right, you're on.*

Wildgoose still troubled her. It had to exist, though it wasn't in the house. She knew it hadn't been *thrown* out; if it had been taken out, it was biding its time somewhere else. Her attempts to rework it had failed. What was the point of an inferior copy?

There were only the lines of the Invocation, which she knew, except the start was wrong. Wildgoose muse? She sometimes ran through them, but they hurt, because they needed the rest of the poem.

The door handle turned. In came one of the guitarists.

'Mmm lovely smell,' he said. 'Would you care to make us guys a couple each?'

'Come in. Join us. Pancakes all round!' said Maeve.

As the newcomer beckoned in his pal she hurriedly put the first pancake on a plate for herself – she used to say that the first one was never the best – and told them they couldn't toss the pancakes; she would turn them with a spoon. The second bowl of batter was ready. She cut a lemon in half and put sugar on the table.

Write another poem! The first one was never the best...

'Have you got syrup?' said the second lad.

'No! This isn't a caff.'

'Sorry, Mrs Carter.'

Wildgoose was the best. She had written other poems, 'ordinary' poems. Buddy was thinking of doing another book for her. *The Geese of Aberlady* had sold out; *Odd Gloves* had sold very well. She didn't want another book with geese in the title. She'd been invited to apply for another grant. Ollie had told her about the analyst identifying groups that were not being equally supported. Women with children were among the target groups. The way Giles was growing, she wouldn't be a woman with a child much longer.

The Library had booked her to talk about her poetry at another round of Literary Initiative events. While a major part of what she had written was submerged by its disappearance, readers had enough to go on. The libraries had copies of *The Geese at Aberlady* and *Odd Gloves*.

She didn't talk about the missing manuscript.

There was no point.

A letter had come from Mrs Susan Percival, Frippy's mother, inviting herself round to inspect the premises where Frippy was spending too much time. It wasn't put like that, but it mentioned 'our offspring having such a touching friendship' and Giles being 'a most determined young man.'

Alarm bells rang all over the blue-inked letter on its Basildon Bond paper, lying on the kitchen bar. Their 'offspring' had known each other for years. Perhaps this was about the band's prominence, or Frippy's development into a young woman, or her constant, almost nightly absence from her home? The letter was a handy mat for the empty eggshells. Maeve considered how to reply. She knew all about Dr Percival. She didn't need a privileged relationship with his wife.

She'd managed to eat three pancakes while dishing out another ten or so to the three young men. You had a party. She would send Mrs Percival a message via Frippy, who wasn't here tonight. Maeve would need to rush out to meet Karen.

Late nights in town, favoured by younger poets, were beginning to tell on Maeve. She still managed an early rise and didn't often see Giles in the mornings. He usually sloped off in the middle of the morning to report to the Refusers' Unit at coffee time, where he met Frippy and other self-selected students of the ever-optimistic Bernie. Bernie liked nothing better than to teach low-achieving teenagers to read, using special books about footballers and shop girls. His second favourite occupation seemed to be listening to Frippy and Giles practise songs. Giles and Frippy were quite good at reporting the doings of the Unit, which was how Maeve got her picture of it.

On this occasion Giles was up bright and early.

'Morning, kiddar,' said Maeve.

'Morning,' said Giles. 'Kiddar's naff. Nobody says it.'

His voice was deep and steady; it had been variable over the last few months.

Maeve picked up a coffee mug and made a place at the table.

'Does kiddar mean somebody young?'

'I don't think so. Don't say it.'

Besides Giles' used plate and the new pot of lemon marmalade, there were tapes and a tape player on the table, tatty music sheets, and an A4 note pad that could have belonged to either of them. Guitar bridges and strings surrounded a mug full of pencils and biros, mainly Giles'.

'We should keep this table clear for eating,' she said.

'Half that stuff's yours.'

'I didn't say it wasn't.'

'Here's the post.' Giles held out three envelopes. One was addressed to Maeve, in her own handwriting with a fold up the middle.

Rejected poems.

'Sending letters to yourself again!' The old joke had survived their years to the point of being companionable. His mother smiled.

The other two were addressed to G G Band and G G Music Enterprises. Raymond, the paperwork guy, could look at them when he came in this afternoon. One was lopsided. Giles opened the package. 'Another of my fans. I wish they'd grow up and get c.d. equipment. Tapes went out with the ark.'

He put the first tape in the player on the table and switched it on, loudly. In less than five minutes he gave it the thumbs down. 'Don't bother showing these to Raymond.'

'If you've finished with it, could you turn it off?' she answered mildly.

Giles obliged. He further obliged by picking up his jacket and heading for the door.

She wondered where he was going. Was there any point asking? 'You're early!'

'See you this afternoon, Mum. Band practice tonight.'

Maeve sighed, briefly tidied the table, and set out for the branch library where she was making a long-term success of her morning job. She reached the leafy corner in which the small, circular building was set, half a minute before the caretaker. By the time she looked round he was sprinting along with the key. Early sun filled the library through modern glass. She should be able to put Giles and her complicated domestic life aside for the time being, as she hunted out Catherine Cookson novels or soothed the caretaker who had asked her to requisition a new doormat. She was the Librarian-in-Charge for the branch, despite working mornings only. She started at 9 a.m. instead of 10 a.m. and she had to take responsibility for things like doormats. But she couldn't forget the situation in which she herself was the only 'doormat' in sight.

Yesterday followed her to the library like an over-loyal dog.

Giles was arranging another big concert. He had defied her to stop him. She'd already had the *Chronicle* phoning for a story. She gave them Johnno's number and hoped for the best.

She had hosted the women writers – her old pal Karen and others – yesterday afternoon and they were in mid-session when Giles arrived, right in the middle of them discussing Karen's poem about parenting. Karen said to Giles, 'You have to practice with your band if you want to be good!'

So Giles said, 'Right, ladies, you can get up and read your poems with the band at the club on Friday, if you can come.' Karen offered, 'I'll come,' and two more said they would. They were meeting at Karen's tonight and tomorrow to practice. Giles reckoned the club audience would love the poets. Maeve could see it would make a change from crooners. She couldn't be there on Friday. Bev was holding what he called a *soiree* in Jesmond and she'd promised to take poems. She could almost see Bev's house from the library windows.

The plump lady chose four books. Maeve took the slips from them, put them in the docket tickets, and pushed the tickets in the wooden slide box. Central Library was going over to computerised records.

Today hadn't got going yet in Jesmond and her mind went back to Giles. He and his pals had been playing the working men's club twice a week between bigger gigs. You bet they paid him well, but they wouldn't be paying the women for their poetry. Karen asked him outright. 'When you've proved good enough for them to book you, then you'll get paid.' That made Karen even more enthusiastic. Something would happen out of turn. Not being there would be one less worry for Maeve.

Eleven o'clock, and busying up a little. The staff room was tiny. They usually took their coffee behind the lending desk. Only Maeve on these mornings. She had a pretty cup and saucer.

Doormats. Take last night. She'd had to cook Giles something, wash clothes he needed for today, find the rosin he had lost, talk to him and listen, since he wasn't surrounded by his usual companions. Their mothers would have been surprised if they'd all gone home for their teas. Then there were her own things to wash and her hair to do, against a background of violin scales. The violin was his newest craze. He'd found one in a junk shop down the Western Road and he was convinced it was a brilliant one.

Raymond, a practical, quiet guy with a Scottish voice, had peered inside the fiddle and balanced it in his hands. 'Aye. Cheap violins can be good. By accident.'

'This isn't a cheap violin that was good by accident,' said Giles. 'It's a good violin that was cheap by accident.' Maeve and Raymond had looked at each other and laughed. Thinking about it, she laughed again in the library. It seemed Raymond was accompanying her to the library as well as her son. She liked Raymond a lot. She was beginning to actually hope he'd be in when she handed over her library to the afternoon staff and returned to the house. He was often there.

The ladies barely survived the working men's club. A male comedian had appeared on the same night, and had been very rude in his act with a model of a willy. While Karen was reading, the joker sat in the front row waving this object around, raising howls of amusement from the audience behind him. No one could hear a word of Karen's carefully practised poem. Karen stopped reading and bawled at the joker. He ran onto the stage and chased her round with the thing. Karen said she had been made to look stupid.

Karen called in to tell Maeve this tale, no doubt hoping also to catch Giles' ear. Maeve gave Karen a mug of tea and tried not to laugh at the story.

'It's the beginning of your performance experience,' said Maeve.

Giles came rushing in.

'Mum – oh hi Karen. Mum, I'll be out till tomorrow. Night club for the band, and I'll crash out wherever I am at the time.'

'Ahem,' said Karen.

'Has she been telling you about last night?' he asked Maeve, then to Karen, 'Well done. You coped well with that nonsense.'

'Did I hell. I shouldn't have had to cope with him. Whatever made you book him?'

'They didn't book him. He gate-crashed because they wouldn't give him a booking.'

'They should have stopped him at the door,' said Karen.

'I agree,' said Giles. 'You should always insist on getting paid, then the club will treat you with respect. Anyway I must run.' He departed. The front door slammed.

Karen looked up at Maeve. 'Your son has a cheek. He said we wouldn't be paid. At least they heard Margo and Naomi. But mine was the best set.'

'Yes of course.' Karen looked at Maeve suspiciously but her face was bland as always. 'He does have a nerve, you're right,' and Karen went on her way slightly happier.

The boy was such a mixture of kid and adult. It became confusing, and Maeve wondered how she would have coped without Raymond. He and Giles barged ahead with music arrangements and Maeve left them to it. Raymond said the only way was to support him. The music was brilliant and for this sort of music, the players had to be young. On this Raymond and Johnno were agreed.

Another thing about Giles' band, and this was why Raymond was working at the house: the G G Band was a lucrative concern. With Johnno in charge while tending his construction business, Raymond had a properly documented part-time post steering the band through success after success. Four or five big concerts a year pulled in huge ticket sales, and there was regular money from their working men's club. The lads, still schoolboys, had take-home earnings from the concerts that far exceeded pocket money, and satisfied the various parents. The boys had their own instruments. Raymond was needed for keeping things in order, accounting the money, controlling equipment and looking out for development prospects. The latest aims were to get the lads kitted out in sponsored T shirts and blazers, and to organise paid exposure for the band on Tyne Tees Television.

Maeve felt both fooled and left behind. The growing lads rampaged round her house, using her kitchen, playing music loudly all night. This was Giles' home too and the band was exciting for all of them, but sometimes all she could do was cry on Raymond's shoulder.

The daily outing was an escape, a breather, a parallel world. It worked one-way: she never thought about the library when at the house. She and the afternoon librarian overlapped properly twice a week. They talked about their clients: the school kids, the lady who gave them Mars bars, the man who read Westerns they nicknamed Louis L'Amour. Stephanie talked about her children and her painting class. Maeve kept quiet about the Band.

On other days, like today, after a quick exchange of messages, Maeve walked home at lunchtime.

She let herself in and sat down, looking weary and tearful.

'Come on lass,' said Raymond. 'You could use this energy writing your lovely poems.'

She did still write poems, but the disappearance of her poem *Wildgoose* came back to her mind, as it often did. It was more than an incident. It was an attack by forces unknown.

'I can't get down to proper writing.'

'Aye, but this won't last forever. Giles is growing up. You'll have the house to yourself again some day soon.'

Maeve looked Raymond in the eye. 'You've forgotten something. Or maybe you don't realise it. This isn't my house at all. It belongs to Giles.'

'He isn't going to throw you out.'

'Not yet, but the time will come. We will part before he is a man.'

True enough, Giles was still a boy. He was in the centre of an organisation that made him seem mature. Raymond was part of that organisation, Maeve only on the edge of it.

Raymond stopped whatever he was doing to a soundbox to make them a pot of tea.

'You'd best have a sandwich, poppet. An egg or something. I had a bacon butty. Keep you going.'

She smiled. 'You are kind to me.'

'Everyone should be kind to you, they have only to look at you – '

'Oh come on Ray!'

'You need a break. Why not go and stay with Eric in Edinburgh for a few days?'

'Eric's working in Aberdeen, you daft bugger.'

'Language, Maeve.'

Maeve laughed. 'Who taught it me? Those boys, that's who.'

'Eric would let you stay, even if he was away. And there's those women in Leith who you stayed with before. I'll tell Johnno you need a holiday if you won't.'

'Leave it to me. I won't admit defeat to Johnno.'

'Nothing defeats you, Maeve.'

'*Wildgoose* defeated me.'

'Well, it matters to you. Do it again. I won't get in the way. Can take you out somewhere inspiring if you like.'

Maeve knew what he meant. Raymond was good at finding 'somewhere inspiring.'

'I can't do it again, there's only forward, not back. But I'd like an expedition. Perhaps I could write something else.'

'That's the spirit. We can't go away before this concert.'

Maeve felt more cheerful with this kind of promise.

Maeve had left the front door off the latch. They didn't hear Giles and Frippy coming in. Maeve was sitting in the kitchen on Raymond's knee, her hair and clothes dishevelled, the lace on her bra showing, her skirt riding up above her knees. Raymond's arm was resting under her oxter and around her midriff. Her face was stained with a trace of wet tears.

'Hello Mum, what's up?' said Giles.

Raymond remained relaxed.

'We're having a cuppa and recharging. I've done last month's accounts for the band. Your mother's not long back from the library.'

'Hello Mrs Carter,' said Frippy cheerfully. The conspiracy of women.

Frippy and Giles were high on their music.

'Frippy sang a *Cats* song, but she can't do it at the concert, only at the club.'

'Aye, it'll belong to old Valerie Eliot,' said Raymond.

'Who's Valerie Eliot?'

'T. S. Eliot's widow – he wrote *Old Possum's Book of Practical Cats.*'

'Who's Old Possum?'

'Like to hear the song?' asked Frippy.

While Frippy was belting it out, Maeve released herself from Raymond's loosened grip, shook herself tidy, and lifted a cake on a plate out of the fridge.

She saw Frippy gazing at the cake, unable to comment since her voice was taken up in singing. Frippy liked cake. They could have cans of coke, make another pot of tea. They could see to that themselves.

'That's beautiful, dear,' said Maeve when Frippy had finished the song. 'I used to read those cat poems with Giles when he was – ' she hesitated.

'Knee-high to a grasshopper?' offered Raymond.

Everybody laughed.

'Do you write your own songs?' Maeve asked her.

'No,' said Frippy, 'I never write them, but I sometimes make them up. I remember them and sing them. They are just songs, you know.'

She launched into another song in her resonant soprano. The song was simple; perhaps she'd composed it. Her voice could be loud but she knew how to match the volume to a smaller room. Raymond stopped talking. Maeve watched Giles and Raymond. Everyone found Frippy's voice astonishing. Whatever she sang, popular, opera snippet, hymn, pub ballad, singing turned her from a child to a woman. It was the confidence, and the attention she gave to the instrument – her voice.

Giles picked up a guitar from a corner of the floor.

Frippy stopped for breath.

'Can't we put the *Cats* song in the show?'

'No,' said Raymond. 'There's permissions.'

'Shucks,' said Frippy.

'Like Giles says, the club but not the concert.'

'Are you rehearsing tonight? Can I stay? Susie knows I might be late.'

'Who's Susie?' asked Raymond.

'My mother. I'm too old to say *Mummy*, except to her of course. I've started saying *Susie*. When I'm talking about her.'

Maeve remembered the letter from Frippy's mother, and smiled.

This was what made her son happy. The house was filling up with drumbeats and tunings up, trials and trilling, guitars and guffaws. Not to mention scroungers in the kitchen.

The boys emerged to the rehearsal space chewing warm pizza squares, then wiping their hands on towels, strategically in place, to continue setting up the various instruments. Raymond was checking sound levels and instilling confidence into the young musicians, reminding them of concert dates and requirements; two weeks (as well as the club tomorrow). Soon. Giles took a demonstration turn with the drum kit, ousting Jake for the moment. He'd be on guitar tonight. 'Like this, see,' he said to Jake, rolling a thunderclap that made everybody jump.

Raymond told them when they'd be setting up and practising in the actual hall and how to get inside through security. Tickets were going and they were reminded to inform their families and friends: tickets didn't sell themselves.

Though G G tickets did tend to sell themselves.

Their noise went on till late in the evening, drums pulsating through every wall. Giles would understand his mother felt some responsibility for the young people; he would notice when she disappeared for a while –he would know the noise would be a bit much for her, but they all knew concerts were the priority.

As the session concluded she re-emerged and hovered around as the lads were collected by parents or went home with lifts. Frippy had a lift from another parent from that part of town, and Maeve instructed him to see Frippy right into her house.

'Thank you, Mrs Carter,' said Frippy. 'Please would you phone my mother and tell her I'll be singing at the club with G G tomorrow and that I'll be okay?'

Frippy was the only one who ever deferred to Maeve. To the others, this house was just the G G rehearsal space. Maeve sternly watched Giles seeing Frippy out of the house.

There was no question of Giles waking early in the morning after a band practice. By the time she was back from the library he had emerged. It had been a good session, that had been obvious last night, but Giles opened today's conversation with a direct challenge.

'Mum,' he said, 'Raymond's married.'

'Well, well.'

'Do you think – '

She interrupted him. 'Why do you think the young people should have it all?'

'You sound like Johnno!'

'Johnno and I are not mortal enemies! We are friends, despite your best efforts!'

She had deflected the subject. Giles had made a point about Raymond, whom he'd seen sitting close with his mother the previous day. He had the courage to raise the matter with her in private. She ought to respond.

'Giles, I need my friends too. You have yours. Raymond is one of mine.'

'Raymond's our manager! We need him. You might scare him off!'

'I won't stymie your manager, I promise. He's a good manager. I appreciate him.'

'I can see you do.'

She looked at her son sharply.

'Don't worry. I'll see he's okay. It's hard for him to work with you youngsters all the time. Both he and I appreciate a little companionship. You'll have to leave it to my good sense.'

'And his good sense, I suppose.'

'We can slot in among people's other relationships,' she added thoughtfully, realising that this was indeed a key to success. 'Like Frippy has a family. You're not a threat to her family?'

He looked across at her.

'It never occurred to me I might be a threat to Frippy's family! Could that be why I'm slightly afraid of Frippy's father?'

'I wonder.' Maeve attended to the coffee maker. 'And why would I want to stop Raymond being exactly the man he is, wife and all, music and all?' She set out cups and milk. 'Have some coffee.'

'Thanks, I will, Mum,' said Giles. 'It's true, it's your life.'

'Don't you forget it.' She passed him his coffee cup, smiling at him calmly.

One-nil.

'You cause arguments every day!' said Giles.

Maeve stared at him in disbelief.

'And there's another thing. I need to go up to Edinburgh soon, to see my friends.'

'Oh Mum, can't you live without Eric?'

'It's all the poets. They are part of my life, just as you are. Directly after your concert. I will ask Johnno to keep an extra eye on you, have you stay over with him.'

'But when will I see Frippy?'

'Don't be ridiculous. You will see her at school. You are both fourteen, you see Frippy in the daytime. Full stop.'

'Do you have to rub it in? And it's not school, it's the Unit.'

'I won't say the Unit is a damn silly idea. It seems to suit you. But are you clear about me going away? You could stay at your father's, but I know you want to play music. Would you prefer to sleep at your father's?'

'I'll be all right here. Raymond will come in as usual.'

'Raymond can't look after you overnight. Raymond is *married*!'

There was a funny side to this and they both laughed.

'I get it; it's only fair. When I'm sixteen, you can go as often as you like. You should do that anyway. Dad and I will make it look okay if that's what worries you.'

Two-nil.

Giles rose from the table and put his cup in the sink. Sun streamed on his face as he passed the window and she noticed a touch of incipient beard. Giles continued:

'Can I have next month's allowance early? There's

something I want in the music shop in the Grainger Market.'

'I can't give you more money just now. You've got enough money. And I know your father chips in. You get your allowance when I get paid and that's it. Kiddar.'

'Why won't you pay me early? I'll lose the chance of my bargain.'

'That's what life's like. It's time you learned.'

'That's mean. It's a cost of my music.'

'This is the electricity bill. It has gone up hugely just from your electric guitars and amplifiers. This is a cost of your music.'

'It can't be all that much,' said Giles.

Maeve still had to make an effort to keep her temper at times.

'Here is the bill. Look at it.'

He took it and read it. 'Surely you're not expecting me to pay that?'

'Don't be silly.'

'Johnno will pay it if you can't.'

'I don't like depending on Johnno. I'll manage without him.'

'But he would bail you out if you were stuck.'

'He would,' said Maeve, 'but I don't want it.'

'But surely knowing he would bail you out, doesn't that make you feel better and less stressed?'

She sighed loudly. She'd have made a good actress.

'What would you know about stress? You do exactly what you like. You ignore the rest of us and go your own way.'

He was still holding the electricity bill, which had red letters at the top: Final Demand. 'ALL RIGHT,' he shouted. He reached for his Parka, and dashed from the room and from the house. Maeve shrugged.

Maeve was reeling from a phone call with Johnno. Her son

had gone out and paid the electricity bill, then taken the receipt to Johnno and complained Maeve had made him pay it. She could hardly believe it. He had extorted the money for a double bass from his father, this being the object of his desire in the music shop. Maeve said there wasn't room for a double base in their house and he could damn well keep it at Johnno's.

'You're losing your temper,' said Johnno.

'Are you surprised?'

'He's gifted. He needs support. This music is a short life, he needs to be in it early. That's been agreed.'

'He's exaggerated what happened. It's nothing to do with him being a musician. I'm just trying to understand a teenage son!'

Maeve never argued with Johnno. Instead, she ended calls. This time she wasn't quite quick enough hanging up, for Johnno said, 'Let me know if you're not managing. I've got plenty of income, I could buy you out if you ever want to move on.'

Buy her out? What was he talking of? She had a flash of inspiration. 'Johnno, thanks for that, it could happen.' She put the phone down.

The phone rang again. She was pleased to hear Eric. 'Oh Eric', she said, 'I've just had Johnno on the phone.'

'Is everything all right?'

'More or less.'

'Look, I'll call round. I'm travelling by car, I'm in Chester-le-Street. I've been to see my Mum who's in hospital. I could take you out somewhere for the afternoon. We could have a chat.'

'Oh yes!' Maeve was surprised. 'That would be lovely.'

'Think of somewhere you'd like to go for a couple of hours.'

What might Eric want? She couldn't remember him ever

trying to organise a chat with her before, though plenty of chats had just happened throughout their lives. Maeve put a pizza near the cooker as a hint for Giles, found her coat and the right shoes, and was ready for Eric at the door.

They went to Prestwick Carr, a little-known bird reservation, a large reclamation pond, not far up the Great North Road. She remembered it fondly from trips on the bus with Giles when he was below school age. She was often isolated in the house with him. This was modest country, with little in the way of contours. Small woods and water spread in all directions, with seats and shelters, easy parking and hardly anybody there. In winter the banks were crowded with her favourite geese, mainly pink-footed, and greylags, bean geese and white-fronted geese. Now the birds who didn't do summer migration were enjoying more space for themselves in the fresh warm air.

Eric didn't miss the geese, for he had never built up a sympathy for these birds. He wandered round following Maeve, admiring the watery Northumberland coastal plain. They found a bench and sat down.

Maeve knew Eric wanted to talk. She waited.

'I think you'd like to hear about my new interest in Sylvia Plath. I'm talking to writers at Aberdeen and they say, *She couldn't be further from us*. She never visited Scotland. Pure Cambridge and the south.

'*There was the north*, I say, *Ted Hughes' family*.

'*Scotland doesn't exist for such people*, says another academic.

'*She was an extremely good poet*, I say.

'All this got me thinking. I realised she went to Toronto and the Canadian wilds, which are not unlike Scotland. I've been back in touch with my contacts, they've come up with some great pointers and I'm writing about Plath in Toronto with a view to putting in for a place on the PhD course.'

'It's a pity she didn't go to Scotland,' said Maeve.

'Why do you say that?'

Maeve wickedly replied, 'You could have titled your study *Thon Quine: Plath in Aberdeen*!'

'You've made friends with Sheena Blackhall haven't you?'

'Well yes, and I've read her Doric poems. I haven't been to Aberdeen. What's it like?'

'Another country. Long streets, long beaches, sparkling granite, and the people have thick hair.'

Maeve laughed. 'You've been having an interesting time. While I've achieved nothing. If you don't get out, don't see people enough – they forget you.'

'No one forgets you Maeve. It's an illusion. I was forgotten while I was in Canada!'

'You came back with higher status – separated from the *hoi polloi*...'

'Nonsense.'

Maeve said, 'But I've done nothing.'

'That's not the case,' said Eric. 'You've written something good.'

'What?'

'I know you have. I'm a poet. I sense things. I know you have something up your sleeve.'

'I'm not an up-my-sleeve person.'

'In this case, yes you are.'

They stood up and walked towards a little beach. A flotilla of grebes, an overgrown family, swam near them.

'All right,' said Maeve, 'I wrote a long poem. It was very good but I lost it.'

'How?'

'It vanished from the house. I think it was stolen, but who would possibly want it?'

Eric stopped and turned towards her.

'Maeve, if that is so, it exists and it will be found.'

They moved on, tossing out ideas about Sylvia Plath's

potential response to the countryside. She'd liked bees, but that meant beekeepers, people. She would sit and write in a hut in the country if she was given one, but she would write anywhere. Had Plath liked the sea?'

They went to a small hotel Eric found for tea.

'This tea room is like the one in Bamburgh,' remarked Maeve.

Eric looked round at the curtains, pictures and ornaments, the fireplace filled with pine cones, three round tables.

'You're right. I wrote the first lines of *High Tide Bamburgh* there!'

Maeve could remember. 'We talked about the wreck of the *Forfarshire*.'

'Only a few men were saved. And a woman. A coaster with passengers.'

'Men need women, perhaps,' said Maeve.

'My sister Sal would say that. Dad's past heavy work and beside himself and relying on Sal who's in charge...'

'And your Mum's health not good. It's hard,' said Maeve. 'Mine rely on each other. They've lost curiosity. They can't keep up with Giles. Only my Dad has an inkling about my work...'

Eric took a slice of fruit cake. 'How long ago was that Bamburgh trip?'

'*High Tide Bamburgh* was the seventies wasn't it?' said Maeve. We were kids!

Eric nodded.

It was a funny sensation, sitting here with the teapot between them, so like that earlier time.

'And other shipwrecks,' said Eric. 'You told me about the *Lusitania*. I told you about the *Iolaire*. Tales of men's lives and deaths to regale one another.'

'In western waters,' said Maeve, 'far from the cities, a liner in wartime off Ireland, a large yacht returning to harbour with local young men. In the one case, victims unconnected with the area, in the other, the island's life blood.'

'The cruel sea.'

'You sent me your *Lusitania* poem from Canada.'

'Did I? It's been on the drawing board for years. The sea is demanding.'

'Even at Morecambe.'

He looked at her thoughtfully. 'Us and our writing,' he said. 'The poem you lost. Can you recall any of it?'

'Only the first bit but not the first vital words. I recited it to the seals at St Mary's Island! ... *fly beyond fear, let moor spread packed river pearls unopened* ...'

'What a nice line,' said Eric.

Maeve smiled. 'I learnt this fifty-line section – the Invocation.'

'How lovely! Have you ever done it in a poetry reading?'

'Never. I want the poem back. I repeat the start to myself sometimes – it's my mantra.'

Eric nodded. 'I believe you. I believe in it – it must be found.'

They were tempted to go on to Bamburgh, but they hadn't time. He drove her back to Newcastle, inviting her to Edinburgh – she could stay in his flat whenever he was away. He seemed to have taken in that she was a serious poet, just when she was beginning to doubt it herself.

She'd always known they were both poets. He'd had that unnerving instinct she'd written something special. Yet, why was she suddenly hit by a conviction that he was bowling up the north road considering her confession about her poem, wondering whether it was very good, whether it existed, whether it would be found, and whether he would be happy if it was?

Chapter Ten

MAEVE'S ESCAPE (1996)

RAYMOND WAS SYMPATHETIC to Maeve's recent problems at work, after ten years of peaceful routine at Jesmond Library. Giles had been six when she started, long before Raymond was around; now he was nearly seventeen, she was putting off the realisation that he no longer needed her.

Perhaps she was leaning on Raymond too much.

The library was 30 years old. The latest thing was to have shelving units on castors that could be moved around to allow other uses of the space. People were beginning to say computers would affect libraries even more in the future, and councils wouldn't have big budgets for books. In a time of uncertainty, the delightful little circular library was holding up well in its structure. Meanwhile the library management were noticing lumps of concrete falling off and crumbling from the main city library's outer walls, and this made them grumpy.

The doormat saga was revived. The caretaker reported the current doormat stolen, probably by a tramp. Maeve had to requisition another one. An inspector came along and made out a special demand for a fancy-shaped mat to fit the rounded doorway, though they'd managed fine with ordinary ones before. He then surveyed the room, trying to push the fixed bookshelves over, making them sway, kicking at the lino, and grumbling as though everything was Maeve's or her colleague's fault. It seemed he was itching to demolish something that was hers.

Echoes from her irrecoverable poem, parts of which had been written right here, sounded among these bookshelves that had seemed so permanent, at the chair and desk this man was deriding. Half-remembered, they ricocheted round the windows and ceilings – before they were written down and after she had lost them. Fragments, lines would come back when she stared at the sky above the Jesmond roofs.

> *cranking pit-wheels pulled men out to light*
> *from under earth they tramped through fields to*
>   *windowed brick,*
> *women, bairns and fire legitimate.*

The inspector put in a report that the whole interior needed a refit. Maeve and her co-worker were summoned to see the boss, who explained that their library would have to be shut for three months. He was sorry, disruption was inevitable, and they would be offered alternative part time work, details of which were in letters that were on their way to them.

She opened the letter the following afternoon and showed it to Raymond. 'A bit of a fait accompli.'

Raymond read it through.

'How long have you worked there?'

'Including before Giles? I came here when the new Central Library opened.' Maeve counted up. 'I've been working in libraries since I left school. That's terrible. Ye knaa – I've had enough!'

Raymond laughed – 'I've had enough!' and they both launched into the *Wings* song.

The letter needn't be answered yet. But as Maeve moved across the kitchen to make tea – and toast and honey (she needed comforting) she realised that a change in her life was in progress. How often it took some small outside event to bring things home to you – not that having to vacate her beautiful little library was minor. It needed refitting because it was a show building, of course, and Maeve suddenly knew she had spent enough of her life in it.

The next day, discussing this situation, Stephanie happened to let on she would prefer full time now her children were older. Maeve said nothing, but sang the 'I've had enough' tune to herself on the way home.

This might work out well for everyone.

Raymond was in again. He looked at the letter carefully. 'You know this gives you the right to leave. You could ask for a pension! I don't mean to be cheeky, but – '

'You are. But it might be a reasonable idea.'

Maeve secretly jumped at this suggestion. She thought it out in private, made the decision, and with two weeks negotiating it was all arranged.

Giles wasn't particularly sympathetic, and Maeve realised that he didn't relish her being in the house all day. But, snap, nor did she.

She enjoyed her last two weeks. It *was* a great little library. She and Stephanie were given boxes of chocolates by the friendly regulars, amid cries of 'Come back soon!'

But she would not return.

Raymond was checking the equipment for a gig on Teesside.

'You need to live in Scotland.'

Maeve was planning yet another trip north, for a performance that was an offshoot of Edinburgh's famous *Women*

Live. She was composing a poem. Her packing was desultory: she hadn't much to take. They had stopped for a bite in the kitchen. Raymond made crunchy toast and cheese without burning anything.

'I can travel,' said Maeve. 'I've been practically commuting for the last two years.'

'There's a limit to travel,' said Raymond. 'In the end it's a whirlwind. You've made all those poetry friends in Edinburgh, and you thrive on them. You need to be there. It has to happen soon.'

Maeve felt more than a little frightened. She wasn't usually frightened.

'I ken,' she said in homage to him. 'I like that you're Scottish.'

'Aye. You are simpatico. You are a Celtic Fringe person. You've developed this affinity with Scotland, you have Eric in Scotland – you're almost turning down England!'

'We don't leave our countries. But we can have more than one country. I will come back.'

His arm round the back of her chair, he gave her a sideways hug. She sighed. 'Time's up for me at Sandyford.' She stood up. Ray stood too, hugged her again. 'You are very brave.'

Inevitably, Ray's and Maeve's association was coming to an end. This had begun and been enabled by several road runs to Scotland. The band had started a series of smaller gigs in a Glasgow club. Ray delivered the equipment in the van, and collected it the day after. No one took any notice when Maeve went with him.

Overnight, Ray would park on some deserted west coast beach or in a glen, and roll out a palliasse, a rough mattress stowed under the boxing. It might be light till past eleven and again from three or four, and they could sleep. Maeve found these adventures exciting, even educational. Scotland was both open and secluded, especially the north.

Maeve almost felt she ought to learn to drive for her future if she wasn't going to travel beside Raymond for ever, and she wasn't, she couldn't.

Besides its countryside, Scotland was full of trains and little cities. She'd manage without driving. She would have years there, perhaps twenty or thirty – at forty-odd, 70 was far enough away. She would meet even more poets and people, she would write more poems. She'd be happy.

She had known this would happen. She was moving to Scotland.

'So I'm going. Just like that. Should I be warning Giles?'

'What's it to do with Giles?' said Raymond.

Giles would be all right. Raymond would be all right. Raymond had Ellen; and he still had the G G band and Giles' concerts, and now recordings.

At sixteen Giles was a man. He'd increasingly been treating the house, the kitchen and its foodstuffs as his; he would come in with a bag of croissants or a takeaway meal; he wasn't handless with a tin-opener or even a potato peeler. For a while Maeve had had to make an appointment if she wanted to cook for him, and increasingly she was eating with Raymond, or rather, snacking with him. Their catering had imperceptibly evolved into snacks for busy and separate people.

Better by far to spring it on Giles. There'd been many a fait accompli on his part: he would be travelling; he would be entertaining a girlfriend; he would be out. She remembered a proverb: The fox has many tricks; the hedgehog has only one trick, but it is a good one. Hers was an excellent trick, and if she was going to refer to Aesop's animals, the wildgoose was migrating. Giles would understand. Raymond and Maeve took their mugs of tea back to the rooms they were working in.

Am I leaving? asked the half-written poem.

I leave my giants laden by weight,
inhospitable shield, peg them recumbent...
failed variable demons, identical graves...
snow or drought... Go, it is time.

She looked out of her window, its ordinary view seared on her mind. It was beginning to look back at her as if it, too, felt jaded with her presence. Giles had grown up, precipitously yes, but decidedly. She was free to choose Scotland and Eric's territory. She had always followed Eric, and yet this step was new.

Giant, I will arise, my elevation terrible, privet
   beanstalk, leylandii bland blank
inimical deathly high cypress   stirring limbs
       mouth   teeth, dangerous brain

This poem was adopting her long line style, where her poetry wanted to go. She would move on in Scotland. Her poems had to follow her life.

Courage, we cross boundaries, rubicons of time
   hedges become bridges, in seven leagues we recede
     hypnotising failures into futures, our options
     determined
       mountain ranges a week's walk distant.

There was more. Her poems were improving.

In Giles' house, the books were communal. Her son genuinely had little time for reading, but he had his favourites, science fiction and *Lord of the Rings*; and in poetry, William McGonagall, Pam Ayres, Leonard Cohen, Bob Dylan. He had music books too.

Maeve picked out a motley heap of books she couldn't do

without. She couldn't carry them all; she'd leave them in a box to go up to her. She wasn't precious about notebooks and publications. She selected a bundle. The rest would be safe here.

Her lost poem about the geese wasn't here. She had long lived with that. Yet it seemed more likely to be here than anywhere else, more likely here than nowhere. After hesitating, she left *Waterbirds of the Northern Hemisphere* in the bookshelf. She had learned everything she needed from it, and she faintly believed it might attract *Wildgoose* in some way, help to keep it alive or bring it back.

She looked through her clothes. She owned disgracefully few decent pieces. Summer or winter, every item stuffed into her cupboard was useless. She saw it suddenly. Well, that made packing easier. She'd noticed a fashion for wearing a summer dress over jeans. She liked this practical and cheerful mode – how she was dressed right now.

She could do it. She was ready to leave this house with a few notebooks, jeans, two more dresses, her favourite coat, her swimsuit, a couple of pictures and that stupid model giraffe Giles had given her. She was leaving sadness and achievement behind. Trying to rewrite the old *Wildgoose* was impossible.

> *Morocco scorches   we breed in arctic light*
> *What had occurred in Agadir,*
> *dwelling under black silt, bones,*
> *French language battles horror.*

All that organised travel, those visions, how had they been patchworked together? She no longer knew.

She would explain herself to Eric. She had stayed with him in Edinburgh often enough; he slept at Richard's to give her more space. With his improved contract in Aberdeen, where he commuted for short weeks (Monday to Thursday), he and Richard were negotiating a mortgage for a bigger flat. When she arrived with her suitcase, Eric saw her as the ideal replacement tenant. Besides, he had come to expect Maeve to follow him about.

Maeve was delighted. She was ready for the change. No more leaving poetry events early to dash for the last train. No more being in the wrong city when anything happened. No more racket of Giles' band half the night, or teenaged barrack-room lawyers whose names she didn't know, materialising from nowhere and asking her to mend their trousers, settle their arguments or make them tea.

She put effort into her new home straight away, early snow notwithstanding. It was almost *de rigeur* for her to be starting adventures in early snow. She was a migrating goose, her reality the air around her. The wide grouping of poets she knew in Edinburgh and Scotland, birds of a feather, were her flock.

It was her moment of triumph, despite the buts.

Triumph, but she would have no partner. Her lover belonged to the life that was ending.

Triumph, but she would have to work. She reckoned on temporary typing. Edinburgh was packed with lawyers' chambers, commercial offices, quangos, headquarters, breweries; all depended on temporary typists. She could type and spell. These were (in those days) skills. She'd been out registering with the agencies yesterday. The Scottish branch of the Farmers Union needed someone: she could start the following week. She wouldn't have to work every week, but she might work extra weeks for convenience.

Triumph, but she would have to write. It was no good sitting in her castle relishing her long-desired world: it was all about having time and space to write.

She went to a big city supermarket and re-stocked her kitchen with the basics, carefully listed. *Her* butter dish. *Her* teapot. *Her* fruit bowl. She would add the frills gradually.

After the kitchen, her bedroom. Eric's Richard, the more domestic of those two, had bought her a double duvet, pillows and linen set. He'd chosen a blue and green pattern; she would soon buy a second linen set, a dashing colour – gold or red. The bedroom had at least as much floor space as bed, a clean warm rug, light walls, a window with shelves beneath it, and a built-in wardrobe.

It was frustrating, having a new bedroom that looked as nice as this when you weren't going to share it with anybody. Would that come? Or was her easy relationship with the dozens of poets in town dependent on there being no favourites? How favourite might a favourite be? Were these abstract questions? As her eyes began to water, she fetched in one of the new small chairs. The clean-looking ironing board would go here too, between the door and the window. Better than in the kitchen. A scarf or two, a paperweight, a mirror on the shelf. Next week she'd start buying more clothes.

Eric's living room, too, was morphing into hers. Her watercolours of Grasmere, Windermere and Morecambe Bay were hung on the walls. One frame had lost its glass. All were carefully placed away from the sunlight. A new, brightly coloured circular rug embellished the floor, and she'd found three small folding chairs put out on the pavements for the binmen. Richard had put her up to the Edinburgh pastime of staking out smarter streets on the nights before rubbish collections.

Her six-foot model giraffe had moved cities. A rare present from Giles, it had been sent from Fenwick's store, a couple of years ago, as a kind of apology after that trouble with the troupe of dancing schoolkids and the band. The giraffe reminded her peacefully of the survived chaos of the past. Raymond had delivered it, along with her favourite small red sofa and boxes of pictures and books, saying Giles had helped Raymond put the items in the van.

Only three days in and she was winning.

Eric was sitting there, exactly as of old, only he was the visitor and she was the host. Neither of them mentioned this was the second time Maeve had followed Eric into a living space. Extraordinarily, since she left her parents' home, Maeve had never lived anywhere that hadn't been Eric's first.

'It feels right to have moved away,' she told him. 'Giles is an adult now, coping with the house, on good terms with Johnno, still busy with gigs. Let's not worry about him.'

'How old is he, sixteen, seventeen? You have a grown-up son.'

'And you have a grown up nephew.'

'I don't think of him like that.'

'Without him,' said Maeve, 'you'd have no interests in the young generation and perhaps that would feel worse. It's just how it all worked out. You could ask how it went wrong for me – my mother does – and possibly my father, though he has the good manners to keep his views to himself, and now poor soul he is waning.'

'You have done wonders. Oh Maeve, I'm sorry. You are important to me, Maeve. But things have gone so wrong for you in your personal life, it ain't fair.'

'It is fair,' said Maeve, 'it is what I have chosen, though I admit the results are odd. I didn't want Johnno but I wanted Giles.'

'Beware of what you want...'

'And Johnno has been totally fair financially. That's the main reason we're still friends.'

'He can afford to be fair.'

Eric looked out at the weather, mild but wintry.

'You're doing fine. I'm meeting Angus Calder this afternoon. Shall we go look for him? He'll be in the Filmhouse, or at home, or in that bookshop on Bread Street. Want to come?'

Eric picked up his typescript article in a folder. They found Angus in his house, looking sombre.

'Eric, have you heard,' he began, without more than a quick nod to Maeve, 'It's about to be announced on the news that Sorley Maclean has died.'

'Oh no!' said Maeve.

'That's tough,' said Eric. 'What a man. What an era. How did you hear?'

'The lines are all hot. Alasdair told me, for one, and then I saw Aonghas at the Scotsman offices. Mind you they will have the obituaries ready. It's a big story. Sorley is known worldwide.'

Today's *Scotsman* lay on the sideboard, already out of date.

'Maeve, would you make us some coffee?' Angus indicated his small kitchen as the phone rang. But she waited, to miss nothing of what was said. The phone stopped ringing before Angus reached it. He ignored this.

Eric asked Angus, 'How well did you know him?'

'Less well than I know most Scottish poets,' admitted Angus. 'He came to Edinburgh more than once a year latterly. He worked here in the university at one time, but the Gaelic poet I know best is Iain.'

'Sorley's history goes way back. No one is sad at an old person dying, except the people who loved them.'

Maeve disagreed. 'But we loved him! Poets love one another! We are all linked, and death is the time we are most linked.'

Angus answered his phone. 'Sorley's publisher. She says the funeral is being arranged on Skye. I'll need to go. Will you drive us up, Eric?'

'Oh yes, I am enough a fan of the man's work myself. He was a very political poet. I will do that.'

The phone rang again, while Maeve made coffee for three.

'I'm to go up on the train,' reported Angus. 'There'll be media taxis from Kyle.' He came across for his coffee. 'Giles has just got in touch with me.'

'Not our Giles?' asked Maeve apprehensively.

'Good god no. Angus' agent.'

'A historic event.'

'I've read the poems in English,' said Maeve. 'Sorley's translation. We've all heard him read in Edinburgh.'

'*Hallaig*,' said Angus.

'My favourite is *The Woods of Raasay*,' she said. 'A friend of mine struggled away trying to translate that, without much Gaelic to go on. She got a recording of it and listened to that and used a Dwelly's.' Maeve could picture the purple and black cover of the most prevalent Gaelic dictionary. 'She made quite a good job of it, but Sorley didn't like it.'

'He wouldn't,' said Angus.

They sat around a bit longer. This was world-shaking news if you were a Scottish poet. A very, very important poet, using a language from the north of the country that had been all but stamped out. Maeve reflected how they had all listened in awe to the music of the Gaelic most of them couldn't follow. No wonder governments traditionally feared poets, sought mealy-mouthed poets, or closely monitored the activity of known and popular writers in their attempts to curb them. Here was a poet in a language spoken only by thousands, yet world renowned. The end of a poet's life mattered, the deaths of poets were tales told far and wide.

Maeve felt honoured to witness the Scottish reaction to Sorley's death.

'We will go up to Skye,' announced Eric. 'Richard will want to come. You too, Maeve.'

'I'd love to go up. I'm needing a break from Ray, you know, but that isn't the main reason.'

'No, it shouldn't be.'

They walked back via a bar, where they left Angus with some students.

On the pub doorstep they ran into Derek from Glasgow and paused for a word. Derek was looking for Suzy who lived in the Grassmarket. They were going to hear Sandie Craigie at the Art College.

'Suzy told me you've moved here. I thought you lived here already!' he told Maeve. 'I'm trying to get Suzy to move to Glasgow.'

'Say hello to Sandie from me,' Maeve said. 'We can't come, we're meeting a couple of writers from London. Richard bumped into them last night.'

'Hang on,' said Derek. 'You're in the programme. You're reading!'

'What?'

'*Women Live*. It's the revival.'

'God, what's the date? Oh Lord! Of course, it's why I was coming up this week! Oh Eric!'

'Your call, Maeve.'

Derek laughed. 'Good thing I saw you.'

'I was excited about moving here – I almost forgot *Women Live*! What's the time? I'll go home and pick out some poems. They'll want funnies?'

'Not a funny night,' said Eric. 'Sorley Maclean died. Angus is in there talking about him.'

'That'll be Angus talking all night. Some of them will never make the Art College gig.' Derek entered the pub.

'Derek's gay, isnt he?' said Maeve. 'Why would he want Suzy to move to Glasgow?'

'Have you met Suzy? Total crossdresser. Can only tell by the voice – and the size of his feet. Unless you watch him walking. Suzy's compering your gig.'

They turned the corner to the familiar street and house.

The television had been accidentally left on. A feature on

Maclean was in progress. You could see the black and white snowy slopes of the Cuillin behind the poet in the video.

She remembered the giants in the snow, and the poem she'd written in Newcastle after that toast and cheese with Ray. She wanted to look at it again.

'Half an hour till I leave for the Art College. You'd better go and meet Richard's writers.' She saw him out of her flat. Not a night for funnies. What about her Invocation, remnant of her lost poem? Should she premier it at the Art College in tribute to Sorley? She still knew it, bar those first lines. It was too much of a risk. Here was the giants poem, unrevised but intense. That would work. Sorley was a giant.

It felt special to be travelling to Skye with Eric and Richard (and Richard's dog), on such an auspicious winter day. Eric's motor was ailing a little and he didn't want to drive too fast. They were overtaken all the way by other cars, hurtling north, on what should have been a very quiet day. All were headed for the Skye Bridge, built and opened a year ago.

The dog, accustomed to car travel, sat in the back with Richard. Maeve was beside her cousin. They had a rare view of the countryside. The further north, the snowier it became. They saw a herd of deer spread over a mountainside. The dog tensed with excitement.

'*Deer on the High Hills*,' said Richard, after Iain Crichton Smith.

'Iain will be there, but we won't see everyone – the place will be mobbed,' said Eric.

They saw no people outside of cars on the journey.

'How empty this country can be,' observed Eric sadly.

At the Skye Bridge, the guy collecting the tolls was having an extremely busy day for winter, and there were hold-ups at which the motorists were grumbling. On the island they followed many other cars round the dark, imposing Cuillin to Portree. The mountains stood out, steep and grave in the snow. They parked the car, leaving the big dog comfortable, and approached the square.

The square seemed to have expanded to allow as large a gathering as would ever be seen on Skye. A sea of winter coats, each enveloping a poet or scholar, friend or official, local or follower, from as far as America, Paris, Germany and London, blocked the driveway to the church, which was filling fast. A P.A. system was in place to bring the service outside. Not being religious, their little party were happy to stand in the square. Although the ground was snowy, the air was not bitter, and they stood around with other proud Gaels and Scots and the view for company.

The Gaelic words came over on the P.A., then the congregation started emerging from the church. Everyone milled about talking. Eric spoke to many poets. Those he didn't know outnumbered those he did. Maeve knew fewer. Scots were prominent but so were the international scholars. Richard saw a friend from Runrig and they all had a chat.

Slowly the extraordinary party drifted and drove to the graveyard promontory and converged at the graveside. Maeve watched with awe as men were called out one by one in Gaelic to take cords to lower the coffin. Family and friends, those who had known him and joked with him and those who had known him on the page, all witnessed this. Bystanders walked across the other graves, bringing another to the number of the dead.

The view lay open across to Raasay in the sun and snow, the sea dark, the land shining in the afternoon.

'No one is surprised to see us here,' observed Richard. 'Any of us, Maeve, myself or you, Eric.'

'There are more people here than just poets. Visitors, homecomers, from far away.'

'We were recognised. I saw people acknowledging Maeve as much as Eric.'

They turned with the mourners and walked back to the car.

'Everyone is equal at a funeral,' said Richard.

Raymond was standing by the car.

'Raymond! It's a wonder you found us.'

Raymond looked sheepish. 'I saw Richard's dog – he saw me and jumped to the window – the car shook.'

'Yes, he does that.' Richard let his dog out and slipped a lead on him. 'Why are you here? Poetry isn't your thing?'

'My Granny on Barra spoke Gaelic,' said Raymond, regaining his composure. 'I know what Maclean's done.'

'Raymond, what's going on?' Maeve asked with concern.

'You have a drummer who is a fan in a van.'

'Och, I know that. It's hard to miss.'

'Maeve, did you say *Och*?'

Ignoring the others, Ray pleaded, 'Maeve, come with me and we'll talk.'

'Okay, tell them you're giving me a ride.'

'Raymond,' said Eric, 'Giles isn't here is he?'

'Mercifully, no. He was heading off to Carlisle when I came away. Oh, and *ciamar a tha leibh*.' Raymond stamped his feet. Excitement made them forget the cold.

'*Tha gu math, tapadh leibh*,' replied Richard, not a real Gaelic speaker but quick on the uptake.

'We're outsiders,' said Eric, 'our only Gaelic is spoken in a gang of Sassenachs. We pay our tribute.'

'*Chan eil mi Sassenach*,' said Raymond. 'Certainly not. But Maeve wants to come out and see Talisker. She was telling me about the white sands in Sorley's poem. But the beach is black. Our personal literary puzzle. I'm gonna take Maeve off your hands and return her to Edinburgh myself.'

'I don't need taking off anybody's hands.'

Richard regarded Eric with a distinct gleam in his eye. 'We're heading down to Sleat and the Mallaig ferry. The

Bridge – but for the Bridge this record-breaking crowd on Skye ...' he shook his head. They all looked back at the heaving dark mass of official and unofficial humanity here to celebrate a language, a literary art, one man, and a threatened culture. It looked less threatened now.

'Okay,' said Maeve again. 'I'll go back with Raymond. It may be too late for Talisker,' she added to Ray. 'It'll be dark in an hour or two.'

Ray had booked into the hotel in Carbost by telephone. They took the walk to the beach first. Snow added to the light. It was a longish trek and darkening a little. Passing near the fang-shaped mountain Talisker, they dropped down to the bay. A waterfall came over the clifftop from a stream. The wind blew it back on itself, a fountain of water in the sky.

The tide was out. They walked briefly on the stones. The beach was white with snow above the recent tideline. The rim where the tide had turned was part way down the beach.

'A neap tide rather than a spring tide,' she said, referring to Maclean's book title. Raymond recited the title in Gaelic. He didn't have much Gaelic but was proud of what he had.

Coming to Skye for Sorley's funeral was one thing, something that fixed you into Scottish literary history, but they both knew their three-year association had to change. Did they want to extend their connection beyond the years of following Giles' adventures and patchy fortunes as he'd careered through his growing years, the nights away in the van? Had they both had enough? This question was easily put in theory but not easily in speech between them. Their quietness on the walk was a sign of this. Returning, Raymond took the lead.

'We have reached an end?'

'Yes, we have reached an end. Do you agree? It's not

about other things, about whether you get on with Ellen for instance. That's entirely your business. Sorting us is our business and we are sorted. You are great. I've had – we've had – it's been lovely, but you know we have nowhere else to go.'

'It has been a very nice affair,' said Raymond.

'I'm glad we did it. We were right to do it properly.'

'It isn't forever.'

'Affairs have a bad press,' said Maeve. 'They are good for people.'

'Seems like we're in agreement, hen.'

Raymond had never called her *hen* before.

'Yes. Thank you for coming up. Too many people don't end relationships properly, especially men. They are terrified of talking. Football was invented so men would have something to talk about.'

Raymond laughed.

'I've gone as far as I want to,' she added. 'I've got poetry and I've got Giles.'

'I've got Giles too.'

'*We met in the heart of an otter,* like Kathleen Raine and Gavin Maxwell – the difference was that they didn't like each other.'

'She was in love with him wasn't she?'

'Maybe she was, but she didn't like him. It was an act of aggression on her part.'

'That's a bit unfair. The old story, wanting to reform him?'

'Too facile,' she said. 'Anyway they've been and gone. Everything comes and goes. No it doesn't, it goes and goes.'

'Are we in agreement?'

'You're right.'

'And Giles is the otter.'

They fetched their bags from the van.

'Who's going to ask for two rooms?'

'Which is the least undignified, me or you?'

They went up to the desk and gave Ray's name. 'We booked a double room,' said Maeve, 'but we've just broken up. Can we have a room each?'

The hotelier had seen everything. He knew to keep cool.

'Let's see. We are busy because of the Maclean funeral. I could do you a good sized twin room?'

They looked at each other.

'That's fine.' They both nodded.

The dining room was bustling and clattery with the full house out of season and waitresses in from the village, but the chef did well. There was a sort of carvery. They chose venison with roast potatoes and carrots (you never got many vegetables on the islands) and a cheese board with grapes and flans. The diners next to them were poets Maeve didn't know. 'A wake for one poet is a wake for us all,' said the elderly one, in Cambridge tones.

In the bay window, a young man sang dreamy Gaelic songs to a guitar. They saw other diners tipping him, and did the same.

'The otter is music.'

When they eventually retired, they found a bottle of hotel grade fizz in their room.

'To celebrate breaking up well,' said Raymond.

Next morning, the sea sparkled. There was one sensible route to Inverness. Raymond filled up with petrol at Broadford.

Beyond Inverness, winter darkened the summits, veiled the dramatic surrounds of Killiecrankie. Then Perth, and a swooping cruise through the lowlands to the Forth Road Bridge.

Maeve sat commenting on the scenery for the quiet parts

of the run – deer on the moors, a flock of geese resting. Raymond stopped briefly near the geese.

Go, geese, gather...

Busier and darker, the drive more demanding, she sat quietly.

'We'll need to eat. We forgot at Broadford.' She inspected the dashboard cubby-holes.

'Yes, and something to drink,' said Raymond. How about the Indian restaurant in Corstorphine?'

'Good idea,' she said.

They drove on to the little high street restaurant and ate jalfrezi, rice and korma. They drank water and cups of tea. Raymond paid out of the G G petty cash. He dropped her at Tollcross with a brisk exchange of thanks, and drove away.

She felt a little shaken but she knew they would both recover.

There was some post.

Her eyes welled when she opened an arty card from Giles. It simply said *Good luck Mum.*

There was also a card and booklet from Sheena Blackhall, who had heard Maeve was on Skye for Sorley's funeral, and had hoped to get along but was prevented by teaching.

Maeve would invite Sheena to stay here on visits to Edinburgh. She could do it now. She had this room, the bedroom and her own kitchen and bathroom. She had privacy. She had her poetry friends. She had books, she knew editors. Eric and Richard were not far away. Eric accepted her these days. He hadn't much option. She was ready for time for herself, for her writing, a home that consoled her, and not being anybody's wife.

She would write, about giants, Gaelic funerals on islands, about loud bands, drums and dulcimers, taped-up letterboxes and Canada, Briggflatts, poets, wide sands, dangerous seas and the moonlight on Pennine fells. The same things she would dream about in her perfect little home, all she had passed through to reach her proper milieu, the poets flocking back and forth over Scotland on their mysterious errands.

She dreamed of the geese too, but she wouldn't need to write about geese again. Lost though it was, her old poem still existed for her. It had not been thrown away. It had not disintegrated. It had been moved.

Chapter Eleven

MAEVE'S RETURN (1999)

EVERYTHING WAS ROSY. Maeve sat on her small red sofa in her Edinburgh home – she no longer thought of this as Eric's room. Her bare feet rested on the luxurious rug, coffee steamed on the small table beside her. A shiny calendar on the nearby wall showed a coming season full of events. Her two books of poems lay with other poets' books in a heap beside the bookcase. Computer and note-books were on a neat desk further away, under the Scottish watercolour – a rampart of mountains, a foreground loch and geese.

She re-read the letter from Giles. She could count the letters Giles had ever sent her on one finger. What was odd about his letter? There was something unsaid in it. You didn't spend your life being a writer without being able to second-guess any letter.

This was an unanswered question so far.

She put the letter aside and picked up her batch of new poems for performance. Which would she choose if she went down to Newcastle?

Eric had warned her not to re-use her performance poems

too often – they were of the moment. Something that could have the house in stitches one year could be meaningless the next.

She was still very pally with Eric – why shouldn't she be? It was widely known they were cousins. The poetry world had expanded hugely in the last decade or more, say since 1985, and was big enough for both of them. Occasionally she was invited to lunch with Richard and Eric. Sometimes Eric met her in town. She knew they held poetry dinners she didn't attend.

She knew, too, she hadn't always been fair on Eric. But then that was mutual. They had used each other. She had never truly understood his gay identity, the way she understood those of Bev and Alice. There had been no sexual interest between them; family closeness saw to that. He had failed to warn her of dangers, forgotten to include her in publications. She was a challenging rival poet in his private world.

The market was falling out of temporary typing, since word processors had become computers. Men in the offices she'd worked in found it quicker to do their own typing these days. One or two decorative permanent typists was all that even the biggest places needed. Maeve hadn't realised that the decorative element had been part of her qualifications. No longer young, she was always well presented, with that calm cheerfulness that makes half of anyone's appearance.

She was doing a week's temping for the Philatelic Bureau, which sent off first day covers to collectors, mainly the army, all over the world. Typing the envelopes was the craziest work, and she could only handle the schoolroom atmosphere of the posse of typists by laughing at it, but it paid.

Now she was a comfortable fifty-something, and at last a contented one, she could see the office comedy and laugh.

There'd been fun moments. She'd made poems out of some of them. She'd made money out of all of them. The office where the whole staff were brought in to walk round a table collating documents until they were dizzy. The office where her first job every morning was to photocopy the crossword.

Returning to Giles' invitation, she read the details thoughtfully. The G G Band was preparing a major concert. Because of the new popularity of poetry, Giles was including three short poetry spots in his concert and he would like her to take part as a poetry character who would appeal to his punters. Maeve thought poetry character an inferior description to poet. What was even odder, he proposed to pay her, and a proper rate.

Her instinct was to say no. Her new life was real; she was busy. Her uncomplicated and now distant affair with Raymond was over, and she didn't want to meet him again; but Giles had reassured her that Raymond would be away on holiday with his wife.

She still thought no. Not many performance poets were over fifty. The concert audience would be much younger. She knew the two women she would be performing with, Karen, of the library and learner writing community, and Frippy, unforgettable early girlfriend of Giles. He should balance them with a man.

There was rain outside and a swishing sound from traffic. She crossed the room to draw the curtains, behind the vase of roses that had come Interflora for her recent birthday, from Raymond, still married to Ellen, still working for Giles.

One way or another she had relented, perhaps because she wanted to solve the mystery behind Giles' letter. Perhaps because her son had asked her a favour. And here she was.

She had accepted the invitation to stay at Giles' house,

aware it was now a true house, including the upper flat, which Johnno had bought and was in process of doing up. She was given an unfamiliar upstairs room, that directly above her old writing room and bolt-hole. The old scene across the Sandyford street looked a little different from higher up, like a life seen twenty years on. She noticed once again the heavy hedge trunks resembling a giant's body leaning along the opposite side of the road. It was merely a hedge; no one but herself would ever notice the giant.

She went downstairs. It was a novelty to use stairs in this familiar house. The second main door to the old upper flat had opened onto the staircase, arranged in such an odd way that the stair cupboard was part of the old lower flat, a cupboard under inaccessible stairs. She admired the way Johnno had opened the staircase. She went through to the familiar old kitchen – her kitchen through much of her life. The ghost of the young Giles, of breakfasts, of... but she must live in the present.

Giles was in the kitchen, with Frippy who was to perform and sing. The atmosphere was imbued with excitement and tension. The instruments and equipment had gone ahead to the venue ten minutes away.

Giles knew she liked coffee. The brew was fresh and aromatic. She sat down at the table, but Giles gestured for her to get up.

'Come with me,' he said to his mother. 'We have found something in the renovations which belongs to you.'

She followed him through the hallway, mystified. Was this to be some awful garment left behind in a former era? A kitchen item? The most ancient of typewriters? What could it be?

Giles turned into her former room, his office. A table, a different one, stood in the place of her old table.

Maeve was shocked. She gasped for air and sat down on the banquette that hadn't been there before. On the table was a paper box, the kind that carried a ream of paper. It was light blue and white. Inside the box...

She reached over, touched the apparition, lifted it. It wasn't light and empty, but full of paper.

'Your poem,' said Giles.

She couldn't speak. The words *Where was it?* wouldn't come out of her mouth. She leaned forward again and shook off the thin card lid. There was the title page. There was the manuscript. Flicking through it she saw it was undisturbed.

'Has anybody read it?' was what she said.

'I remember you losing it.'

'I'm not surprised,' said Maeve. 'I was distraught.'

'Do you want to know where it was?'

'Where?'

Giles led her into the hall. He opened the stair cupboard. Maeve looked in at the jumble of shoes, umbrellas, guitar stands and cardboard boxes, very little different from how she recalled it five years ago and more.

Giles stepped into the cupboard. He pointed up to the top of the cupboard, its ceiling under the risers. She looked in and up.

'Here.' Giles indicated a small ledge in the woodwork high up where the stairs turned the corner at the top. Maeve had never seen the ledge before. She gazed at it, remembering her thorough search which had included the floor of the stair cupboard, to the very back.

'How did it get there?' she asked.

'I was only ten,' said Giles.

She looked at him. The tears came, and with them the silent words.

Soon she'd be able to recite the poem.

Her Invocation was no longer a road to nowhere.

As she shook with emotion her son held her.

'We have to do the concert now,' he said gently. 'You can sort it all out in the morning.'

'Can I have it in my bedroom?'

'It's yours. We'll be tired tonight. Let's leave it till tomorrow. It's not going to vanish again.'

But Maeve took the package upstairs to her room. She hid it under the bed, looked in the mirror, took off the Paisley scarf that was obscuring her raw silk plum-coloured two-piece, and added her chunky silver necklace. Before going back down she took out the poem once more, lifted the title page, and looked down at the first lines she hadn't been able to recover. She sat on the bed, reading. The coffee could wait. *Goose muse*, not *Wildgoose muse*. There was the answer. The next page or two. Yes, they were in her brain. *Goose muse*. The rest, her *packed river pearls unopened*, were below.

Frippy clearly knew something about the poem, for she was very kind to Maeve, whom she addressed as Mrs Carter, plying her with her coffee at last, and making sure she ate a fresh warm croissant, which helps in any shock. Giles was completing his own preparations.

The people carrier collected them on time. Frippy got in the back seat with Maeve, put her arm round her and hugged her, which Maeve was not in a state to analyse. She hadn't the headspace to be angry with Giles. She accepted Frippy's comforting gesture. There was little else she could do. They drove down to the Criterion, an old, old cinema below the Armstrong Bridge at the foot of Ouseburn, a popular area for Geordie youngsters. It would be mobbed. *Goose Muse*.

As ever, the music was dreadfully loud. She could see why it was called heavy metal. Sound equipment sprawled everywhere, and a massive new speaker stood at the front of the stage. This was the big speaker's first outing, surely a bad idea in Raymond's absence. Everyone was excited, the vast crowd of supporters mostly teenagers.

Maeve waited with the two other readers. She wasn't listening to the music properly. She wasn't thinking about the lighter poems she had intended to read. She was away with the rediscovered poem. Her mind was all over the place. This had been a central symbol in her life, the loss of this key achievement of hers. It made her think about how you might have to live without something that was necessary to you and why.

After the efforts to replicate and rephrase and remember what had vanished in the trauma of loss, the despair all those years ago, the secret of *Wildgoose* was unlocked. ... *retreat to tundra, fly beyond fear, let moor spread packed river pearls unopened...* Her poem was restored, and so was she.

Giles had decided the three would read one after another in an interval, and that Maeve as the guest would read first. He seemed very slightly worried as he introduced her personally. 'The one and only Maeve Cartier,' declared Giles.

She went up beside the big speaker to begin. She'd done plenty of stage work and had a sympathy for the young. She was a well-kent name to the audience. Some of them knew she was Giles' mother but it didn't matter – they didn't all know and she had a different name.

Goose muse, wild art spur thy retreat... She had it now; thinking it began with *Wildgoose* had thrown out the rhythm. The lights were up. She could see the kids' expressions, including some who were spaced out. There were lots of drugs in this community.

How could she be professional? She suddenly knew that tonight she could make no one laugh. The two poems she had selected would not seem funny to her and she would not be able to present them as funny. Her jokes would fall flat.

Silence. They were attentive and it was her moment.

They had paid for this concert: she had to give them value. Without introduction she launched into the Invocation of her poem.

> *Goose muse, wild art spur thy retreat to tundra, fly*
> *beyond fear,*
> *let moor spread packed river pearls unopened, beyond*
> *human invasion*
> *yearly spin life from rock's barnacle skies,*

No problem with the words. She could summon them all. They weren't fusty. They were fresh. Nothing wrong with their reception: the punters listened surprised and spell-bound. Never mind Giles, she was doing the concert proud. There were another twenty lines of the Invocation, when the first geese in the poem would whirl down to land....

> *Go, geese, gather, let feathered beat of goosewings herald*
> *visitations.*
> *Grise-grey down fluffed below pinions, low within a*
> *shoreside walnut grove,*
> *leaves engraved with autumn veins...*

She couldn't reinvent such words. Beyond the Invocation, she now had the power to unroll the whole poem, months and months of savouring and weighing phrases, all recorded again, translatable from the pages in her guest-room, pages she would never lose again.

There was only one thing she'd forgotten: her tactic wasn't very fair on Frippy and Karen. They weren't expecting this. It would affect the reaction to their performances: they had expected to follow frivolity with more frivolity. It would be impossible to rescue the atmosphere after this poem.

As she drew to a close she was aware of Karen and Frippy

moving in behind her, very near, beside the speaker box. She could hear them whispering urgently about who would follow her. Neither of them wanted to be next. She heard Karen saying angrily, 'No. You can sing,' and hitting something for emphasis.

What happened then was cataclysmic. The speaker wasn't attached to the floor, as it should have been. The top-heavy box tottered, distracting the audience and of course Maeve. As she paused to look over her shoulder, the box lurched over in the direction of the three of them on the edge of the stage, and crashed on the floor where they had all been standing. The two women cannoned into Maeve and she fell.

> *...where sand-dunes made by wind protect from wind,*
> *they land.*

In a split, irretrievable second, Maeve went right over sideways into the old-fashioned orchestra pit that lay below the stage. She caught sight of a piano before she hit her head on it. She dropped painfully down some metal-edged steps and collapsed into rusty music stands.

She heard shouts, wails, cries, applause, requests for a doctor, ditto an ambulance. She had a certainty the poem had been well received, stronger than her pain. Faces peered down above the pit. Then she blacked out.

The white room was in a hospital. Smaller than a ward but it had to be a hospital. Nowhere else could be so clean and empty. The bed was high. She wondered where she had been. She couldn't move.

She tried to wiggle her toes. Nothing. Her arms and hands wouldn't move. They seemed pinned to her side. She could feel the hard aches of broken bones, and her head began to hurt as she entered awareness.

A nurse came by. Maeve tried to smile, but couldn't. She needed to speak. A squeak only.

'Last night –' she managed, faintly.

The nurse looked doubtfully at her. 'You've been out for the count for three days. Glad you are back with us – but take it easy now!'

The nurse had a Geordie accent. She was in Newcastle, that was right.

'RBI?' Maeve's faint voice sounded.

'Yes, you're in the R.V.I. I'll get the ward sister to have a word with you. And I'll bring you a drink.'

The sister came to the nurse's call. 'Water,' she said to the nurse, 'but she may not be able.'

The sister sat down and regarded her shrewdly.

'Well done, Mrs Carter. You must be calm. We're not out of the woods yet.'

'What day?' Maeve could only manage a word or two.

'I'll tell you a little of what I know. If you are upset, close your eyes and we'll let you rest.'

'What?'

'You were brought in last Saturday night, very late. I'm told you fell at a concert. If so, it was a very bad fall. Your broken bones should heal, but your head took a knock. Doctor doesn't think you are stable. It's best to relax and sleep.'

'Visit –?'

'Your family want to visit you. We'll allow them in when you're well enough.'

'Visit – who – now' said Maeve.

Maeve made an effort to drink water from a cup held by the nurse. She managed to raise her head and take a sip. Her lips were numb and her jaw hurt as she raised her neck. Her face felt bruised.

'Good,' said the sister. 'We'll let someone see you, but don't try to talk. You must rest.'

Quiet again. Maeve was beginning to remember the concert, her poem that existed after all, and how she'd recited the first part, but Karen hadn't liked it. Karen had pushed over the speaker. Perhaps only Maeve knew that.

Her old survival instinct kicked in, but how could she relax? She squinted round at the part of the hospital room she could see. No shelves for flowers, no cards, no colour. It was a side ward, nothing but light new brick showing outside the window. Her head hurt. Something electrical hummed.

She shut her eyes. Everything went velvety black. Her brain was running through the lines of her favourite poem by Eric. He usually wrote modern verse, which didn't run with metres and rhymes, but he'd had a sonnet phase, when he was back from Canada. It started:

> *So much is lost, so much is always here,*
> *a sight once seen, we never could let go,*
> *a power once known –*

'You fell at a concert.' The black velvet dissolved as that night's external sounds re-entered her consciousness. She heard the ambulance, sirens, the music halted. She felt hands lifting her out of a black pit. What a lot Giles would have to smooth over.

The sister was entering the room. The man behind her was too tall to be Giles. 'Please do not upset her,' the sister was saying. 'She is in a very frail state.'

'Eric...' Tears came although Maeve could not sob or control them. Her eyes were wet in her face. She could see her cheek swollen under her eyes, beside the familiar shape of her nose.

Eric looked worried.

'Maeve,' he said, 'I am so glad you are... I came here on Sunday. Today is Wednesday. As you can see I have waited for you.'

'Giles –?'

'He's been here, but there's all sorts going on. Health and Safety are going spare, and the Press, the police are interviewing everybody, and...'

'Not supposed worry me,' said Maeve.

'You'll get better, that's the main thing.'

She couldn't promise. Her head was banging again.

'Giles – my poem,' she said.

'Yes,' said Eric. 'I've heard about your poem.'

'Publish it?'

'I'll read it first.'

'Have done it – at concert.'

'I know. Giles told me on the telephone to Edinburgh.'

'Oh.'

'Giles will come soon.'

She heard, but could not respond. Her eyes were closed. There was a tinnitus of music in her brain. Faintly it sang:

> *Giles will come, Giles will come,*
> *when I am goose I will be dumb.*
> *Let Mary Weylan speak instead*
> *of Eric's plight when I am dead.*

She didn't know who Mary Weylan was.

She slipped in and out of consciousness, lost track of the days.

She was with the wild geese, their cohorts in flight, the white geese, brown geese, patterned geese, returning to their tundra in Canada, their old cliffs on Shetland, their lochans on Islay, their feeding grounds round Aberlady and on the Carse of Gowrie, their sea-washed sands on the Solway. Her poem had been saved in this country of the north. It would reach Scotland too. It would be published.

Eric couldn't promise. He never could promise.

But the poem itself promised it.

Perhaps she would turn into a goose. She could picture her bruised face changing, an unfamiliar bony beak. She'd have feathery wings, and a bird-brain, instinct in place of words. She could imagine becoming a goose on her death. She could follow the fortunes of Eric, her poem in his keeping. She could come and go in the skeins of migrants, be the goose of her poem and range the whole hemisphere, in Canada and Scotland, north-Pennine England, Scandinavia and Ireland. Or she could shadow her people, eavesdrop in houses and meeting places, a ghost goose to frighten the house-dogs and loiter in pubs. But who would believe her, who would capitulate to such reality-defying imagination?

There was only her poem.

The rest was ended. Being dead was not being at all. All would depend on Giles and Eric. Her mind ran effortfully round her parents, her family, Ollie, Alice, Eric's Richard, and her poetry friends. There were people who relished her poems, even her published books or those that had been performed. Buddy and Deirdre had published her books of poems. Deirdre had moved on from Durham, was fighting her fights in her actor's apparel somewhere else unknown. Deirdre would like the poem. Maeve had been a feminist, if entirely by accident.

Would Buddy publish *Wildgoose*? Could that happen in the end? She wasn't thinking very straight, but she knew she would not be there to see it printed.

'Maeve. Come on Maeve, can you take a little water? Can you wiggle your toes? Try to grip my finger!'

The medics and nurses were faint, distant, further away.

She heard Giles' *Hello, Mum*. She couldn't speak as she had almost spoken with Eric. She was glad he had come. He would be all right. One look at Giles would tell anybody he'd be all right. She couldn't open her eyes.

But she saw geese in the skies, the geese settling at Aberlady Bay, biding on the Solway, masses of snow geese rising in Canada from a creek on their way to the tundra, more geese than anyone could count, it was said a hundred thousand at once. Their balance in the dimension of air, their utter neighbourliness in the closeness of flight.

She saw the concert. She saw Bev with a camera, while she was waiting to read.

She saw snow, the fallen tree-trunk, the laid hedge-stems, old cold images of slain giants. They were larger, less powerful, less numerous, than the geese.

The giants were her menfolk. They had hindered and helped her.

She did not wake.

She would fly out to Morecambe Bay.

Coda

Chapter Twelve

ENTER MARY WEYLAN   (2002)

MARY WEYLAN WAS SCARED.
The publishers of her first book of feminist poems had fixed her a reading at StAnza Poetry Festival in St Andrews. She had done a few readings before, mostly in Bristol and always with feminist groups. She was a feminist before she was a poet, and a sociologist by occupation.

She had never been to Scotland before. There hadn't been time. She'd worked full time on her university courses and in her vacation and evening jobs paying her way, then she'd married a Welsh boy, refusing to change her name to his, then they had fallen out and he was trying to divorce her, and she'd suddenly found she had a whole book of poems on the doomed marriage, and the book had been accepted and published in a whirl of being told what to do. Her book was the latest feminist sensation, and now she'd been told to go to Scotland.

She was only twenty-five.

An academic and a researcher, she had this week turned up, almost by accident, a small film of a poetry reading in Newcastle upon Tyne. It had been filmed by an obscure photographer called Beverley Batey, who had sat on it for two years then deposited it in the Northern Poetry Library in Northumberland. No one had looked at it since. But Mary had learned of it, and sent for it, and the library had provided a digital copy. She was studying this on the train on her laptop, with earphones.

The film was of a concert for youngsters when a woman poet had fallen from a cinema stage to her death. There had been a big fuss about this, especially on Tyneside, a few years ago, but things had gone quiet. Mary was interested in how this had happened, how the woman fell. She fast forwarded to the interval, and saw the three poets climb on stage. She heard the name of the one who was reciting first, a pleasant looking, quite tall woman, neither young nor old, wearing a plain dark shirt and skirt, fashion boots and silver necklace – formal compared to the two behind her, both dressed in more youthful style, dolled up, in jeans.

Concentrating on the grainy picture she suddenly caught the beginning of the poem. The recording was clearly and firmly spoken. Mary saw yet again how arresting the poem was. She had listened to it twice between Darlington and Edinburgh.

Looking at the video she saw one of the women give the speaker box a sharp shove – she heard the sound like a high drumbeat. The huge box spun to the ground, the performers fell against each other and the slightly older woman disappeared over the stage front as she finished reciting the poem. There was a roar of applause, concern, excitement and horror.

Mary stopped the recording and looked out round the train.

She'd seen no mountains yet, only the landscape of Fife after she changed trains in Waverley for Leuchars, the strangely-named halt for St Andrews, where she'd be met by someone from the Festival with a car. Nor had she seen any islands, except Lindisfarne, and that was in England.

She saw snowdrops in a wood, lambs in fields, cold-looking sea.

From Leuchars, Brian Johnstone, the poet and Festival Director, took her to her hotel and explained the short walk to the Byre Theatre.

Mary Weylan was waiting in the Green Room to go on stage. She took deep breaths, imagined a marble in her mouth, shaped consonants and vowels silently. She hadn't anticipated such a big theatre, such an impressive audience. Her experience of poetry events up to now had been Bristolcentric.

There had been quite a long interval after the applause for the very well-known poet who had preceded her, and the punters had finally returned to their seats.

Her minder had gone on ahead and introduced her. She walked to the lectern in an overwhelming silence. The force of gravity pinned her to the stage.

She began. She couldn't read everything from the book, otherwise no one would queue up to buy it afterwards. She read a group of poems that had been well received in Bristol, and had been described in a review as 'frankly feminist, exhilarating in their honesty.'

Mary was sensitive to her listeners. That sensitivity had made her marriage impossible. She had disguised her short-term husband – she was not vindictive, but in disguising him she had made him an everyman as she was an every-woman. It was her wholesale rejection of marriage as a viable institution for this new century, that she had managed to express in this drama or pantomime of a single marriage, that had turned her book into a cultural event of 2001.

As a sociologist she had understood that poets and people faced not only a new millennium, but also a new century. She averred – through her poems – that as a society, everyone was blinded by the significance of the millennium, and had not prepared for the century. This was played out in the disasters, pitfalls, and sometimes miraculous efficiency of marriages. Her poems were disputes, arguments or flytings between two poetic voices, meant to represent female and male.

She was confident she looked good tonight. She'd been coached with recordings of her voice: it was light and clear and carried well.

After the first two poems, she knew her audience was with her. After four more she began to feel the argument was becoming too linear for them. Listeners needed a change or they'd go to sleep, just when she might be winning them over. She pulled out a sheaf of new poems, written in the excitement of the reception of her book, in the flush of realising the connections between poetry and feminism, and the way her work related to that of other feminist poets. She thought she was identifying a movement.

Mary began reading dedications to other women writers. She read a poem inspired by Carol Ann Duffy, a poet then working in London. This was well received.

She read a poem about Sylvia Plath. She thought it had something new to offer, but as she read, she realised it was not going down well with the audience. Women in the nearest rows, whose faces she could see, glanced questioningly at one another; she was aware of shuffled feet, of tiresome sighing by the men.

Mary dropped the sequel to this poem.

'My last poem,' she said, 'is for Maeve Cartier. She may not be familiar to this audience' – there was a murmur of dispute – 'but she is the only known poet ever to have been killed by a fall from a stage while reciting poetry.'

Now her audience was awake. Some of them gasped, others tittered. People glanced at each other.

Mary was not a stupid woman. She realised something had gone wrong. Wasn't Maeve Cartier from England, from

Newcastle? The poem was contentious, because Mary's poetic style was contentious. It was only a poem. She believed in it. She carried on.

The audience saw she had finished her reading, and duly applauded, but it was no longer of one mind. As she moved from the stage and the listeners rose from their seats, she could hear the susurrus rising as discussions began in the auditorium.

'You certainly got them going,' remarked her minder as she returned to the Green Room to pick up her cardigan and bag. They were barely inside before the door swung open again and a tallish, slim man whom she assumed to be a poet rushed in, followed by a more compact young man who looked like a businessman. The taller one was patently fizzing with anger.

The angry man (or poet) almost shouted, 'Where did you get the story about my cousin?'

'What?'

'Maeve Cartier's my cousin. Your story was wrong. On nearly every count.'

Mary's helper tried to intervene.

'Sorry, Eric. We have to go for a book signing now. Perhaps you can talk later or tomorrow?'

But Mary Weylan could fight her own battles. 'No, this is important, I'll sort it out.' She turned to the man called Eric.

'Maeve Cartier's cousin? I didn't know she had a cousin.'

'You don't know very much about it at all.' The man was still raging.

'That's as may be. Maeve Cartier doesn't belong to you, she belongs to poetry. She belongs to women poets.'

Eric interrupted angrily. 'Poetry should be truthful. Your poem was a total invention. *Feminists of uncouth hue – bilious lavender – the rest swaggered on* – the rest did NOT swagger on! This has NOTHING to do with Maeve Cartier!'

'Calmer, Eric,' said the other man – or did he say *karma*?

'Speaking for women poets,' argued the Bristol one with spirit, 'when I say *Goddess, Poetess or Muse*, I'm asking what men ask of women. Maybe they only want women as poetesses. The woman poet is killed. Look at Plath.'

'I'm doing a doctorate on Plath,' said Eric stiffly.

'Proves my point! Men setting up as experts on a woman poet! Plath, Plath, Plath, it is always Plath! What about the rest of us?'

'Maeve Cartier was my mother,' said the younger man unexpectedly. 'I'll thank you not to spread nonsense and political twist about this incident. My mother was a very good poet, not a political chancer. But I see you'll need time to be informed. I'll get my legal people to write to you. I'm grateful for your interest but it needs to be grounded in the real situation, in what happened.'

'It was unfortunate, wasn't it?' asked Mary.

She was handling their unexpected onslaught as well as she could. She wished they would appreciate that she was tired, that she'd just come off stage from a taxing performance.

'For instance, this was a music concert. There's no mention of that in your poem.'

'Poem?' began the tall one, Eric, belligerently.

She put her glass of water down and picked up a soft jacket or cardigan and wrapped it round her. She was listening, thinking. The younger man was Maeve Cartier's son? This was ridiculous!

It was time to drop her bombshell. She hoped it would prove to be one.

'I do know what happened. I have a video recording of the concert.'

'Impossible,' said Eric.

His companion seemed less incredulous. 'Where from? Whose is it?'

'The Northern Poetry Library. I borrowed it.'

'Who took it?'

'They sent it. Oh, you mean...Someone called Beverley Batey.'

'Who?' Eric was still incredulous.

'Bev!' cried the other man. 'I know Bev, he used to visit my mother.'

Mary Weylan had found time to play the rest of the sequence. 'Quite a disaster, wasn't it? It showed Maeve Cartier falling. It showed the rapturous applause mixed with the calls for help, the panic...'

The two men listened, silent.

'... the police arriving and trying to clear the theatre, kids screaming and hiding ecstasy pills, people demanding their money back. It was like some crazy movie.'

'It was disastrous,' agreed the son.

'I wasn't there,' said Eric.

Mary turned on him. 'If you weren't there, what's your problem? Who the fuck are you?'

'I'm sorry,' said the young man. 'I'm Giles Grysewood and this is the poet Eric Grysewood. I'm surprised you've heard of my mother without the connection to Eric Grysewood.'

'Oh my god,' said Mary Weylan. She looked at these Messrs Grysewood in confusion. Her StAnza minder was tutting with impatience.

'Okay,' said Giles. 'We all care about poetry. I appreciate that you found this a significant story. However it is about a real person, a real poet, and if you use her name you must be faithful to the facts.'

Mary capitulated. She delved in her bag. 'Here's my card. I'll talk to you about it.'

She then ran off with the StAnza lady to the waiting book table.

Their arrival in the foyer caused a mini sensation. Helpers crowded round, scandalised that Eric Grysewood had chased Mary across the stage after the reading. Mary's minder apologised and tried to calm them down, which Mary appreciated. They settled her in beside the bookseller's table.

Seamus Heaney had been signing books earlier, in the interval, before leaving to go for a train. That would be the reason he'd read before her. She'd missed her chance to speak to him through not understanding this. He'd given her a gallant smile when they did the sound checks. She could still see a pile of his books.

But she had other things to think about, and she used her short chats with book buyers to try to find out what had gone wrong in her reading. Mary had thought the Cartier story a niche interest, something feminists kept to their chests in England, an arcane grievance. What did these people know that Mary Weylan didn't?

Some of her book buyers were happy to talk. Less than three years ago, their cheerful acquaintance Maeve Cartier had met her death, in an unlikely and frightening way, while performing on stage, in the ad hoc, unregulated, haphazard manner of most performance poetry. It had shocked them all. Some had known her in Edinburgh or Glasgow. A gay man remembered her at a party in Roslin Glen, with her cousin Eric Grysewood, who was at StAnza this year. Did she know?

A woman, almost as young as Mary, had spoken to Maeve Cartier on Skye, in the mid-90s at Sorley Maclean's funeral. 'I didn't know who she was then,' this woman confided, 'but I met her in Glasgow later. We read at some protest on Glasgow Green.'

'Was she political? What was the protest about?'

'I cannae remember. We were always protesting. We went to Cornton Prison to protest about young women's suicides. We read our poems on the grass outside. She was good friends with Sandie Craigie. You ought to catch up with Sandie. Sandie wouldn't come to StAnza, but Maeve would. I met her here once.'

Mary signed the book.

'If you write your email under your name, I can put you in touch with her son, if you're interested.'

Mary added her email address. 'The son – he invited her back to Newcastle, I heard? Makes it much more poignant.' Mary didn't say she had met the son. That was, if he and the cousin had not been fooling her. Eric Grysewood was kosher, the StAnza staff had commented on him when she was late for the signing.

'I liked your poems.' The girl thanked her and left.

Mary wondered what Mr Giles Grysewood was doing at a poetry festival. She understood he was a well-known musician, but she had not thought poetry was among his interests.

Next in the dwindling queue was a musician and poet, who told her. He hung about till there was no one left but him.

'Giles Grysewood is here with two women who are performing in the cabaret. One is a woman poet called Karen. Nice woman who can sing. The other is Frippy Percival. She has a popular dress shop in Newcastle called Grey's Anatomy and she's a grand singer. Giles is rich – from the concerts he manages, singers too. They'll be holed up somewhere smart.'

'Oh,' said Mary dumbly.

'Giles would've wanted to hear Seamus Heaney, he'll have heard of him.'

Mary glanced across the tables to where Seamus' books were being packed away.

The young man proceeded, 'No flies on that Giles. Everybody in music knows him. If he was older he would be Sir Giles Grysewood, and that's a fact.'

Mary Weylan signed his book.

'Fancy a drink in the bar?'

They took a lift down a floor, and entered the hubbub of pre-cabaret gossip. Mary saw Giles and Eric, together propping up part of the bar, and tried to go to another part for their drinks. But her companion pushed her right up against them. She couldn't avoid Eric. She smiled at him. He glowered back before returning his attention to his whisky glass.

Naturally she had picked up that he was gay. Flirting was pointless, but perhaps at some point he would be willing to be friendly. Somewhere in her mind she had formed the wish to revive and detail the story of Maeve Cartier. Maeve was receding from memory even as people had told her scraps of the story this evening, three years after Maeve's death. Mary Weylan was impulsive: Maeve Cartier was her next subject; the book would not be poetry. The struggle between men and women mattered to Mary.

She stood there, waiting beside the long bar with its rushing servers, shouted orders and flailing hands offering banknotes. Glittering glasses and upside-down bottles of spirits flanked a cabinet of orange and lemonade and coke; coffee could be acquired in a neglected corner.

Her companion appeared to have a flair for being last in a queue.

She waited.

Beside her, Eric was gulping down whisky. It smelt much better than the usual whisky in the bars of Bristol. It must be the Scottish stuff, single malt. Eric couldn't half knock it back. But he was also becoming unsteady and maudlin. Mary wondered if it was wise to stay for what might happen next.

Her book fan finally bought her a drink, and since he immediately started chatting to Giles, Mary had no option but to stand beside them. Presently Giles began to include her in the group. He knew damn fine who she was, since he had laid down the law with her in the Green Room not much more than half an hour ago. She thought it gentlemanly of him to chat again.

Mary Weylan cut the cabaret. Eric Grysewood was sprawled across a chair. He came under the category of inebriated poet, if not common drunk. Giles had gone across to greet a glamorous and regal young woman, who came in with a happy-looking middle-aged woman. Mary recognised them. They were the other performers from the concert video.

Only the poet who had bought her drink was still hanging out with Mary. She picked up her bag, said, 'Excuse me,' and headed for the street doorway, where she left them all behind.

But she had not left the story of Maeve Cartier behind.

The email came the week she returned to her desk in Bristol. Giles Grysewood wanted to see her again. She looked out on the cityscape of Bristol, and beautiful as it was, it suddenly seemed Welsh and southern in a dinky sort of way. She wrote a prim reply:

> *Giles, I have been thinking about Maeve Cartier.*
> *Researching her would fit with my academic interests.*
> *I would like to co-operate with you. However the*
> *insurmountable problem is distance, in terms of cost. I do*
> *not know how this can be done in a reasonable time.*

A pity, because Mary hoped to take on this project about the woman who had fallen from a stage and left a cut-out shadow of herself, a shadow that had torn her own poetry scene as if it were an old rag of parachute silk. The strange touch of dirty white dryness. A snow goose landing that one time in Cardiff Bay.

The poet's son would be a highly convenient ally.

The university library had borrowed Maeve Cartier's and

Eric Grysewood's publications for her. She started reading through them, looking for the gender categories she was an expert on. Her other research had been put on the back burner. The flame in the burner was dimming to nothing. She needed to read herself into something new.

There'd been that business with Maverick, 'Literature's Banksy,' as he was known in London. Against all odds, she'd managed to contact him last year, seeking a newspaper interview, but he had sent her a message:

I do not exist. Please write about Maeve Cartier.

She hadn't known who Maeve Cartier was. Life was weird.

Maeve Cartier's poems were vivid but short and miscellaneous, as though searching for something to hold them together. Gloves, calves, damson trees. No sign of the long piece from the film.

Shuffling Maeve's books across the desk, she turned to Eric's poems, expecting less. She was pleasantly surprised by the bulk of his work. Honest, direct, and clever without being shallow, his poetry was cosmopolitan, in contrast to Maeve's country interests. The poet he reminded her of most, among the limited number she'd read, was W. H. Auden. Auden also claimed County Durham heritage. There was a touch of ancient mist mixed with sophistication in Eric's poems, too.

To the Uninitiated

When for example you have studied
a mithraeum excavated in mist,
held in your palm a scrap of ossified wicker,
dusted mole hillocks with fragments

of baked Samian pottery from fingers,
spruced for the opening of this pageant,
have shared pale copies of dissipated extremes,
offering only dried fresh ink, frail jetsam,
then you roll aside, relying on lyric,
the shards of your love immortal for a day.

Two of Eric's later poems, in a pamphlet by an arty pub-lisher in London, were *Lusitania* and *Iolaire*. *Lusitania* was a human tragedy told by the seabirds that flew above the ship. The poem on the *Iolaire* was more intense. The *Iolaire* had sunk in Lewis harbour in 1919, carrying half a genera-tion of Lewismen back from the war, and drowning 200, to the extreme distress of the islanders, and little other ear-lier attention. The *Lusitania* had lost 1200 voyagers. People couldn't even pronounce *Iolaire* ('Oolar,') outside northern Scotland. Grysewood's *Iolaire* received much praise. This time the birds who witnessed the disaster were geese.

Mary liked these poems and could imagine Eric's height-ened sensitivity arising from his cousin's death. He'd ar-ranged for a Gaelic translation of his *Iolaire* poem.

Mary turned to Eric's other work. He'd published a se-ries of sonnets. They were a little different from most of his work, but then so were the shipwreck poems.

Mary had friends in various aspects of feminist scholar-ship. Some of them had started a website a year or two ago: Women in Refrigerators. If you didn't know what that was about, then you didn't read graphic novels, which of course many people didn't. Women in these stories frequently died in gruesome ways – some involving refrigerators – at the hands of men, whose plot would then develop based on the removal of the female lead.

It was a great line with a heap of applications for feminism. Mary wondered if Maeve's real-life death might fit this category. It had impinged heavily on Eric, the one person close to Maeve who had had nothing to do with the fatal stage event. From Mary's limited experience of Eric, he'd been in a bad way after Maeve's death. But how much had Maeve Cartier's whole life affected him – the presence of the female lead?

The phone call was unexpected. Giles was in Bristol and offered to lunch with her, the next day or the day after. She accepted at once. Then she went out and bought a pretty dress.

She hadn't been to the restaurant in the hotel where Giles was staying. Everyone in Bristol had heard of it. She looked nice. Looking nice mattered to her. Maeve Cartier's son met her in the lobby.

'Mary! Call me Giles.'

He asked whether she had enjoyed StAnza – she had – and asked if she ate much for lunch. She said it depended. He led her to a small private dining room.

'I know it's fun to watch other diners,' he said, 'but we might want to talk about Maeve quite extensively. I don't want us to be inhibited by people listening.'

Mary took her seat, surprised. Was this an interview?

A manager came with menus. Giles Grysewood chose the hors d'oeuvres and fluffy omelettes with asparagus and fries. She could have a herb or truffle omelette. She suggested both. Giles grinned. He obviously approved and she began to relax. He asked for a white wine. She picked up her glass and said, 'Cheers!'

They had a completely open chat. Mary felt in charge of the conversation. She persuaded Giles to talk about his mother. His reserve fell away, if he had any reserve: Mary wasn't sure.

'How much did you understand your mother as you grew up? Did you know how much work she put into her poetry? Did she talk about it?'

'We were both artists in a wide sense. I had to stop making music late at night so she could work.'

'You knew she was a poet?'

'I think we said writer. Some people said poet. She had a job, too. I was exceptionally busy for a kid, we both worked our socks off. We hardly had time to consider what else was going on.'

Mary said, 'She'd be a poet rather than a writer – she didn't publish much, only poetry. Writers churn stuff out, don't they? A poet can be a poet all their life, and publish two books.'

'Which is what Maeve did, yes,' admitted Giles. 'I prefer Odd Gloves.'

'Her second. Swing Bridge Press. I bet Eric was jealous.'

'He was, a bit, but he hid it. He's a good man when he isn't upset.'

'But there's this third book, the lost poem, isn't there?'

'Eric has it.'

'Is it wise to entrust it to him?'

'Eric's all right, usually.'

This was sensitive ground.

'But he has been very upset all along,' Giles conceded. 'Guilty that he didn't help her. You have a point, we should get hold of her book and have it copied. We had a hell of a problem with him the day after your StAnza reading.'

'Oh?'

'It started with our hotel. Eric was brought in drunk and incapable in the night, by St Andrews police. The hotelier was furious. Eric couldn't remember where he was booked, and they mixed him up with me, because I'm a Grysewood.'

'How's that? Why aren't you a Cartier?'

'Simple,' said Giles. 'I'm Giles Grysewood Carter – she made up Cartier, and I dropped Carter – for my music and my name. My uncle –'

'Still in Aberdeen?'

'He still has contacts there, but his partner has managed to steer him into a local job teaching writing at Heriot-Watt University. Not quite the status, but doable, and on the doorstep. He'll be more okay at the Watt...'

'In what way wasn't he okay?'

Giles hesitated. 'Angry? Paranoid? Richard has been at his wits' end with him. Perhaps I shouldnt say this. I don't see them often, we're all too busy.'

After his omelette, Giles went back to the hors d'oeuvres platter, which he'd asked the waiter not to remove. 'Eric was terribly disruptive on our journey back to Edinburgh. A dangerous passenger. I had to stop the car in a lay-by and tell him where to get off. He's upset by what happened to Maeve. Blaming everybody including himself. The rest of us have been trying to excuse everyone!'

'Aren't poets supposed to thrive on crises?'

'It knocked me sideways... threatened my music career which my mother facilitated. I owed her a lot. I was the most important person in the house. She had too little time for such a competitive business as poetry.'

'It isn't competitive,' said Mary. 'There's nothing to win.'

'It's competitive for Eric.'

'That's what gave Maeve the edge over him. It went to her core – not just a career.' Mary smiled across the table. 'Eric's poetry is very good. He ought to be important.'

'I doubt that's how it will end up,' said Giles. 'There are too many players in the game, and Eric knows it. He was terrified I was going to leave him in that lay-by. Thank goodness I was able to deliver him to Richard Calm in Edinburgh. Never a better-named man.' Giles chuckled. 'I've been looking into how poetry works. There are the big publishers, the government – the universities –'

'And the people, surely?'

'Yes, the people will be on my mother's, on Maeve's side,

if we can get her poem published.' Giles found a chocolate mint on a side plate, handed it to her. 'Buddy will publish it. Swing Bridge in Newcastle. He'd have done that already if I'd let him.'

Somehow it was half past two. They headed out into a wide lounge area. Giles indicated a sofa.

'Could you stay on? A cup of tea?'

'You didn't bring your singer with you?'

'Frippy? She's much too bright to trail round after me... she's my singer. My marital status is that I have singers. What's yours?'

Mary hadn't expected this. She laughed. 'I can't dissociate myself from cultural expectations, even though I'm in the business of writing about them. It doesn't help.'

'You're a damn sight too clever,' said Giles.

'... for a woman. Go on, say it, I dare you.'

'For your own good. And perhaps, for a poet.'

'Some poets are very clever. They're not all clever. But not all clever people are poets. I'm not a poet.'

'I admire you for seeing that. I saw it,' said Giles.

'You saw it because your mother was the real thing.'

'You're a brilliant writer – don't get me wrong.'

'But poetry isn't in my soul. I know. I've told the publishers there won't be another book.'

'I bet they weren't pleased,' said Giles. 'But I am. One woman poet is enough to have had in my life.'

'Don't push it. A cup of tea. You can tell me about the years with your mother.'

The tea was served in a little window table in the foyer. An hour had been quite enough for the concentrated discussion, and their second hour was more laid back, with Giles willingly reminiscing on Sandyford, school and not-school, and the band. Mary egged him on to talk. He wouldn't realise she was using professional tactics, but her interest was real.

Mary didn't have answers to all her questions yet. She could only guess what the relationship between Giles and his mother had been like. Had Maeve been a detached, uninterested parent? Was Giles an impossible child? Very slightly Mary's junior, and clearly a highly successful young man, entrepreneurs didn't they call such people, Giles had come out of it well.

She wanted to understand Maeve. She pushed the discussion, persuaded Giles to talk about himself, over that extra cup of tea. He had spent several years at an alternative school that wasn't a school at all, had grown up in a congenial environment of school refusers, the least ambitious youngsters around, and a small group of unconventional adults, the closest to him being Maeve. As a sociologist Mary had learned to process information, but there was no way she could send him a questionnaire! She would have to hang around with him, at least for a while. He wasn't dull company.

When they eventually parted, Mary promised, 'I'll investigate your mother's poem. We'll see it published one day. For this, I need to get closer to Eric. It may take time.'

'And then?'

They were still in their twenties! 'If I want to go on pursuing Maeve Cartier's poetry, I will. Or I could retire, live by the seaside and bake, read novels, sew quilts...'

She could see Giles' surprise, which she had intended. She was going to tread carefully with this new man friend, but she wasn't going to let him go.

Chapter Thirteen

DURNESS   (2007)

NEITHER MARY NOR GILES had visited Durness, a Scottish outpost that was putting on a Beatles Festival, or to be accurate, a John Lennon Festival. Giles was enthusing about it.

'Will you come up there with me?'

'Why? Where is this place?'

Mary's journalism was keeping her occupied. She sent off articles and did interviews weekly. Big newspapers paid her to travel the country. She was often in Edinburgh. Giles was busy too and was currently in Scotland. He wasn't Sir Giles yet. Perhaps it was her fault that this remark had slipped round his friends and become a joke. He was identified with public music events and acted much older than his age, which was heading for thirty. Surrounded by smart people, finger in every pie – young but not struggling. Mary remembered the musician and poet at St Andrews with amusement. He'd still be struggling. She might write an article about when and whether to give up.

She was still hoping to meet Eric again. If she could ask him about Maeve's poem, she'd get somewhere. She was convinced there was something he knew, suspected there was something he couldn't face. She'd obtained his email address with difficulty, but he hadn't replied to her approach. A letter to his home had also gone unanswered. Even in Scotland, he was avoiding publicity. Though she glimpsed Eric once in the silent hall of the National Library, he either affected not to see her, or, more probably, didn't notice her.

Yet the years had been kind to his reputation. He was still producing work and was well known as an argumentative critic in poetry journals. Eric had written on Maeve's work here and there. The cousins' names were linked, to their joint advantage. The question of her long poem's whereabouts was sometimes mooted by people in the know.

Mary kept up with his scattered publications, which the Scottish Poetry Library were obligingly cataloguing online.

'Durness?' Mary wondered. Perhaps it would just be a break, but breaks often led to something interesting, led to work, led to... for a journalist like Mary they were often *leads*.

'Where is this place?' she asked Giles again.

'The far north-west coast. There's one road, one hotel, some B&Bs, and magnificent scenery. Cliffs and a massive sea cave.'

'You know it all.'

'I've been selling it to musicians. It's remote. Lennon spent summer holidays there as a schoolboy. There's a Lennon Memorial Garden set round a Millennium Hall, built with millennium money. People want to see it used.'

'Okay. You're mixed up in this, aren't you? I'll come.'

The Festival at Durness was a lot of work for Giles. Complicated plans included transporting a concert piano from Inverness for Sir Peter Maxwell Davies to play. Giles had helped secure the services of the Quarrymen, all in their sixties, for whom hotel beds would need to be found, and musical instruments ferried from Liverpool.

Mary looked up the festival on the internet and discovered that poets, also being shipped there, included Eric Grysewood, Carol Ann Duffy and Richard Calm. There was method in Giles' madness.

It was a chance of finding Eric more relaxed.

She suggested a B&B.

'We're staying in the big hotel. You're my official partner.'

The narrow road round the corner of the mainland swarmed with life.

A thousand ageing Beatles fans had arrived.

Everywhere was full, campsites overflowing, car parks crowded, every conceivable meeting place packed out. People trailed up and down to the Millennium Hall, and to Smoo Cave where events were being held practically in the water.

Highland Police cars cruised around, apparently in shock.

There weren't any Beatles. The headliners were John's ex-wife, John's half-sister, and John's elderly uncle. Giles was concerned with the music up in the Hall, and left Mary exploring the Quarrymen's pub. Mary hadn't mentioned she'd seen Eric on the list of poets. The poets were not Giles' responsibility, but he would know. And he'd know she knew – that was the joke, the delegating. Music was Giles' job. Eric was hers. Mary scanned the big parlour and saw him, standing with another man by one of the windows.

She was greeted by the sound of a smashed glass. Eric had seen her and promptly dropped his wine.

Despite this embarrassment she was impressed he had recognised her.

His companion looked round, confused.

She grinned. 'Great to see you, Eric Grysewood. How are you?'

There was a pause.

'My partner, Richard Calm.' Eric indicated the man beside him. Richard nodded, enquiringly.

Perhaps Eric had forgotten her name. 'Mary Weylan – we met at St Andrews one year.' To Eric she added, 'I've been enjoying your poetry!'

Richard said, 'Aye, we had ructions after St Andrews that time. Eric was unhappy and drinking too much.' He glanced at Eric.

'I hope you're better now,' said Mary.

'Well, that's a glass of wine I didn't drink!' Eric answered, as a girl from the bar came with brush and dustpan. 'Are you reporting us for the papers, Mary Weylan?'

'I'm a tourist for once,' she said. 'Off to Smoo Cave. And I'm researching Maeve Cartier.' Because she was.

Richard and Eric looked at one another. Richard spoke.

'Maeve never came here, as far as we ken. You're welcome to chum us to the cave.'

Eric and Richard picked up their hand luggage, and the three of them left the big pub and headed down to the shore. Everywhere was up or down in Durness. Sometimes both, as the road battled the contours, pedestrians causing motors to slow and creep.

'Have you booked in somewhere?' Richard had a small rucksack, while Eric was carrying a capacious and heavy-looking cloth book bag with folders of typescript sticking out.

'We can sleep in our car,' Richard answered. 'We'll make ourselves scarce along the coast. You?'

'I'm staying at the hotel.' They knew she was a journalist.

Eric seemed more relaxed. 'You like my poems?'

'I like your sonnets.'

'An aberration. You have read my cousin's books?'

This was what Mary wanted to hear. 'Yes, except her unpublished poem, *Wildgoose*.'

They were moving down the stepped footpath to the shore, towards the opening of the sea-cave onto the bay. Beyond the cave were high cliffs, liberally splashed with white painted graffiti: local slogans and love equations, for whose edification no one knew.

'Of course. You wrote that ridiculous poem about her.'

Mary decided not to disagree. 'You're right, it was ridiculous, but it shows I cared. I've read Maeve Cartier's work, and yours, since. I've grown up.' She looked hopefully at the difficult man. Eric looked back at her, unimpressed.

A stage was set up in the cave. The audience space had a floor of stony sand and rippling water. Some people were sitting on bigger stones among trickling streams. A walkway at the side led to an underground waterfall. Light came from the shoreside entrance and a round hole above, in the cave's roof.

'Nowhere to sit,' said Eric. 'I need to pick out some poems for my reading. I can't put this bag down, everywhere's wet!'

'You're a deadline crasher?' asked Mary.

'I had no idea what this would be like, what sort of people would be here. It's certainly different. I'm trying to get the feel of what to do.'

They wandered out of the cave again like water turning with the tide. They set off to climb the path they had come down, back onto the land mass. 'Maeve would be countin' the geese up there,' said Richard. 'She'd be wondering where further north they'd be liable to fly.'

Eric went off the path towards the clifftop.

'The signs say *Stay on the Path*.'

Eric turned to Mary and said, 'Poetic license.' He moved quickly up a narrow track round a curve in the cliff.

Richard and Mary stopped.

'We can't leave him, can we?'

'I dinnae see why not,' said Richard. But after a minute they followed him.

'There's that hole in the clifftop,' said Mary.

'Stick to the track.'

When they rounded the corner, Eric was moving well ahead of them.

'Is he all right?' Mary asked Richard.

'He wanted to come. He likes being called to read at events. We ken he's conceited. But I wonder – he sometimes wonders, if he's really as good as all that.'

'Oh, he's good,' said Mary. 'I want to ask him about Maeve. Will he let me?'

'He doesn't like feminist scholars. Men poets are interesting too! And he's rooting for the gay scene.'

'I understand this now,' said Mary. 'Not just me, we are all growing up together.'

'Yes, I agree.'

They walked on amicably. The air was soft and fresh. They came to a cliff edge at the far side, the one where they'd seen the graffiti. Eric went untiringly ahead and they followed towards the headland where the ingress joined the sea. They found Eric sitting on the grassy clifftop, not many yards from the edge, books and folders spread on the grass. The view was spectacular.

While Richard gazed over the northern blue, seemingly unconcerned with Eric's papers, Mary sat down beside Eric and asked what he was doing.

Eric pointed to his folders. 'These are my performance pieces, some of my best poems, and this is new work. The Beatles fans won't have heard my work before. They'll want easily understood poems, like tablets that quickly dissolve in water. They'll want references to the Beatles but I have none. They'll like a laugh. On the other hand the top poets and Maxwell Davies will be impressed by more ambitious work, perhaps Scotland-related, and I believe our Literature Director will be here, the guy who decided who would come, so...'

'What's Richard going to read?'

'Richard reads whatever he's written last.'

'What will you choose?' asked Mary, grabbing a stray paper that had swirled onto the grass, and giving it back to him.

'I don't know. Shipwrecks? I have troubles. I am concerned all the time about Maeve, whom you didn't meet.'

Mary had no idea what to say.

'She was better than me,' he continued. 'Much better. And in my recent work, I have used some of her technique I learned from her long poem. The poem young Giles wants to photocopy because he doesn't trust me with it. What's all that about? And Mr Giles Grysewood, why he isn't Sir yet the way he is going on...who but Giles would be arranging all this music? Sir Peter Maxwell Davies no less...'

'...who lives on Orkney – you can just see Orkney from here...'

'Anyway,' he said belligerently, 'I've brought Maeve's poem for Giles to copy. Here it is!'

He pulled out a hefty pile of typescript, almost an inch thick, and waved it in the air. Mary watched him, thunderstruck.

'Here are my troubles,' he said. 'I'm going to throw them away. Over the cliff.'

'No, you can't,' said Mary impulsively.

Eric stood up, leaving the rest of his things lying on the bookbag. He paced towards the drop.

'Richard,' called Mary.

Richard turned from watching the sea. At that moment Eric flung himself to the very edge of the cliff and hurled his papers out and down. In unattached sections they fluttered and bombed out of view.

'That's done it!' cried Eric. 'No more troubles – they've gone!'

Richard came to Eric and pulled him back from the edge, drove him further back.

'What was that, Eric? What was it about?'

'Maeve's manuscript. That's it sorted.'

'No, it wasn't in your typescripts. These are book versions. And work you did on the magazine. Do not tell us porkies.'

'A ship sunk! A parachute! A snow goose!' Eric ranted.

'Maeve's book was in a box,' Richard shouted back. 'Boo-ox' the sound carried on the breeze. 'Last time I saw it was ages ago. You've never touched it!'

Eric grabbed his book bag and ran further from the cliff. He collapsed in the rough grass as if in despair. Mary watched in horror and silence. How little she knew about Eric; she must leave this to Richard.

Richard had his arms round Eric. The loon was crying, great heaving sobs. Mary turned and sat down looking away from them, facing the sea. How totally dreadful! The typescript was down in the sea now, sea that slapped at the sheer rock round the end of the bay. It would float away to nowhere, and geese would take the papers for their nests. She was beginning to think like Maeve! Let it not be Maeve's manuscript. How terrible that her approach to the two men had ended like this. She sat watching the ocean.

Richard tapped her on the shoulder, nodded, 'Carry these for us,' passed her the bookbag and gave her a hand to pull her up from sitting. 'We're going back to the car, then we'll see about this evening's performance. Come with us.'

Eric was standing a little away, looking done in. They started back, Richard holding Eric by the arm, and then by the shoulder as they returned to the proper path. The afternoon wore on. They came to their car.

'I'm going up to the Millennium Hall,' she said, turning to go.

'We'll come with you if you like,' Richard offered; Eric had still not said a word.

'I'll see you up there,' said Mary.

The first person she saw in the Hall was Giles.

'All set. Time for a drink.' He took her to a makeshift bar, with hall tables and chairs set out near it.

'I need a drink,' said Mary. 'I have something to tell you.'

When she had given her account, Giles said, 'You didn't have lunch? You'll be famished.' He went to a kitchen and came back with a beef and salad sandwich on a plate, and a pint of her favourite cider.

'So we can expect his lordship along here to read as though nothing had happened?' mused Giles, as she ate. The sandwich and drink were much needed. Eric and Richard showed up at that moment. Eric disappeared into the cloakroom. Richard came up to Mary and Giles.

'Mary, you've met Giles?' he began.

'Eric's Richard,' Mary reminded Giles.

'Go and talk to Eric,' said Richard to Mary. 'Now's your chance. He's gone into the men's loo. Wait in the lobby. He needs to talk. You're good at that.'

'She's a professional,' Giles admitted ruefully.

'She's honest,' said Richard. 'That's the important thing.'

In the exposed northern garden at the end of the world, it grew cold. Mary was glad of her reporter's style windproof coat. As on the cliff, Eric's smart light coat was thrown over his suit, with his usual strong shoes. Had he left his book-bag in the car? He had nothing to do with his hands, and he looked neither comfortable nor happy.

'Come on in,' she said.

'No, I need solitude. There's none.'

Mary turned to a small bench in the lee of the building. Eric sat down beside her. They could see little but the garden's prickly, sharp looking wind-resistant shrubs. The background of sea had darkened to emptiness. Weak light came from the lamps at the door.

Words had not deserted Eric, if reason had. 'Mary Weylan, I think you can do as little for me as I can do for you.'

'Try me,' said Mary. 'Trust me.'

Eric surprised her by laughing. 'Trust a newspaper writer with a secret?'

'Everyone has secrets. I'm a book writer, this isn't gossip.'

'I don't need a book writer. I don't want to be fodder for the next generation.'

'That seems reasonable,' answered Mary. 'We only have our time here, that's all. We must make the best of it.'

'Sorry but I've never been slightly interested in women.'

Mary's turn to laugh, taken aback. 'That's not what I meant, as I think you know. What's the problem? What's upsetting you?'

Eric turned towards her. He spoke flatly. 'Mary Weylan. You can't remember the pop revolution, the angry young men. Life was real then. I was an angry young poet. Now I'm past sixty, and everything's ruined. There's no reason to go on living.'

'Talking is going on living,' said Mary, alarmed. 'I thought you were upset about Maeve Cartier.'

'Maeve Cartier was younger than me! And you are younger than her. You are pursuing me, not because of me but because of her! I don't belong in this discussion at all.'

'I'm not pursuing you,' said Mary, stung.

'Yes you are. Emails, letters, looking for me in the National Library.'

'I wasn't,' said Mary. 'I have other work to do than hunt for your cousin's poem. If you have it, be honest with me and fair to her.'

'Give over! She's usurped my life. Women poets have trodden their brother poets into the ground, pushed them into the sea – you've followed me to the farthest corner of the land. There is no end to your chase.'

'Your Richard sent me to talk with you – not to listen to insults,' said Mary. She was breaking all the rules of counselling but this man was too many steps ahead. Only a direct tackle would work.

He responded. 'I have no insults left – but I'll tell you this. Maeve understood this. Her poem exists. It has been moved. This time, I have moved it. It's not in the water. I advise you to let things be. Maeve's poem has had a reader – me. She belongs to me.'

'I said at St Andrews that she belongs to women poets. Was that wrong?'

'She belongs to poets. I'm her nearest poet and relative. She belongs to me until I say otherwise. Until I die, which is going to happen, Mary Weylan. Do you accept that?'

'Only under duress. And Sylvia Plath, you were studying her? What did you conclude about her?'

He was silent. She waited.

'I concluded the PhD,' he said with finality.

He slipped his arm round her. This was a gay man, a man trying to connect. A smudge of light, orange and greenish, moved across blackness behind the spiky shrubs. 'That's a tanker,' said Eric. 'A tanker at sea. Quite a sight, in the daytime.'

'This is an extraordinary village. Crofts built into banks, a few animals, passers-by. Life goes on in the hardest of places.'

'The hardest places are the most beautiful,' said Eric. 'You are only a kid. The men on that tanker know hardships you've never imagined. Being intellectual doesn't help us.'

Mary looked up at him, trying to fathom him. 'Nothing helps us.'

'That's about it, nothing helps us. We are what we are. Same with Plath.' They watched the tanker's lights move on and his arm fell down from her shoulder, sensibly.

'Plath – she had first world problems,' suggested Maeve.

'And last world problems.' The tanker's lights disappeared round an invisible headland. 'I've seen too many sights,' he said. 'Shall we go in?'

They were getting frozen and she rose thankfully. They joined Giles – just after Richard had read poems in Eric's place when he had not appeared. Mary smiled doubtfully at the others. They could not tell whether her parley had gone well or badly. Nor could she. Eric was quite biddable and, oddly, made no fuss about missing his reading. He went off to fetch them a drink, started talking with someone at the back of the hall, and did not return. John Lennon's uncle spoke about the ten-year-old Lennon, how he'd tinkered with music in their cottage down the hill. Everyone went quiet for a piano moment with Sir Peter, who played something he himself had written when aged ten.

One of the police cars was waiting on the road outside. A local young couple were calling urgently, 'This way! We found him here.' The police followed with a torch. The garden lights were switched on from the Hall and the couple repeated, 'Here!'

The slim man lay collapsed on the gravel. Richard moved forward. 'He's my partner.' A policeman knelt down to look for a pulse, and said, 'Wait – his wrist is slit. We need an ambulance.'

Unfortunately, the ambulance supposedly on hand had been spoken for. It had attended an eighty-year-old Lennon fan with a broken ankle and broken ribs at Smoo Cave and had headed off with the patient to the hospital at Inverness. The first-aiders had gone back to their crofts. Giles Grysewood had to go onstage between songs of the local choir, to ask if there was a doctor in the company.

The doctor, a woman from Liverpool, collected two tea towels and the washing-up bowl from the kitchen, and the legal first aid kit. She made Richard and bystanders pull the unconscious Eric onto a blanket in the light, cleaned up a lot of blood, strapped up the wrist properly, checked his pulse. When the doctor was told the hospital was a hundred miles away by the shortest road that was so narrow and twisty it took two and a half hours, she shook her head.

Mary was badly upset. People noticed how she sat on a wooden hall chair and shivered and shook. When Eric had been fully attended to, the doctor gave her a cup of sweet tea and asked whether she'd be seen home.

The police were on their telephones and announced they were taking the casualty to Inverness. They adjusted the back seats and the doctor strapped the patient in prone. He groaned – a good sign. With Richard and the police driver in the front of the car, they were waved off on their journey by the crowds exiting the festival event. One local policeman stayed behind.

A bus came for the tired performers and staff. The hotel had hot soup, croissants, and coffee for the late contingent. Giles and Mary took a tray to their room. They calculated when they might phone Raigmore Hospital. 'If you don't mind,' said Mary, 'I need to sleep in the other bed.'

In the hotel breakfast room, Mary rang the hospital. 'He's stable and will pull through.' Other musicians and poets came in, asking what happened, or how Eric was. A subdued Giles headed off to Smoo Cave. Mary, still upset, took her coffee back to her room.

Richard called the hotel that afternoon. Mary picked up the extension. He sounded relieved. It had been touch and go, the journey was interminable, and the hospital used to be a lunatic asylum.

'He's going to be all right?'

'Two or three days in here. They're letting me stay as a relative. We'll go back to Edinburgh by train, and pay to have the car returned. Good thing Billie's looking after our dog.'

'He told me he didn't throw Maeve's poem away?'

'He nearly threw himself away,' said Richard.

She'd have to leave it there. She wished them well and ended the call.

She relayed Richard's news to Giles.

'I've remembered the last two lines of that sonnet.'

'Is it by Eric or Maeve?' asked Giles.

'Good question. I'm dropping Maeve Cartier's poem for a while. But the hostile pastures... will regenerate.'

'Let's hope so,' said the poet's son. 'You'd think studying Plath would have taught him respect for Maeve.'

'He cares too much about Maeve, not too little. His message was that I shouldn't intrude. He has taken possession of *Wildgoose*.'

'We're at the end of the road?'

It was no longer their road. It was Eric's. But the geese would return:

from skeins in skies we drop to earth and feed
on hostile pastures plump again with seed.

Chapter Fourteen

PALACE GREEN   (2015)

THE NEATNESS OF Durham's Palace Green struck Mary as she came blinking out of her allotted space in the Archives building into the bright sunlight and orderly ancientness of the precinct. She'd been reading Maeve Cartier's *Wildgoose* all morning. Pencils only, but she simply read today. The fabled box had acquired a library ownership tag but it felt like Maeve's private property and took Mary closer to Maeve than she had previously been.

The demise of Eric just before his seventieth year was old news now. Dramatically, his body had been found on a snowy moor in the Lake District, getting on for two years back. Giles was embarrassed by the bad publicity, particularly since some of the newspaper reports alluded to his mother's death. Mary wasn't going to think about it all over again. She shivered.

She had read Eric's obituaries as a poet – in fact she wrote a very small one. Much later, she sussed that he might have an archive in Durham University. Mary had come here looking for *Wildgoose* among Eric's papers. She had found it.

She crossed the Green in the sunlight and instead of

heading for one of many student cafés where today's young people gravitated, she continued to the great doorway of the cool, quiet Cathedral and went inside. Amid tiresome rows of chairs she walked under the stone forest of decorated pillars. She tried to shake off her excitement about her fresh reading of Maeve's poem.

The poem clung.

This interior had power, but there was power in Mary, too. All of a sudden, she felt changed; no longer cool and collected, no longer a 'young scholar' or 'rising star,' 'new arrival' or 'influential journalist' in today's hasty assessments, but a guest of the centuries, like Maeve, alive and sentient for a flickering moment in the light. Maeve's poem brought music into this place of music. Yet the more Mary learned about Maeve, the more she realised one could not entirely separate the cousins.

Beneath and behind the Cathedral, there'd been a time when men could wander the country carrying bones of a saint. A shrine to St Cuthbert behind the altar, a coffin of St Cuthbert, now somewhere private, a display in the Undercroft. Maeve had carried Eric with her as closely as a saint's old bones. Some of her lines hinted as much:

> Geese overhead, procession on a road,
> between high trekking wheels old men cart Cuthbert...
> haloed thoughts   who crave their crown
> years flown

Maeve's description of a secret orchard in the slopes behind a castle, a goose blown off course, hung strongly in her mind like incense in a side chapel, a curtain between reality and time. *History* had nothing to do with *his* or *her* story, as some today pretended. It was more like *Hidden story*. When Mary recovered herself, she could write a column on this.

The Cathedral held hidden stories of those who had

come and gone through the ages, bad-tempered bishops, gifted stonemasons, mothers and children, miners, soldiers, cooks and historians, people of words and people without words. Priests with Latin as their familiar tongue, speakers of Anglo-Saxon, Geordie, Pitmatic, and English of the northern kind.

Dappled light fell through some of the windows into the vast, silent, vault-like area where she stood.

Mary came out of the Cathedral before the chill of the past overwhelmed her. Maeve had changed her. This had not come from study and reading. Mary now had the wisdom of feeling. She could sense the life of the dead.

She went to a café. She sat among voluble students in their youthful excitement and summed up the end of her youth. Things had happened to her, important things that came from a closeness to other people's lives. *Wildgoose*, the manuscript, placed back in its library sanctity by that well-dressed curator, had affected her. Over a hot drink and a mass-produced, freshly grilled toastie, Mary slowly returned to the present world.

The archivist had made a point of meeting Mary. He had heard about 'Grysewood's little sister,' the one who died at the G G concert – it wasn't clear whether this was a stigma or a distinction. With Mary Weylan wanting access, he was proved right to have accepted Maeve Cartier's papers. Mary was benefiting from the offer of a college guestroom. She knew she was welcome. It was her privilege to read the poem in the box.

> *Restored to our point of departure, above, beyond action*
> *rugged cliff with a nest for repair*
> *strong bird bodies determine our promise, entail*
> *quilled words,*
> *release pen-feathers, trail driven*
> *beyond scribe's nib.*

Mary felt Maeve would not have minded this fate, her work being connected with Eric's. Mary had a new certainty about Maeve's inner life. Part of the change in Mary was that she could now look backwards in time.

One of the students in the café shouted over to Mary, 'Aren't you Mary Weylan?'

She pulled out her standard variant answer. 'How lucky! You can give me your impressions of Durham University for an article?'

The student grinned in defeat. The others turned back to one another. She smiled faintly.

It had been raining on Palace Green. The whole place was dwarfed by the north Cathedral wall. The long wooden benches were occupied, one loafer per bench, even when wet. She got one to herself, spread a plastic bag over it and sat down in the shining light. She'd spent yet another morning in the library with *Wildgoose*. Seeking permission to copy it for publication was going to be complicated and would involve others: publishers, Swing Bridge she still hoped, and owners, advisors – Giles or Richard. It would be handy to see Richard again, because she liked him, but he lived in Edinburgh, a day trip away by train. The trees of Palace Green sighed and rustled faintly in the drying wind.

Day followed day. Durham followed Durham. Routine was how longer poems got written. Mary began to have a better impression of Maeve writing this poem, in Giles' youth.

In the Archives room she had read the poem three times at least. She wanted to make a précis of it to help explain it to publishers. She had to fill in a form stating her purpose in copying from it, which she managed to fix. She admired the structure and drive of the poem as she unpuzzled it. She'd decided she wasn't a poet, but by god, she was a reader. A digital clock overlooked the quiet room. She preferred analogue clocks. Time was the circling of Maeve's geese round the sky.

> *sun, dawn, noon, hide from heat, sun, rain,*
> *evening shortens flight   daylight to feast,*
> *we scramble, corn, corm spread to sprout,*
> *sprout to stem and seed*
> *voracious beaks seek tidbits.*

The River Wear's most remarkable stretch wound past Durham Cathedral and Castle on the east, south and west. Mary soon figured the complicated geography, walking down a lane then a path to a college boat-house on the east, a shorter, less favourable 'windy gap' among buildings on the western side. Down on the riverside path, little but the plop of a small fish or water bird, or a swift student row-boat, disturbed the silence. Beyond the western side the river entered the city, with bridges and places to eat, before it departed, less glamorous, towards Sunderland. Mary was busy in the library and wanted quiet between sessions. This was ideal for her.

For the moment, she herself owned *Wildgoose*, a woman working on a woman's work. The poem was romantic and she loved it.

> *morning's air over edge of land, sea's comfort dawns*
> *on safe machair sea-otter, seal party by lighthouse,*
> *illicit distillery skirted under wing.*

But it wouldn't stay like this, would it?

By now Mary knew it had reached Durham from Gryse-wood Farm twenty-odd miles away, where Eric's work up to his Canada year had been stashed in his old bedroom. Sal, a woman farmer, she understood, was Eric's sister. She probably wore wellingtons and had straggly hair. After

Maeve's death, Giles had entrusted this Sal with two cartons of Maeve's papers and letters, including the correspondence with Eric, which Eric had wanted to keep. Sal had slung Eric's parcel containing *Wildgoose* into one of the cartons, and in due course it had arrived at the archive centre for sorting out. The poem had lain like yeast quietly bubbling in the dark, stronger than anything that tried to contain it.

> *Go, geese, gather, let feathered beat of goosewings herald*
> *visitations*

Five white geese pottered on a spur of bank across the river. Domestic geese – one appeared to be nesting – not migratory. The gander arched his neck towards her, his open yellow beak emitting warnings. Here were no small irregular fields, no shed or crate or housewife to feed them potato peelings. Perhaps they flew or swam to some haven upriver, beyond these concealing bends. On her side of the river chaffinches hopped, feeding on picnic crumbs.

She followed steps up to the town. She'd eat in that nice little place she found yesterday. Even the newer town, banished from the citadel in the thirteenth century, gave a sense of history. Quiche and a glass of wine, ice-cream, a brownie, happy on her own. She could make coffee in her college room.

She couldn't forget Eric and Richard. Her discovery of *Wildgoose* was about a woman's achievements, a woman's perspective. Yet Eric was part of Maeve's story. She thought with amusement and a little pain of how she'd come up against their personal tensions, at least the fall-out from them. St Andrews, Durness. Mary and Richard were not strangers. She imagined him, living alone after Eric's death, in the Edinburgh apartment. She smiled wryly at the waiter, who'd been making eyes at her, not very seriously. She paid, and went back to her college corridor.

An elderly graduate of Durham University had requested access to *Wildgoose*. She'd seen him at the front desk, over-looked by the staff, where they often put one-off visitors. Maeve's blue and white box, with the fat sheaf of papers Mary had been regarding as her own, sat proudly in front of him. A librarian came over to her, and quietly explained. 'He's an old friend of the Archives and he's over from New-castle. Could you come back in the afternoon?'

Inconvenienced, but fascinated that someone else was seeking the poem, Mary headed outside, momentarily at a loss. Palace Green was empty and quiet. The French-sound-ing 'Place Green' of early times had been smaller – with shacks and businesses set around it, no doubt. Clerics out for a breather, travellers' gossip, somebody hanging onto the sanctuary knocker at the Cathedral door. Perhaps those medieval citizens had sometimes sloped off to the river as she was doing now.

On a seat by the towpath she opened her takeaway cof-fee and two morning rolls. Unerringly the Durham woods towered above her. She began to feed the chaffinches. Over-head, below clouds, flew three greylag geese.

The seasons were passing.

The geese arrived noisily on the water as though they had noticed her. She threw them lumps of her last roll. More characters in her life. She was in a phase of living monastically right now.

She envisaged two books: Maeve's published poem, and a book on the cousins, perhaps not written by her. Perhaps this secondary book wouldn't happen. It was too much to think about with her other work. She was always several weeks ahead with newspaper columns, allowing for imme-diate topicality at times. She'd write something one morn-ing about the student boat clubs.

As she sat at the edge of the trees on the sunny grass, a hawk shocked her by descending onto the chaffinches and lifting one away. It shocked the chaffinches too – all disappeared in a flurry. The geese had seen worse things, and, finishing the bread, flopped their way to the further bank, mingling with the white geese.

She climbed back to her work.

The elderly graduate nearly bumped into her outside the Archives. He looked about eighty. He wore a dark suit, his trousers supported by braces across his non-existent waist, and incongruous white trainers as though these were his only comfortable footwear. He recognised her and his eyes were twinkling.

She risked it. 'Did you enjoy Maeve Cartier's poem?'

'Indeed I did.' He moved aside from the footway. 'I was a friend of her family.' He hesitated. 'And of the poet herself. I am sorry if I claimed your kill this morning.'

'Apology accepted,' said Mary. 'I'm happy to share the kill. I hope to see it published fairly soon.'

Further hesitation. They both wanted to talk, but they were strangers. Mary beheld a formal, old-fashioned man who probably couldn't be dragged into a café on a whim. She took another risk.

'I'm Mary Weylan,' she said.

The old man smiled. 'I thought so. I'm going for a train, but I need sustenance first. Would you care to accompany me to a little joint I know?'

'I'd be delighted,' said Mary.

They went to a nearby club room Mary would never have found. He bagged a table, ordered a drink and one for her (she chose lager) and added, 'My usual Ploughman's sandwich, no, the Picasso sandwich, thank you.' He put a business card on the table, saying, 'Northold, this is me. I knew Maeve Cartier for twenty years in Newcastle, before she went to Scotland.'

'I never met Maeve, but her son Giles is a friend. Perhaps you knew him.'

The Picasso sandwich came, containing onion, olives,

salami, peppers and cheese. It was divided into quarters. He offered her a quarter, but she declined.

He asked her, 'You got onto this story through Giles?'

'On the contrary, I met Giles through my interest in Maeve. And the poem is a delight. Especially after we feared it was lost. Richard thought Eric had lost it. I met them all, and I liked Richard. Did you know him?'

'Still know him,' said Northold. 'He was obsessed by the fact Eric had missed some sort of poetry gathering at Buckingham Palace that winter. Apparently Eric received an invitation – not Richard – on the day he disappeared. He hadn't looked at his mail. To Richard, that gave colour to the timing of Eric's death. As if the one thing shed light on the other.' Northold drank his beer. 'It seems a harebrained idea but it was all you heard from Richard for months – plus how his old dog was getting on.'

'I thought there were things I needed to ask you,' said Mary, 'but they've evaporated. The poem was at Grysewood. It was brought in here and we have it. In a nutshell.'

'I persuaded the Archives to send for the boxes from Grysewood,' said Northold. 'But I didn't realise her poem was in them.'

'I imagined them trundled through green lanes by monks on a cart...'

'Like the bones of St Cuthbert?'

Mary laughed. 'But why here? Maeve and Eric were in Edinburgh and Newcastle.'

'Why did you come looking here?' he asked her.

She thought back. She didn't know. This was weird: she should be the one asking the questions. Had he really known Maeve Cartier well?

'There's something else', said the old man suddenly. 'Basil Bunting's archive is here. Puts Eric's papers to shame, but... Maeve thought very highly of Bunting.'

They didn't stay long, having much in common but

little more to say. They bade one another farewell, and she watched him totter off towards the town and station.

She walked back to Palace Green thoughtfully. This old fellow had thrown her some wheat and some chaff. Surely Maeve wouldnt be as old as him, if she had lived? Was it worth asking Giles about him? No. And she didn't quite like that story of Eric and the poets at Buckingham Palace. It sounded fishy. Did Eric rate London and the establishment? Eric was difficult but not shallow. He was despairing but not insecure.

Mary herself had been to the Palace in London when Giles was awarded a C.B.E. He'd invited her as a guest. London was part of Mary's life, though she had gained such a lot in the north, pursuing Maeve Cartier and learning the culture. The south was more foreign to Giles, though he assimilated it well. It was not part of Eric's, or Richard's, background, and would not be within their compass. In its stead were the splendour of Durham, the grandeur of Edinburgh, the strength of Aberdeen.

She found the wheat when, back in the reading room, she asked at the desk for an introduction to the Basil Bunting archive. She worked even longer in the archives and spent less time on the river banks, which with the autumn were becoming leafier at ground level and barer in the treetops, as lines of student rowing boats pulled by. She read about the suburban Tyneside train journeys on which Bunting slowly wrote his poem *Briggflatts*. That was the routine in Bunting's construction, as she envisaged it in Maeve's *Wildgoose*. Mary's précis of *Wildgoose*, its demystification, its clear countenance grew.

Mary discovered how much Maeve had revered Basil Bunting's work, his beliefs about poetry, music and sound, his trust in the northern background and culture. She saw influence and inspiration. Maeve never attempted to use Eric's laconic style. Maeve's work was pure romance.

Go, geese, gather, gather then separate again
weave cradled sky, fly sleepless air,
readers of northern texts, wise maps

She never plundered Bunting's lines. Maeve's geese flew over Briggflatts terrain; Maeve's cadences had drawn on Bunting's distance. Lindisfarne, Morecambe and other northern haunts had been shadowed. Scotland had welcomed both poets and geese.

Wildgoose was the work of a woman artist, who had found a voice of her own, but she wasn't a woman who hadn't depended on men.

Over sand passages high waters surge, swirl, part, lunar
tide's tricks.
On plotted routes, travellers consult in whispers, halt
without wings.
Horse-backed Quaker pilgrims tour by moonlit fells
on chosen nights –

Maeve was a sucker for long lines.
And here was the précis:

'Wildgoose by Maeve Cartier.
'Wildgoose is born in Canada. She taps her shell of egg.
Soon she is flying round the world, across the Atlantic
Ocean to Scotland, the west coast and the east, without
boundaries to England, Aberlady, Lindisfarne, Edinburgh, where with inherited navigation she thinks the
glass roof of the Station is the Nor' Loch. The Pennines,
Lancashire, the Western Isles, present and past. She flies
over shipwrecks where grown men perish, the Iolaire,
the Lusitania, over one-time tragic towns, Agadir in
Africa, Aberfan and Dunblane, she lands among popula-
tions and in isolation, among large congregations of geese,*

*and alone over waters, countrysides in their various
aspects. She interprets the sounds of geese, follows their
music as it resonates over land, she is with the Beatles,
with Beethoven. She is not restricted in time. She may fly
across Roman-occupied Northumberland and Third Reich
Germany, she ventures the African interior before and after the first explorers. She follows women's communities
and countries where women and men do not experience
the world alike, and she seeks communities where the
genders are integrated. She derides unshared wealth. She
rides low over the waves, almost touching the heads of
fishermen in cobles, or high in the blue. She weeps with
those weeping and sings with those singing. She is sometimes alone, sometimes in groups of migratory geese. Most
of the denizens of the ground never notice her. Immortal
as a goddess, she never dies and she often wishes to.
'Passing through seven cantos for season and distance,
the past, the future and theme, there is an ending in
circularity and the deeper and deeper understanding she
achieves gradually and with effort through her quest.'*

Mary had said her research came with a man. The whole
connection had gone on longer than she or Giles had expected. She wound up work at the Durham archive, reading *Wildgoose* once again, in hopes of her own printed copy,
with her own introduction, at some future date. She arranged to meet Giles in a hotel in Morecambe. They hadn't
met for a while. He'd been travelling more widely. He was
renting a house in Manchester, handy for the BBC. This
week he was seeing managers and singers in his Lancaster
music hub. Mary vacated her room, collated her precious
papers, reduced her luggage to a small case by throwing
away some worn clothes and broken sandals, and struggled
for the last time across to Durham Station. Before she left,
she went to the Cathedral and looked again at the sanctuary
knocker. They didn't let you touch it nowadays.

She met Giles in the late afternoon on a windy day, and she told him about *Wildgoose* and how publishable it was. They walked on the sandy prom with the tide swelling over the bay.

'Work done,' she said. 'I'm going back to Bristol. I still have a desk there, and a colleague who'll rent me a room in a flat.'

'When are you back north?'

'It's permanent.'

'But –' Giles stopped.

Mary knew he wouldn't argue. He wouldn't let on he was surprised.

'So what shall we do this evening?'

'I'd like a walk by the Lune estuary, at the end of Morecambe Bay. I'd like to see the geese.'

A little further than the end of Morecambe Bay. Giles hailed a taxi on the prom. Then they were on a shoreside footpath with trees and flocks of geese. Mary had been right, though she hadn't expected all this grass. Widening now, the Lune's fresh water from Briggflatts met the sea. Fields of geese, pink-footed mainly and the odd bean goose waddling on the grass, and in the water, on the swelling tide, were geese, a large party of swans, and a variety of other water birds, including ducks.

Neither Giles nor Mary had much to say as they strolled, like the birds, round the path. Goose land. Deserted but for these noisy returning geese, rough pasture ran on for miles down the coast, southwards into the distance where Blackpool guarded its long stretch of beach.

'Perhaps I'll find some odd gloves,' said Giles to himself. He led her into a pub where they would eat for one last time.

Giles could run off his mother's poem on the office machines for his concert goers. His staff could produce a book. However Maeve's old fans were no longer hippies but parents. 'We need a poetry imprint,' he decided.

'I can write to Swing Bridge Press.'

'I'm told he's retired,' said Giles. 'Age, and he's spent his money.'

'Pity, he liked Maeve's work. I'll find someone,' said Mary.

She suddenly thought of Maverick, the Banksy of Literature, and how he had asked about Maeve.

'Here's to your mother's poem!' She raised her wineglass. It seemed a happy conclusion.

Giles raised his glass too. An excellent wine for an outcome. 'To *Wildgoose* after all these ups and downs! To Maeve Cartier!'

'And to Eric Grysewood.'

'And to us. What on earth can have happened that night?'

'We have to trust,' said Mary. 'We've done our bit. We've found *Wildgoose*. We can never know all of a story. We'll never understand it all.'

'I figured that out at Smoo Cave,' said Giles.

'I learnt it on Palace Green.'

Chapter Fifteen

ERIC'S LAST JOURNEY   (2013)

In 2013, after holding out for so long, Eric and Richard had bought a television, to celebrate Richard turning seventy. They didn't need the change of routine, and the programmes mainly disappointed them. They sometimes watched films. Absently Eric flicked the TV into life. A feature on snow-holing in the Cairngorms. He was absorbed by the pictures of the snow. It didn't seem to be typical Alpine snow, smooth and crisp as cake icing, against a cobalt sky. It was flurried, uncertain, Scottish snow, with trails over the summit moors showing dark edges of rough rock outcrops streaked by the ski routes' wavering swathes of snow. The sky was white, almost indistinguishable from snow.

Strong men climbed into their snow-holes and settled down to sleep. They would wake warm in the morning.

The damsons boiled up in the saucepan and hissed on the hob. Eric watched Richard lean back and turn them down. The moussaka was good and the wine went with it well. It ought to be cheering him up, but it didn't dispel his lethargy. They had coffee and cheese, left the too-hot damsons for another day.

Richard suggested a visit to the nearby gay club they often looked in on.

'I couldn't. I'm not up to socialising.'

'If you dinnae write, that can get you down.'

'What's the point? Writing's overvalued. Literature died with the twentieth century.'

'Oh come on. You've done well enough out of it. You have the ear of editors. You can still place poems. The young people know who you are.'

'No. The young people don't know who I am. Why should they? They were all born in the 1990s or the 2000s. There's no place for dead white European males in their definition of literature.'

'You need to come out and let your hair down.'

'I have hardly any hair left.'

There was a pause.

'Richard, you go out, and I'll write this thing I've been trying to write, and then maybe I'll follow you down.'

Eric fetched his writing pad and settled on the sofa in the drawing room, without even glancing at the dishes, which Richard put under water in the sink. Richard tidied himself up and went out looking sprightly and, as Eric acknowledged unwillingly, nothing like seventy years old. Provided you didn't ask Richard to run.

Eric's retiral had left him low-spirited. Heriot-Watt University had helped him to feel involved in an actual profession, instead of this mish-mash that was poetry in the modern world – poetry in any world. The work had kept him too busy to stare hard at the head of the gorgon of what he had given his life to. Western poetry, European poetry, Scottish poetry. Would he be better off turned to stone? Maeve wouldn't have given up.

Look at *Common Room Poetry 9*. He had edited and

published it two years ago – the last paper issue due to the mounting cost of postage, and a gloriously confident exegesis of European poetry and the translation industry. The academic rumpus which his magazine had caused had delighted Eric and warmed his heart which was now so bare and bleak.

Common Room Poetry was supposed to relocate to the internet, but Eric hadn't done it yet. He didn't know enough about websites. Richard might show him some of the online poetry journals.

But Richard had gone out.

Eric could have replenished his wine and sloped off to bed, but there was yet another problem to contemplate. He and Richard were no longer lovers.

Friends yes, family probably, but if there was one person's fault, and there may not have been, it was Eric's. In his last patch of depression, when he had had to go to the doctor (and thank goodness he had gone), he had expected to sleep at such odd times, and the nothing that was happening in their bed was so embarrassing and unbearable, that Richard had split the bed, which was one of those zip-up-the-middle ones, and put half in the third room, the one they hadn't used much, and announced that he needed undisturbed sleep.

There followed the only major shouting match that had ever happened between them. Not because Eric couldn't see that they required separate rooms, but because he felt guilty and thought he should have the smaller room. He kept yelling, 'You keep the bedroom, I'm not up to it' until a neighbour indicated he could hear the noise and requested they make less of it.

This huge rumpus helped calm Eric down. He did recover, with medication, and a little contemplation along the lines of 'We can't get it right all the time,' (Richard) and 'Few people have ever changed the world, except for the worse!' (Eric).

Soon he would have been fifteen years without Maeve. How everything had changed. It wasn't just computers. Edinburgh had become his life. Where was everybody? Hamish Henderson, Sorley Maclean, MacDiarmid, all the leaders dead. The students spoke of them and sought their books. Were they still communicating somehow from that nowhere they all were not? The evenings they had spent in Sandy Bell's. He took Maeve at least twice, the first time when he'd met Hamish Henderson. It came back to him for real. Many people used to call him *Wildgoose*, now only Richard.

The trattoria which Richard said had gone. No, he said had gone. The old chef, vanished. He recalled the old man's first conversation with him, word for word and clear as day. *Poeta, eh? You live round here? You from Scozzia? You eat here tomorrow eh?*

From the land of Italy. The land of Dante and Vergil and Hadrian, the empire builders, the writers. Their international language, that had affected all generations until now.

Caedmon, countryman of the East Coast, Whitby. The beauty of being famous for poetry that wasn't extant. Caedmon was an inspired shepherd invited into the big hall to pronounce eleven lines of vernacular support for early Christianity. Poetry wasn't an overcrowded profession then. And Bede wrote a vernacular death poem. Were death poems a thing? Eric sighed. Then as now, if you were famous your poems became known. Richard had found Hadrian's fabulous little death-verse, the Emperor who had such a fascinating life staking out these northern provinces, the Latiniser back in imperial Rome. He had flourished before Caedmon, if Caedmon could be said to have flourished on his gale-swept patch of coast. Hadrian's short verse, turned to Scots, was the only thing of Richard's that Eric had published. Hundreds of translations existed if you looked round Google. How weird was Google. The universe of microelectronics was still a surprise to Eric. Maeve might just faintly have heard of the internet.

> *Gin Ah'm deid, spirit, ye'll no care,*
> *alane Ah topple doun thon stair,*
> *nor rise nor breathe wioot ye there.*
> *'Tis thus we share oor tide thegither,*
> *We're naehin wioot ane anither.*

Baboom! He liked it. Richard wasn't bad. It didn't matter to Richard what he had done or not done. Eric preferred his own version, practically a limerick. He couldn't find it or remember it. He amused himself sometimes transporting these ancients to the twenty-first century. Caedmon on Facebook. Hadrian on Twitter. Bede using instant translation into bad Anglo-Saxon. *Whisht, lads* (Beowulf).

He was sitting on the sofa where Richard had left him. This was, what, 2013. He looked down at his paper. The page was pristine. He pocketed his fountain pen. He couldn't even write a letter. Not this kind of letter. He'd never tried a novel, despite those chancers churning them out by the month – what was that project NaNoWriMo? A novel in a month, by people who had read all of two novels in their lives?

He did better by his students than that. He made them read properly, he made them obey a few rules. Once they knew them, they were away, provided they had imagination and could write without spelling mistakes. But who knew nowadays if anyone could spell? And they did write – everybody did. All this change and development interested him. Perhaps he should delay his retirement?

But would he ever write another poem?

He decided to go to the club where Richard would be. He put his jacket on and sauntered down through the cool evening air, past the railed-in grass and trees, up the few steps to the mid-terrace building, nodding to the doorman as he entered. The rooms were quiet, the atmosphere relaxed. Music was playing as he peered round, looking for his friend.

Richard was dancing with a very beautiful black man Eric had never seen before. It was amazing that Richard could dance, considering his stiffening legs and complaints about the stairs, but while his movements were unambitious, his sense of rhythm was excellent. His partner in the dance was flamboyant and they were trading off each other well.

Eric watched them for a few moments then asked an attendant for a Laphroaig. An acquaintance gave him a look with no interpretable meaning. Eric waited for the dance to finish then caught Richard's eye as he came off the floor with the stranger. Instead of them moving apart, Richard brought the man over to Eric.

Eric was ready to flip but he wasn't sure how. In theory they were free to make other social connections. When Richard introduced the man, Eric said 'Howdy' and then stopped, not prepared to assist conversation.

Richard looked at him for a moment. 'We're getting a drink, will you have another?'

'No.' Eric was curt. 'I'll be driving.'

'Driving? Not till tomorrow? What's tomorrow?'

'Nothing. Just losing my temper.'

'Aye well, tomorrow.'

'If bad temper could be measured, it would be illegal to drive in one.' The stranger spoke in beautiful English (from Oxford?) and headed for the bar, where Richard, after a helpless glance towards Eric, followed him.

Eric left the club alone, walked home, collected another whisky (Glenmorangie), his block of writing paper, fountain pen and paracetamol and proceeded to the bedroom.

Why wasn't it okay for Richard to relate to another man? A dance and a drink, no more...

But what if Richard felt lonely despite living with him, when they'd stopped, well, stopped needing to say anything that way? Was this going on secretly? It would be a secret, wouldn't it? Richard would not want to upset him, sharing a home as they did.

How had this ceasing of intimacy with Richard become irreversible?

Eric should pull himself together. He ought to do another *Common Room Poetry*. It was much easier nowadays. You emailed people you wanted poems from, they sent the poems in files, and you slapped them on the page. But it didn't feel such an achievement as before.

He leaned his pillows onto the headboard. He would sit up and write what was bursting his head. It wasn't a poem, no. It might be a suicide note if it turned out like that: I see no point in sitting in this home? No future? No "usness" left. Richard will be better off without me. Eric couldn't write it, couldn't crystallise it, couldn't believe his own story. He threw aside the small block of letter paper and screwed his pen cap back on. He lay back, trying to sleep. If only he could dream.

He was a throwback, unable to watch today's confident women on telly, in programmes he and Richard didn't rate. He was a Beatles fan. Born before 1950, this elderly sector, from Liverpool and Manchester, London and the small towns, had flocked to the north of Scotland in their – hundreds, only hundreds left, a thousand all told, those few years ago after time had stopped mattering, after the internet started spoiling literature, after the awful death of his cousin Maeve. And the folly, the hubris of all this poetry. The great poets of their generation were under their noses. Lennon and McCartney were the greats. A matter of opinion but that was his. He was tired of the stuffy poetry echelons. The young Beatles, playing Newcastle, playing Glasgow, starting out when he did, 1963. Maeve seventeen, 1965. Maeve dead 1999, and in 2007 he barely survived Durness. Life was very long.

Graffiti on the cliffs at Smoo Cave, on the far north coast by Durness. Who made the effort and why? Did the Merry Dancers descend with moonlight paint? Paul and Linda had lived near Campbelltown, beyond the long, long roads and the seas for sailing. The young poet fiddler met them there. The old dame Naomi Mitchison hung out at Carradale, her books overflowing her rural house, Linda's kitchen pottery overflowing hers. Mitchison dead, Linda dead.

Lennon a boy in Durness, his lone holiday journey on train and bus to his uncle's house. Sea, cliffs, fields. Uncle in the cottage, an envelope of John's letters in his jacket.

Rounding the north of Scotland in a small car the tourists collided with a larger car on the far north coastline among the rocks. Out of the other car stepped John and Yoko with two rich kids. Lennon's money smoothed things out but not their shock, their story to dine on, relief none were hurt. The Beatles crashed their car in Golspie on the east coast years earlier. In the small local hospital they spoke to a wee boy having his tonsils removed. The boy, the poet and fiddler, told his tale. The poet and fiddler was in Sandy Bell's, bought Maeve a drink. *This* life was the afterlife, life without Maeve.

In Durness the poets assembled. The ageing Quarrymen, the Poet Laureate, and the last ever beat poet known to man. They sang and performed in the vast, watery arena of Smoo Cave. On his computer he viewed Smoo Cave from his home. Google maps had come in. Yet it was distant and difficult – vast tracts where you couldn't use a mobile phone. The concert grand, trundled, nursed from Inverness to Durness in a special removal van. In the big hotel at Durness behind dark curtains, poets missed the Northern

Lights. Campers saw the Dancers. Eric and Richard's car awaited its police tow. Eric in a northern A&E a hundred miles south. He couldn't survive without Maeve. He had already lost.

Richard was making breakfast. Eric looked in and said, 'I'm going out today after all.'

'Where?'

'North of England.'

'Okay. Will you have some toast?'

Richard's old dog eyed him up. Yawned.

'Thanks. And a cup of coffee.'

'There's some mail.'

Eric picked up the letters doubtfully. 'Those are mine,' said Richard. Eric's packages included *Poetry Review* and associated leaflets, and *Acumen* with whom he had a reciprocal arrangement that went back as far as *Tynescript*. He shoved them aside in a tray. Richard had been out with the dog. Today's bread, today's milk.

'You're not tired of it all, like I am.'

A few minutes saw Eric through his toast and coffee, then he went into his box-room study. It was tidy. He picked up his car keys and left the flat, banging the door latch.

The east coast was less popular, the safer option down the west. Some of the busy staff at the Watt, especially the women, had talked about 'me time.' Eric wanted some 'me time.' He was driving away from Scotland to the bits of his life he had carelessly left in the north of England. Places he needed to see. People would say 'before you die.'

Everything crowded in on him, starting with Grysewood Farm. He wasn't going there. He had abdicated in favour of Sal and he wouldn't interfere. He wasn't going back to Newcastle, to Sandyford, either, because of the terrifying grown man Giles.

Glimpses of sea. What made him think of Durness and

the badly cut wrist, the familiar scar under his hand on the steering wheel? Richard had taken that seriously and tried to send Eric to a psychiatrist, but the problem was, Eric had no idea why it had happened. And that woman Mary, how and where did Giles find her, Maeve not long dead?

Eric was fantasising about his early days, places he associated with poetry, his family and Maeve, his lifelong fight with words and how he could make them sing. He was going further south, though it wasn't 'south,' the Pennines and Lakes and Tyneside were not 'south.'

He felt he had lost. Billions of words were written and published, his own, Maeve's, Richard's, everyone's. They sat there in books, these words, reading their music to themselves. Who else read them? Students, who could as well take the next book from the shelf? One's loves and lovers?

Crucially, Maeve's main poem wasn't there. It wasn't in those thin shiny volumes of recent poets' work, it wasn't in university libraries, nor in his own study. It was at Grysewood. Eric knew that, but it would never be found there. Nothing would be left.

Buddy was furious at the manner of its loss, yet Swing Bridge Press had Maeve's *Collected* ready for publication without it. Eric had not been invited to write an introduction. He'd heard a rumour that Swing Bridge Press was short of money, and would only be publishing quick earners, and not too many of them. He hoped it wasn't true.

Eric rolled across the border from Scotland to England, the North Sea stretching to his left.

Maeve had never had the same sort of wishes, although she wrote so well and sometimes unfashionably, never quite melding with popular feminism. Yet feminists were trying to piece together Maeve's history, treating her death as no accident, but a flag of warning, a rallying banner, for their factions. Like that woman Mary what *was* her name, suddenly such a friend of Giles – that was heterosexuality for you.

Mary Weylan was better known than when he first met her at the poetry reading. She was a respected social commentator, writing in the Sunday papers, often about gender, a matter of increasing interest to readers. What had Mary Weylan tried to say – that Maeve belonged to women poets, not to him?

Maeve belonged to herself – supremely so. All her life she was solitary despite her men and her child, her library jobs and her women's poetry crowd. And he, Eric, was close to her. But she was gone. How had the years of the new century fled by as they undoubtedly had fled by? Was it only older people who found this so?

This and more in his mind, a lifetime of feeling through his own and others' experience, he cruised down the narrow and dangerous sections of road around Lindisfarne, turning left at Beal.

He had only visited Lindisfarne twice, but he loved both the place and the idea of the place. He needed physical contact, his feet on the strand.

He paused by the concrete pillboxes in marram grass and gazed over the flooded causeway, imagining Cuthbert, Aidan and the other saints, with such different despairs.

He drank the remaining coffee in the card cup from the petrol station, while studying the tide table under its raggy perspex. A wait till afternoon.

Year on year, Maeve's flocks of geese had come, while the saints ran Lindisfarne Abbey, while monks illustrated the Gospels, using goose feathers from the long green links in the lee of the tide race. Birds of the air, untroubled by the tide, part of the tide, they came and went with the swing of the world.

Bees for wax for candles.
Geese for quills to write.

It should have another two lines. He couldn't do it. Turning the car, he drove on. Farewell to Cuthbert, the Abbey and silent beaches, waves swelling, sinking and falling around the isle.

Beside the last patch of old road north of Tyneside, he passed rows of red-berried holly trees. Greengrocers' lorries cut masses of holly for sale in Newcastle's markets before Christmas time. Men stood on top of lorries, harvesting berried stems, trimming the high trees for colour and beauty. Maeve had written about them, thirty years ago.

He silenced the car radio, responding to crackles as Radio Scotland packed in. The road became the bypass, widened to multi lanes, the sweeping lie of the land round the Tyne unchanged by new bridges or the iconic Angel on the fell.

He felt detached from his life. He was a stamp fluttering from its envelope; a holly berry on a tree. It was growing colder. He turned up his car heating but it didn't respond. He rolled up the passenger side window, inch by inch. He needed Maeve the writer.

Much as he admired her he had never wanted sex with Maeve. If anyone hadn't noticed, he was gay. He couldn't *politically* want sex with a woman. Maybe if it wasn't about sex it didn't matter?

Up country beyond Darlington, he shot round a bend and pulled up sharply as a car slowed in front of him. The distance between the cars shrank.

He should phone Richard. Phone Maeve. YOU CAN'T PHONE DEAD PEOPLE. He pulled into a hedgerow verge, stopped the engine, put his head into his hands and shuddered.

The intensity of being alone, his mind as free as he wished to make it. Sedbergh. His old school stood away from the road, not somewhere he cared to investigate. He stared at it, slowing down. He hadn't talked about his school to Richard, although Richard had spoken of his. It was a question of what bugged you, and school had not generally bugged Eric. At Sedbergh he had fallen for a boy who died climbing a mountain in Switzerland. All that was left to him, for quite a while after, had been poetry and Maeve.

Sedbergh, roads not built for modern traffic, scenery unique and superb, town at the back of nowhere, the north-western corner of the dales.

Eric seemed always to have known about Bunting's tiny Quaker hideaway on a tributary of the Lune. Bunting and MacDiarmid – the provocative pair who'd been present when he and Maeve first stepped into this dance. There was a story about Maeve and Briggflatts. It would come back to him.

Pleased with his navigation he reached the hamlet. The place was more beautiful than could possibly be imagined, even in the inauspicious weather, the leaflessness, dusting of snow. A graveyard, Bunting's memorial at the foot, near the gate. All stones identical – Quakers these.

One of the small group of buildings in Briggflatts was the meeting house. Its careful carpentry, its gallery of documents and books, quiet centuries of being small and hidden and sought. Local congregations with local voices accentuated through time. And in recent decades, poets from all over the world. Eric knew quite a few poets who had talked about visiting here. Many others had come, national and international scholars, devotees of the stony Pennine language of this poet, now absorbed into the academic priesthood of poetry.

Maeve and Ollie too. It had come from Ollie's esoteric knowledge. On that far-off day when the schoolgirl Maeve came to Newcastle, hadn't she met Basil Bunting while he, Eric, had bombed off to Leeds with his early lover, Dr Joe, his first book publisher? Eric recalled Bunting's funeral.

He'd been present, alerted by another poet, not long before he went to Canada, while the scourge of AIDS was decimating gay friends. Dr Joe had died of AIDS while Eric was in Canada, infection befalling him long after their time together. Eric shivered.

He grasped at what he could see, the brown joinery, doorway into the kitchen, surviving ancientness, a small jar of simple flowers. Eric looked into the visitors' book thinking of Maeve. He could visualise her here so clearly. The room looked into its own centre, but the whole world could come in inside someone's head, as Maeve was here in his. Who had she come with? Ollie, Alice and – some woman Alice knew, whom he hadn't met.

This visitors' book only went back three years. The first entry said *Last here with Jon Silkin*. The signatory was from Cambridge. Jon Silkin had died in the nineties, as Eric knew. Silkin had become his correspondent, an advising editor, a literary uncle. Eric's first *Common Room Poetry* had been a tribute to Silkin. Sixty-seven years, Silkin had lived, less than the Biblical blessing of Threescore Years and Ten.

Eric had hoped he would make it.

He forgot to sign the book.

He went outside and crossed a field. It led to a steep drop down to a river, below a green railway embankment. Briggflatts had seen the railway come and go.

Who wanted to be anywhere else?

Eric didn't. To say he had no purpose in this expedition did not explain the short length of hosepipe in the back of the car. If he stayed, he would stay here forever. If he went on, he'd never come back. He had hidden Maeve's poem, not destroyed it, but certainly she was lost. What were his words against these realities?

He strode past every leafless herb, each trickle of departing water, with no one to exclaim to as he turned each corner, over-conscious of those who had come here, entirely excluding him. His disappointments began to pile up, clouds over the tributary becks and the Rawthey as they ran towards the Lune.

He returned to his car. He began to fix the pipe to the exhaust.

The fresh sweet air hit him and he suddenly felt guilty. For the environment. How could he pollute this air from the deep hidden country, perfect air that allowed lichens to form, mosses to thrive? He couldn't. He'd be polluting a sanctuary, a place of pilgrimage if he went on with this ritual – it had hardly been a plan but there it was. He wasn't thinking clearly either. He recognised – awkwardly – that he wasn't destructive enough.

To be or not... To go on being sorry for himself. To withstand mental pain, await physical pain while ageing.

Didn't he have a mobile phone? He would phone Richard. He felt in his pocket but the phone wasn't there. He rummaged in the car. Nothing.

He went back into the little stone building with the oaken interior, the church-like meeting room carpentered in 1695 in the manner of wooden ships. He wasn't sure if Friends prayed. He wasn't sure he could pray. He just sat there.

He was going back to sort things out with Richard. They had hit age and change and they needed to deal with it. He wouldn't walk out like this, not merely away from Richard but out of life.

And Maeve. Someone must look after publishing her poem. He couldn't hide it till he died, that could be years away. He might become a grand old man, though he doubted it. Fodder for the next generation? No, Maeve's poem, his work too, they were not fodder but succour, contributions to the craft they had both tried to serve.

He took the piece of hosepipe from his car and stuffed it into the prickly heart of the hawthorn hedge.

'What the fuck are you doing?' said a voice.

He turned, red-handed, red-faced, caught in his guilt. A woman stood there. Not very young. She still had the cheeky, confident look of someone young. Her neck wasn't young. Despite the cold weather it was exposed above a low-collared jacket. Her shoes were light and summery. She reminded him of those Tyneside women who went pubbing on winter nights without a coat.

Attack was the best defence.

'What the fuck are *you* doing here?'

'I'm Janey. I want to get away from here, I've been living here too long. Will you take me?'

'Take you where –what are you talking about?'

'I need to go to Newcastle.'

'I'm not a taxi driver.'

'Wait for me, ten minutes.'

'What the –'

He sat down in the driving seat, riffled through the glove boxes in another half-hearted, fruitless search for the phone. What... maybe he should clear off quickly.

She was back in five. She had a coat now, and a shoulder bag. She climbed in the passenger side.

'What are you doing?'

'Will you give me a lift down to Sedbergh, at least, preferably further, any town.'

'No. I don't know who you are, and I'm going the other way.'

'I telt ye, I'm Janey. I need help.'

Eric knew about needing help.

'Okay, I could take you to Kendal or somewhere. If you'll explain as we go.'

They headed west, refuelling the car at a tiny petrol station a few miles up the road. Travellers thrown together. Better for him. He could take her to Newcastle and then, what, two hours to Edinburgh?

All this had been a mistake. It started to snow. It didn't take long for snow to pile up in these perilous lanes.

'Courage begins to wear out as well as strength,' said Eric to himself, as he began to negotiate the western Lake District roads, small and curving past Coniston and Ullswater, back towards Ambleside. All this was Maeve's territory, or perhaps old Charlie's, the father of the little girl who would become the poet and go beyond her father, beyond her cousin too, though they had progressed through their life of words together for much of the way. His memories of this area were powerful. He was quite glad of Janey, to tone things down, berate him for the exact present circumstances, his madness.

Janey stopped rabbiting on after a few miles.

He passed a slope they had climbed as children, covered in bluebells on a late spring day. Then a young boy had been killed by an adder bite. Eric had never been back. The slope was white with today's snow, under the slate-coloured sky. 'I grew up partly round here.'

A lost image from Maeve's poem came to him: *the V on the adder's head leading its push across hillsides as geese spearhead skies.*

The weather was foul, the going hard, night was falling and he was driving through a northern storm.

'The drawback of dying is you can't know what happens next. If you died the day after me, I wouldn't know.'

'You what?' said Janey.

He had spoken aloud.

'Don't mind me.'

'Sorry.'

His mind turned to Richard, who was uncomplaining, didn't make Eric think about anything beyond their basic home, where they lived in a day-in-day-out routine that never seemed existential, for it was simply existence. Richard didn't fill up Eric's brain with problems: one psychoneurotic was enough in a household of two.

Richard, to whom he was driving home.

He and Richard had written together and apart, but always differently, nothing in common between their output of poems except that it was poetry. Richard never relied on outside publication for validation, but published his work himself in pamphlets whenever he felt ready. This gave Richard's work an integrity which Eric had always emulated, an integrity impossible to undermine. They were never rivals.

Maeve had been the rival. Was it because she was family, because she was woman, because he had known her all his life? Or because they loved one another in a different way? Maeve had loved him, he knew. Did he love Maeve more since she had died? He suspected he did. There was more gratitude, less fear.

He drove on up the pass. He wasn't expecting it to be so slippery as the bad weather hit, wind and sleet. Slippy, northerners would say. Higher, it was settling as snow, white among rocks, until there were no more rocky outcrops to see. Beyond that it might be sky or might be snow. It seemed endless.

The cars ahead of him had gained distance. One car could be seen struggling ahead uphill.

He was glad Janey had shut up. It gave him back his thoughts. He looked sideways at her. She was sitting quiet. She had got what she wanted, he guessed, a lift, and he didn't expect her to pay with a story. Though she couldn't not have one.

There had never been jealousy between himself and Maeve. Not jealousy of the poems. It was only about placing them, becoming known and acknowledged in this strange field of egos and spirituality, selfishness and seriousness, reading, despair, desire, scholarship, intuition and downright craziness.

It didn't get easier. He could no longer see the other car. He was driving too slowly. The track was increasingly covered with falling snow, the going no better. Nothing had been coming the other way for a while.

There was a part of this road called *The Struggle*.

Seventy was simply too old for him, he was a forward-looker being forced to look back. Why couldn't oldies just conk out these days, why was his mother in her nineties in a nursing home being fed by others because she could no longer feed herself? Why hadn't she simply fallen on the dairy steps like his grandmother, died and been done with it? He would die here, poets would come to the pub above *The Struggle* and remember him, look at his unimportant books on a tatty corner shelf. No, please no!

The car stuck. The wheels had no purchase, they spun. Only just touching, just beginning old age.

Jon Silkin had succumbed, still struggling with his poetry projects. Lucky him. Sorley in a blaze of glory for rescuing a language, then Iain Crichton Smith. Maeve had been right, there was no litany of women poets' deaths.

The wheels made a whining noise. The car sputtered and stopped. He turned the ignition again but it flooded the engine and the whole thing choked.

'We've met before,' said Janey 'I've worked it out.'

'Where?'

The woman looked at him. 'Up the Tyne. Basil Bunting's funeral.'

He hadn't told Maeve. He hadn't got round to it.

'What use is it now? We're up shit creek!'

'Shit!'

'Can't get it going again,' said Eric, trying.

'Shall we wait to be rescued? Keep each other warm? Give us a kiss!'

Eric was horrified. Maeve turned from her seat and reached towards him. Hugged his shoulders.

'It would do you good. Keep you warm. Don't you want to sleep with wi?'

Eric hadn't often been in this sort of situation. The snow flurried quicker outside. Now he said weakly, 'We're more likely to die together than anything else, if we don't rescue ourselves. Do you want to die in the cold?'

'Heck, naw,' replied Janey.

'Then we'll have to get out and walk. We must be near the pub.'

'Naw!' said Janey.

Eric pushed his door open and stepped out. They hadn't passed the high pub at the top, and the land hadn't started going down. Did the pub have a name? It was well-known, but hardly famous. The same as him.

He had a coat and a scarf, but no gloves. He put his hands in his pockets against the sleet. He was wearing his soft driving slippers. He thought of Columba and the old monks' seagoing coracles. The coracle used the energy of the sea it was crossing. The car was powerless.

'What aboot me?' cried Janey.

'Your coat's no good. Take this car rug. Stay here. I'll get help from the pub.'

'Naw!' said Janey. 'Where's the pub? There isn't a pub!'

He would go to the pub. They needed shelter, a fire and food. But why was there nothing on the road? Something must have happened that he didn't know about.

Janey got out of the car. She was following him.

This woman wasn't Maeve. What caused any accident? Her young musician had never wanted his mother to die. The stage layout, the speaker box, the orchestra pit.

The accident of Eric being out in the snow, in the cold. 'Maeve!'

He saw that the woman had useless shoes.

He stumbled. Maeve followed. He fell into drifted snow, a ditch beside the long stone wall, behind a boulder.

'Come on man,' she said.

Eric knew that thing about the Ning-Nang-Nong, how we always used i, a, o, as the order for fun, nonsense, sound words, shilly-shally, ding-dong, pitter-patter, ping-pong. He knew about the lovely big round heavy silver whisky tray, and how it couldn't be the big whisky silver round heavy lovely tray, and all those grammarians trying to tell us why the hell it couldn't. Because it was our language, we made it, we changed it very slightly, and moved on to where we knew not. That was all any writer could do, the same thing as any child. We moved on to an end. The snow had got worse. He felt colder. Scareder – more scared – more frightened. Slumped in the ditch, in the snow.

'Get up, man.' The woman was frightened too. Maeve wouldn't be afraid – that wasn't right.

The woman was crying. 'Them lights a bit further up the road. Is that your pub? The pub you were on about?'

'Maeve!' He was desperate. '*Wildgoose* is at Grysewood Farm.'

'Do you mean Maeve Cartier? I'm Janey. Hurry, man.'

Should go back to the car. Untreated road. Not maintained in winter. November already. November, winter. No little wild daffodils. A goose in the sky, on its unknown business.

'Maeve!'

'Maeve's dead,' said Janey, angrily.

Not spring. Not summer either with tourists. Cars bumping on twisty busy roads. Boats, bicycles, roof-racks. Nothing. Cold. *The Struggle*. The snow dancing – now hail. The birds down where there were hedges. Tiny stings of hail. The adders would all be underground.

'*Wildgoose* is at Grysewood Farm! Tell Mary Weylan.'

What was he on about? 'Come on man!' she screamed.

'*Wildgoose* ... Grysewood Farm... Maeve, no, Mary...'

Wouldn't somebody hear? Couldn't Maeve go to the pub to get help? A cold snowbound fellside in the Lake District – what was he thinking? Even more dangerous than Scotland – sneaked up on you. Should never have left the car. But car gave little protection – find the pub. Sleet, rain, brain slowing down. Snowdrift. No one's coming.

'Oh no, he's collapsed! He isn't breathing! He...'

So many words: snow, bury, unseen, fire and ice.

He felt a cold hand against his freezing hand. He had a witness.

'I'm scarpering. Sorry I've gotta save meself.'

His wrist – was she feeling for a pulse?

'Them's the pub lights. I've telt ye. He's a goner. I've gotta gan.'

Fire, ice, mountains, beacons, bens, tops. A cold fusion: the beauty, instability, snowing right into his collar, his hands stuffed into his pockets. Trying to swear, but no words. Toes, fingers icy. Pressure on the chest.

The careless fall, the dark pit. Books you couldn't publish. Promises you couldn't keep.

Bones on the fell like a sheep.

Grammar, syntax... rows and rows of words, but nothing to beat the pictures, and no pictures to beat the moors and mountains covered in snow.

Darkness, pain in his chest.

A single goose flew off towards the west, a mournful image in the grey, silent whiteness of sky.

Appendix

Fictional Books by the Fictional Poets in Wildgoose

Grysewood, Eric John (1945–2013).

Grysewood, Eric. *Distances*. Leeds, Northlines, 1966.
Grysewood, Eric. *High Tide Bamburgh*. Newcastle, Swing Bridge Press, 1971.
Grysewood, Eric. *Open Secrets*. Swing Bridge Press, 1975.
Grysewood, Eric. *Selected and New Poems*. Swing Bridge Press, 1980.
Grysewood, Eric. *Homage to Auden and Other Longer Poems*. Pamphlet Series. Aberdeen University Press, 1997.
Grysewood, Eric. *In Western Waters*. Winner of the 2000 UniVerse Pamphlet Competition. London, Tapocketa Press, 2001.
Grysewood, Eric. *Columba: Trinity and Coracles: How Words Survive.* Pamphlet Series. Aberdeen University Press, 2003.
Grysewood, Eric. *Plath in Canada and the Potential of the Wild*. Research Papers Series No.9. Aberdeen University Press, 2005.
Grysewood, Eric. *Interim Poems*. Edinburgh, Marchmont Press, 2010.
Grysewood, Eric. *Selected Poems: Edited with an essay by Richard Calm*. Swing Bridge Press, 2017.
Grysewood, Eric (ed). *Pride: Gay Poetry of the Eighties, an Anthology*. Edinburgh, Marchmont Press, 1996.
Grysewood, Eric (ed). *Poets Plus*. 1–7. Swing Bridge Press, 1981–1987.
Grysewood, Eric (ed). *Common Room Poetry,* 1–9, 1997–2001.

Cartier, Maeve (Maeve Carter, 1948–1999).

Cartier, Maeve. *The Geese at Aberlady,* Durham, Mad Women Press, 1977.
Cartier, Maeve. *Odd Gloves and other miscellanies.* Swing Bridge Press, 1982.
Cartier, Maeve. *Poets Choose: Maeve Cartier,* 1992.
Common Room Poetry 4, Maeve Cartier Memorial Issue, 2002.
Cartier, Maeve. *Maeve Cartier: The Last Poems,* edited by Eric Grysewood. Swing Bridge Press, 2004.
Weylan, Mary, and Bridget Brown. *Cartier and the Demands of Poetry.* Bristol Feminist Papers, No. 6, 2008.
Cartier, Maeve. *Collected Shorter Poems.* Swing Bridge Press with G G Productions, 2017.
Cartier, Maeve. *Wildgoose.* Durham University Library, Special Collections. Typescript MS with holograph amendments in paper box. in Eric Grysewood Archive. Publication rights released to The Maverick Trust, a division of Random House, December 2019.

Acknowledgements

Writing *Wildgoose* has been an adventure, and many people are due heartfelt thanks for their advice along the way. It was written as part of a PhD project at Lancaster University Department of English Literature and Creative Writing, still ongoing. At Lancaster I gratefully thank Eoghan Walls and Zoe Lambert, my two supervisors, Eoghan for his robust approach and Zoe for her kindness; both for professional expertise. Also Prof. Jenn Ashworth, and many more, including fellow postgraduate students who helped to reduce the isolation of the covid year, and the librarians of Lancaster University Library. Thanks also to the Scottish Poetry Library for answering some unusual queries.

Among writer friends, John Bolland and Greg Michaelson helped me enormously by close critique of my work at different stages. As did in various ways Kylie Murray, Morelle Smith, Rebecca Bilkau, Richie McCaffery, Angela Topping, George Walker, Susan Castillo Street, Eileen Carney Hulme, and Martin Blades. Tom Kelly advised on spelling the Newcastle dialect. Sheila Wakefield, Founding Editor, Red Squirrel Press and Colin Will, Editor, Postbox Press went far beyond publishers' obligations on my behalf. To these I must add Richard Livermore, who died before getting a chance to read the book.

My husband Ian King offered full support for the project, and my brother Stephen Evans made the university course possible with finance and accommodation. My other sibs, Paul Evans, Liz Collins and Ann Story, believed in me throughout, and Liz Collins read an early draft. Cohorts of facebook friends watched my lone craft crossing the seas; 300 answers were given to my question, *How might a poet die?* and I am indebted to Elizabeth Marino for uniquely suggesting the fate of Maeve.

Sheena Blackhall, Brian Johnstone, Liz Lochhead,

Hayden Murphy and Tom Pickard kindly gave me permission to put them or their concerns in the story. 'As long as it's obviously fiction,' wrote Tom Pickard.

Maeve's poem *The Sun God* (in Chapter Five) was first published on Richie McCaffery's website *The Lyrical Aye*, with a short explanation, on 3 April 2020.

The frontispiece map was drawn from my rough by Geoff Sawers, the originator of this style of map. His flying compass intuitively caught the essence of my novel and became the header motif.

I have written Briggflatts with the double g, Bunting's amendment, throughout. It is Brigflatts, near Sedbergh in north-west Yorkshire in the other reality.